Dear Miss Horncastle

I hope [   ] he
Book. My [   ] [   ]
wrote it.

Thank you for everything
this year.

from Alfie Bramley 2020

Year 5 rules!!!

THE SAPPHIRE SOCIETY

L. C. SARLL

Matador
9 Priory Business Park,
Wistow Road, Kibworth Beauchamp,
Leicestershire, LE8 0RX
Tel: 0116 279 2299
Email: books@troubador.co.uk
Web: www.troubador.co.uk/matador
Twitter: @matadorbooks

ISBN 978 1838592 325

British Library Cataloguing in Publication Data.
A catalogue record for this book is available from the British Library.

Printed and bound by CPI Group (UK) Ltd, Croydon, CR0 4YY
Typeset in 12pt Baskerville by Troubador Publishing Ltd, Leicester, UK

Matador is an imprint of Troubador Publishing Ltd

MIX
Paper from
responsible sources
FSC   FSC® C013604

For my darling Savannah,
the root of my inspiration and adventures.
L.C.S

CHAPTER 1

MARGALE HIGH

Despite its disproportionately large size to the rest of the school, Margale's hall was hot and sticky, and the saccharine sweet whiff of ice lollies clung to the air.

It was the end of the school day on the last day of the summer term and Savannah Wood stood alone in her bus queue. Her short, cropped ginger hair and slight build made her seem fragile in contrast with her peers.

While the rest of the children squealed in delight at their approaching summer holidays, Savannah struggled to catch her breath in the oppressive humidity of the hall. Her private thoughts were rudely interrupted by a large dollop of ice cream hitting her left ear and slowly slithering down her crisp white shirt. Sniggering erupted from the gang of girls standing behind her, but Savannah knew better than to react. The perpetrator was Kirsty Sharp, a rotund girl with a cruel disposition and greasy brown hair which stuck to her forehead, causing her already-oily complexion to appear as if she had a daily ritual of slopping lard onto her face.

"Oi, you lot, listen to this joke!" Kirsty hollered. "What do ginger kids have to look forward to later in life?" She stood smugly, waiting for her gang's response. "No ideas?" She looked around, holding back on the punchline until she was sure she had everyone's attention. "Going grey!" she howled. Kirsty roared a mucus-laden nasal snort then smashed her rucksack over Savannah's head, forcing her face down onto the wooden parquet floor.

"I've got more," she continued, standing over Savannah, dribbling yellow-tinged frothy saliva onto the back of her head. "What's the difference between the Loch Ness monster and an attractive ginger? Come on, any guesses?" She stood back to face the gathering crowd. "They have pictures of Nessie. Do you get it? Because there are no attractive gingers!" She roared with laughter again.

Savannah lay down on the ground; her cheeks began to blotch red and an uncontrollable weight of nausea lifted down through the ground and into her stomach. She gingerly sat herself upright, giving a sideways glance at Kirsty's shoes as her gangly legs were finally persuaded to stand. As luck would have it, the incident was drawn to an unusually swift conclusion as Mrs Back strutted purposefully towards her bus queue and bellowed over the loud hum of voices, "Those for bus 11 to Sloathe may now board the vehicle but do so quietly."

The queue of children moved slowly at first but soon developed great momentum in the race to get to preferred bus seats. For Kirsty and her gang, the back seat was their goal. For Savannah, it was near the front, away from the back-seat bullies. With a spluttered rev, the rusting orange school bus trundled out of the school car park, allowing Savannah the chance to take a final look at what had been her school for the last two years. The dying weeping willow covering the pond, the rickety bike sheds with a large plume of cigarette smoke seeping out the front. It was not a pretty sight. Margale Secondary School was a miserable institution with grey walls, disinterested staff, bored and unruly children with exam results in the doldrums. But, she wondered, was it better the devil she knew? Three months ago, a letter had come in the post offering her father, Theodore Wood, a new job. Theodore had been an engineer and junior inventor for the local gas company since Savannah was born twelve years ago, until last month, when a Scandinavian wind farm company called Froowind offered him the position of Chief Inventor. As with everything the Wood family encountered, the new job was far from routine. In fact, it was also far from home. Froowind's head office was located in the

Faroe Islands, a group of eighteen small islands in the Atlantic, no less than 1,602 miles from her current life in England. Eysturoy, one of the Faroe Islands, was also the place where her mother, Martha, was born. Martha lived there with her parents until she met Theodore, while she was visiting her friends in London, and they married and moved to England. In a week's time, the whole Wood family would be on the 11.30 Scrabster ferry, bound for the islands' capital, Torshavn. Savannah knew very little about her new home except that Strendur, which was the name of the town they were moving to, was actually a village. It was small and sparsely populated, even by Faroese standards, although it did have a church and a school, the latter of which Savannah would be attending.

The short bus journey home from Margale High passed without further altercations with Kirsty and her gang as they smoked their cigarettes and amused themselves by taunting a dumpy boy with high-waisted trousers. Shouts of "See ya, Ginger!" echoed as she stepped off the bus, and as the smothering diesel fumes caught Savannah's breath, she watched the bus splutter on its way, a wave of bare bottoms mooning from the back-seat gang, disappearing further into the distance.

With moss squeaking under her rubber-soled school shoes, Savannah skidded into the back door of her home, nearly banging her head on the kitchen door in the process. She was welcomed by a smile from her mother, Martha, who stood by the long rectangular kitchen table of the farmhouse.

"Last day finished then, darling, how does it feel?" Martha enquired with a tilted head and thoughtful expression. Savannah didn't know what to say. Her little brother, Tom, balanced awkwardly on Martha's hip and gurgled in her direction as if trying to speed up her response. This was tricky. Savannah didn't want to upset her mother by showing her lack of enthusiasm, but she knew only too well that her weak smile was not going to cut it as a reply. As she inhaled the summer air, trying to force out words of fraudulent enthusiasm, she was interrupted by an enormous crash and smoke engulfing the kitchen, quickly followed by her father, Theodore, racing through the garage side door which led into the laboratory (actually, the garage, but her father insisted it was not a garage; it was his inventing lab).

"Martha, call the fire brigade, we have had an unexpected little research incident!" he shouted. Gasping through the smoke but grinning in equal measure, Theodore hopped up and down while quickly scanning the kitchen. "Savannah, we have a breakthrough, you have to see this!"

As Theodore ran back into the ensuing chaos of the garage laboratory, he appeared oblivious to the fact that the hair on the back of his head was on fire. Calmly, but walking most definitely with a purpose, Savannah walked over to the Belfast kitchen sink, filled a used mug from the draining board up with water and proceeded to calmly stride back over to her father, pouring the contents of the mug onto his head, a used teabag slopping unceremoniously onto his shoulder. Tom squealed with delight at the spontaneous performance and began lunging for the lab door, testing Martha's balancing skills to near breaking point. The Wood household was, as was often the case, in chaos. Martha tried to maintain her best telephone voice as she spoke to the emergency operator on the other end of the telephone line, while explaining the required service and address. Martha's softly spoken voice was no match for the volume of noise in the house and the emergency operator was clearly struggling to hear her, when another slightly larger explosion brought stunned silence to the room for just long enough for Martha to be heard. "Fire brigade, please," she stated.

Whatever the cause of the explosions, they seemed to have subdued and Theodore reappeared, hair extinguished and gasping, "It's fine, all under control now," with a wide grin over his blackened face and his hands placed triumphantly on his hips.

The Wood residence was well known to the Sloathe fire brigade after twelve years of dealing with Theodore's minor research incidents. They were now on first-name terms with them, and Martha contributed cakes to their Christmas fundraising fete every year in a vain attempt to thank them for their continued service. The firefighters promptly appeared at the door, but far from being concerned, Savannah was experienced in the art of surviving such an event, and past incidents had taught her the best way of maintaining her sanity and sense of humour was to head for the haven of her bedroom upstairs.

Savannah's room was a botanical paradise. All of the plants were carefully chosen to be medicinally useful, from the lavender next to her bed to the old aloe vera bursting out of its pot in the far corner. Savannah's room reflected her lifelong ambitions. Her aim was simple: to use plants to make people feel better. She hadn't actually tested her very limited knowledge out yet for fear of poisoning an unsuspecting patient, although Tornado the farmyard cat's flatulence had greatly improved after she prescribed him some chamomile and fennel seeds mixed into his usual bowl of cat food. The windowsill spilled its lush emerald green foliage down from the ledge and onto the radiator, proving to be useful camouflage as she peered at the fire crew extinguishing the last remaining sparks of smouldering plastic which Theodore had accidently ignited. Emergency dealt with and disaster avoided, she slumped onto her bed, her chest rising and falling in quick succession as her eyes glazed over and she stared into a black hole of nothing.

"I find a nice cup of tea can solve most worries, you know." Martha leaned her head around the bedroom door, with an offering of a steaming mug of tea in her hand. "Wait until you see the house. I had the most perfect childhood growing up there. It looks straight out to the fjord and wait until—" Savannah interrupted her mother by hugging her tightly as a way of postponing the inevitable. "Okay, I'll stop telling you, but I know you'll love it." Her mother winked, forcing the blue and white striped mug into her hands. After all, it couldn't possibly be any worse than Margale High.

- ▼ -

The following day was the beginning of Savannah's summer holidays; however, yesterday's minor research incident was still on Martha's mind. She was, after all, the person clearing up the consequences of the explosions with a cloth and bucket of soapy water. Tom was helping by splashing the washing-up water onto the floor and chewing the scouring pad, much to his intrigue. Savannah began the arduous task of packing the contents of her bedroom into boxes but found herself getting distracted by curious items. Old photos, a love letter Jason Smith sent to her when she was five years old. In fact, it was the first and last love letter she had ever received, so she decided to keep it safe and packed it into a box ready for its new home in the Faroe Islands. Other items of peculiar interest included a tarnished gold and blue stone necklace, found in her mother's sewing box. She had no recollection of seeing it before.

"It was Grandma's," said Martha, with one eye on the necklace and the other on the cutlery drawer. She temporarily allowed herself to be distracted and gently took the necklace out of Savannah's hands into her own, looking at the dirty item with fondness, while untangling it from old yellowing sticky tape and pipe cleaners. "Grandma gave me this when I moved to England and married your father. I even wore this on my wedding day, but to be honest, I only wore it for Grandma; I don't really like it." She placed it back into Savannah's palm and closed her daughter's fingers around the bedraggled jewellery. Savannah opened out her fingers and inspected the necklace more carefully. The years of dirt had made the colour of the chain hard to distinguish, but she thought it looked like gold. The centre of the pendant was a filthy blue stone, surrounded by individual swirls of metal. "It's yours now, darling. Grandma would have been pleased that you want it, although I can't think why you do want it, grimy little thing, if you ask me. Pa will find you some metal polish to clean it up a bit, but try not to distract him anymore today; he's already struggling with the concept of having to throw some of his lab rubbish away."

She knew her mother was right; Pa was as distracted by peculiar findings as she was. With this in mind, she put the necklace safely into her cardigan pocket. Tom looked at her pocket while leaning over and giving a faint smile before starting to cough and gag quietly on the scouring pad he had inserted into his mouth and nostrils. A sharp pat on the back from Martha sent the now suspiciously coloured scouring pad out of the offending orifices, and it hit the wall with a squelch, much to Tom's annoyance.

The packing continued as did the ongoing finds of weird and wonderful objects. Martha found a tooth, possibly feline, in the umbrella stand, and Theodore found a World War 2 German submarine clock in the toolbox. After a week of boxes, farewell cups of coffee with her mother's friends and getting Tornado vaccinated for travel, the Wood family were finally ready for relocation. The first week of Savannah's summer holidays had been unusually tame, so she was looking forward to the travelling ahead of her the following day, which distracted her from inevitable thoughts of what her new home would actually be like.

"Fish and chips," Theodore roared as he jogged through the kitchen door. With no furniture left in the house apart from the beds, they sat on the cold kitchen floor tiles and tucked into the food straight from the paper, something her mother wouldn't usually approve of.

"Did you know fish is the Faroe Islands' biggest export?" Theodore exclaimed. Savannah didn't care; she was enjoying her last moments of England and revelling in the vinegar fumes wafting from her dinner warming her lap as she sat cross-legged on the floor. One by one, the Wood family members drifted off to bed, ready for the early morning alarm clock. Savannah wondered how on earth she would get to sleep with so many uncertainties ahead, but she needn't have worried; it only took her head to fall gently onto her sumptuous feather pillow before her weary mind and tired body were in deep slumber.

- ▼ -

Honk, honk, honk. Savannah woke from her peaceful sleep with an abrupt involuntary jerk and an overwhelming feeling of complete disorientation. The sun was pouring in through her bedroom window. "Aagghh. We're late!" Theodore Wood yelled from his bedroom, interrupted by a loud banging on the door from the removal men, who were collecting the last of the furniture. Savannah was tipped out of bed by her father and a bullish-looking man with tattoos up his arms and halitosis, which was so offensive, it burnt her nostrils. With no time to change her clothes, Savannah grabbed yesterday's cardigan and threw it onto her shoulders over her pyjamas, picking up her fresh clothes to put on *en route*. The rusting Volvo estate was loaded with all family members, including Tornado, and the car screeched out of the muddy driveway, without giving Savannah the chance for a backward glance. This was just as well, because the speed with which Theodore was driving had sent the neighbour's chickens hurtling into the air, sending feathers and excrement flying into the atmosphere.

With minutes to spare, they arrived at Scrabster Port just in time to board the ferry. After the performance of getting the tatty car onto the clinking steel ramp, they boarded the ferry, with a tentative cheer from Martha. Savannah and Tom were still in their nightwear and looked decidedly dishevelled after leaving the house without as much as a cup of tea. The car journey was made even more unpleasant by having to roll down all the car windows to counteract the flatulence from Tornado, who seemed less than impressed at being squeezed into a cage. Animals were strictly forbidden on deck, so Tornado had to remain caged within the safe constraints of the car. After a stomach-satisfying full English breakfast, Savannah set about exploring the vessel. The warren of corridors meant the large ferry was a good place to lose time. Most of the corridors looked the same; industrial-patterned garish carpet and grey steel walls with an unappetising odour of damp and vomit, but as Savannah walked up the claustrophobic stairwell to the deck of the ship, the view was different altogether. Although still looking industrial, the outside deck looked rugged and military, proudly displaying rust corroding at the exterior. She stared vacantly at the mass of water surrounding her. The bitter wind swiftly penetrated through her cardigan, causing her to huddle her posture to retain some warmth. Splashes around the stern of the boat caught her attention and she grasped onto the cold steel rail to look down to see what was causing them. Bobbing and diving with great energy was a pod of seals. They chased in the ferry's wake as if race competitors, their fine, silky whiskers trapping sea water droplets like a spider web catches spring morning dew.

Savannah tugged at her cardigan, wrapping the collar around her numb ears and while shoving her hands in her pocket, she felt her newly acquired necklace, which she had accidently left there the day before. Holding it up to the clear livid sky, the centred blue jewel was caked with dirt, and despite the chain being dirty, she unhooked the safety latch and placed it around her neck for safekeeping. She slumped lethargically over the rails and peered down into the sea, but the frolicking seals had gone.

Without warning, her contemplation was interrupted by a gush of seawater hitting her directly in the face. Her facial muscles contorted as the saline stung her eyes and burnt her cheeks. Stunned and quickstepping in reverse, Savannah moved backwards, rubbing her eyes and checking the vicinity for any witnesses to her soaking. Before she realised what was happening, another spurt of water hit her on the back of her head with a force so violent, it knocked her sliding down across the textured metal floor, grating the skin away from her shins. The sea wasn't calm, but waves of this proportion were not something she was expecting. After her rushed morning and bidding farewell to home, Savannah couldn't control her eyes, beginning to bulge with saltwater of their own.

Cold and wet, with bleeding legs, Savannah looked to the stairwell door to make her exit back down the stairs to the cafeteria below but quickly realised the daylight had dissipated and the previously blue sky had turned instantly ebony black. The saltwater and sudden change of light impaired her vision, but something in front of her was so colossal it couldn't be missed. Another wave was heading towards the boat. A wave competing in size with that of a tsunami, which would easily swallow the whole ferry in a flick of a drop. Terror lent speed to her limbs as she began running to the stairwell. She had to warn her parents and get inside off the open-air deck to safety. Her tatty trainers skidded across the slippery wet metal floor as fast as her bleeding legs would carry her. The wind swept her tears racing into her hairline, obscuring her vision and making it nearly impossible for her to see where she was going.

She made a lunge towards the stairwell door; her short fingernails scratched at the handle, but it was too late, the rogue wave had outrun her. Instantly, Savannah was blasted from all directions as the savage wave crashed over the unsuspecting vessel. She clung to the stairwell door handle but was overwhelmed by a painfully high-pitched screeching sound which drowned out even the sound of the thrashing water pummelling her against the door. The ferry shook frantically from left to right, like a fairground ride with no health and safety precautions. Despite needing to retain her grip, the noise was so piercing that she thrust her head into her shoulder to protect her ears. She momentarily opened her eyes and was faced with a huge black cloud looming on top of the water and skulking onto the deck.

A stench engulfed her lungs. She gasped and felt the offending gas travelling down her trachea and burning her lungs and chest, causing her to slump down the doorway in oxygen-starved confusion. Her head whacked against the door and, while clutching her throat, she watched the black cloud moving slowly over her as if to evaporate and consume her confused and coiled body. As she watched, the cloud slowly stalked over her and the light of the sky regained its delphinium blue tinge, sending the offensive black cloud seeping through the railing in front of her and submerging down into the water. In the surrounding sea, she watched the cloud engulfed by a large spurting fountain which exploded into the ferry's path, almost drowning the vessel into submission. Her eyes could stay open no longer, and as her tender eyelids finally surrendered shut, her feet began hitting the roof of the stairwell entrance, the vehement force of the water bouncing her body around like it was an unwanted toy. Savannah shrieked for help as her body was launched upside down onto the roof, the oasis of safety glimpsed through the cafeteria skylight window beneath her. Seconds in time dragged on for eternity until the pace of her battering began to slow and the deafening high-pitched noise softened. Theodore catapulted through the stairwell door and manoeuvred Savannah off the roof and into his arms, continuing to carry her down the tiny stairwell into the cafeteria below.

Inside the cafeteria, pandemonium reigned. The suffocating shrill of panic was etched in the air as passengers bellowed and whimpered across the furniture-strewn room. Theodore carried Savannah past a blood-splattered wall, next to which an elderly man lay covered in blood and unconscious, with several other passengers kneeling next to his battered body, trying to help him. Injured people were scattered across the room, sitting and lying on the floor and being comforted by other passengers. An announcement came over the tannoy speakers: "Ladies and gentlemen, this is your captain speaking. We have experienced some unforeseen technical issues. At present, we do not believe the vessel to be damaged but as a precaution we are collating a full safety audit before we restart the engines. I would kindly ask you to remain in your seats and keep calm. The on-board cafeteria will not be opening as previously scheduled for the rest of the voyage."

"The captain clearly hasn't been in here; how could anyone sit on those seats?" Martha choked, pointing her gaze up to the ceiling, where a selection of chairs had been smashed and one was hanging precariously by a spindled leg to the light fitting. She gazed across the carnage and saw Savannah and Theodore. "Darling, where on earth have you been? I thought you'd been dragged overboard!" Martha embraced Savannah tightly and with a handkerchief began wiping the blood from Savannah's cheek. Martha's protective arms were tightly constraining Tom, but he was clearly enjoying the drama which had occurred. He leant towards his father with outstretched arms, but as soon as Theodore tried to scoop him into an embrace, the toddler took his opportunity to hurtle himself towards the dangling chair, swinging from the ceiling light. Much to Tom's annoyance, he missed his grasp for the chair and settled instead for picking up the remnants of breakfast strewn across the table. Martha sat herself opposite Savannah and with watery eyes started to assess the severity of her injuries. Savannah's right arm was bloodied and one side of her face was cut and beginning to bruise. Her right ankle was a mottled purple colour and had swollen to the size of a tennis ball.

"Can I help?" Another passenger intervened. "I am trained in first aid and would be happy to help with your daughter's injuries." The lady spoke to her mother in an accent Savannah recognised as being Faroese, like her mother's. She was similar in appearance to her mother, although she was younger. Her hair was chocolate brown in colour and styled in a side chignon that had perhaps been perfect before the wave hit but now resembled a squashed silk pincushion. She wore leather trousers with a hand-knitted jumper and beautiful jewellery which clinked and shimmered as she gesticulated. Martha gratefully accepted her offer of medical assistance on Savannah's behalf, so the Faroese lady reached towards a chair dangling from the ceiling light, effortlessly guiding it down to the floor, for which she earned a ripple of applause from a small crowd of onlookers. The mood of the cafeteria was beginning to lighten. The engines restarted and a loud cheer erupted from the passengers. The lady pulled the chair to a quiet corner of the cafeteria and beckoned Savannah to sit down.

"I am Mai," she smiled.

"Savannah," she whimpered. Mai carefully inspected her eye, face and ankle. Her cold hands poked and manipulated Savannah's afflicted limbs until she finally announced that all her bones were intact.

"That's a relief," Savannah sighed. "So, you're a doctor in the Faroe Islands, Mai?"

"No, I do live in the Faroes, but I'm not a doctor; I am a medical herbalist," she replied.

"A hedge witch?" Savannah blurted out, excitement sparkling in her eyes. Since she could remember, she had obsessed over plants and their healing properties. Herbalists were practitioners with this specialist knowledge, and Savannah's goal was to one day train to become a herbalist herself.

Mai grinned. "Yes, some people refer to us as hedge witches, but I only use that term in circles of others in the same profession. It makes people nervous," she giggled. Savannah giggled too, with an acute sense of understanding.

Mai lowered her head and moved in closer to Savannah, whispering, "Your necklace is beautiful, Savannah. Where did you get it?" Savannah looked down and glanced at her grandmother's necklace dangling shabbily around her neck.

"Really?" Savannah squinted dismissively. "This was my grandmother's. I only found it when we were clearing our house in England to move. She gave it to my mother, and now my mother has given it to me. It needs cleaning, but we haven't really had time yet, what with the move." Savannah blushed.

Mai looked at it intently. "It is a very special piece of Faroese jewellery, Savannah, did you know that?"

Mai was interrupted by Theodore, who crouched down to their level. "What's the verdict, Doc?" He looked to Mai for a response.

"Well, as I discussed with your daughter, I'm not actually a doctor, but I think she got off very lightly with a nasty sprain and some impressive cuts and bruises."

"Thank goodness," he said, tousling Savannah's hair. "Did you see anything, Savannah? What on earth happened up on deck?"

Savannah recounted the incident to him and Mai in as much detail as she could remember. Perhaps too much unnerving detail, since Mai didn't offer friendly chit-chat after that but fixed her gaze on the ferry window, staying seated with them until safely arriving at Torshavn Port.

CHAPTER 2

FOROYAR

Safely on shore at Torshavn Port and reunited with a nervous Tornado, the Wood family left the vehicle compartment of the ferry. Savannah was patched up with plasters, her right arm was hung in a sling and bandages supported her ankle, which imitated a misshapen aubergine. The tired rusting old Volvo estate looked like Savannah felt, chugging and groaning at the effort of manoeuvring down the ferry ramp. Torshavn, the islands' capital, lay before them; its clean, narrow streets and homely architecture was distant to any city she had ever encountered before. The buildings seemed squashed and stout, with rooftops of corrugated iron and grass giving the impression of a patchwork quilt being thrown amidst the sky. They gratefully waved goodbye to Mai and began the final leg of their journey.

On the road leaving Torshavn, the weather became more and more precarious. The charcoal-coloured clouds enveloped the horizon and swallowed up the landscape. It was 10.30 at night, yet still daylight due to the island's northern latitude location, meaning up to nineteen hours of daylight in these summer months. The winding roads felt as if they were leading to nowhere, with sheep grazing on grassy hills and unexpected waterfalls dripping out of mountains, like the rock had inadvertently sprung a leak. Savannah could not help but be drawn in by the country's bleak beauty, despite her exhaustion. She wound down the car window and indulged in a deep breath of the crisp, fresh air, which engulfed her lungs and made her dizzy with satisfaction. They passed yet another waterfall, its crystal-clear water trickling out of the mountain, saturating the wild flowers below, which a herd of sheep contentedly nibbled on.

"Ahh, Foroyar, it's good to be home," Martha muttered affectionately.

"Who's Foroyar?"

"It's not who, Savannah, it's here. Foroyar is the local name for these islands," Martha replied.

"Well, since you're a native, Martha, which way do you suggest?" Theodore asked expectantly. They were at a crossroads, with no road signs in sight.

Martha's first language was Faroese, the Faroe Islands' main language, but as she rightly retorted, "Theodore, I haven't been back to Strendur since

I left with you, thirteen years ago. I don't know the way from the city, and if there are no signs, I cannot translate nothing into directions."

An elderly lady was walking at the side of the road, so Martha wound down the car window and asked for directions. Although Martha had always had a slightly different accent to English ladies, Savannah had never really heard her speak in Faroese, and she quietly marvelled at how beautiful and gentle it sounded. In fact, her mother really was quite demure. She had a tall, slim build with long golden hair that wafted in the wind, much like she should be appearing in a perfume advert.

She didn't speak Faroese to the woman for long, since most people spoke English. Luckily, the schools taught in English, too. "*Tusund takk.*" Martha waved to the elderly lady. "It means a thousand thanks. Right, so it's left, then right at the big waterfall, then straight ahead to Strendur."

"Okay, Strendur, here we come!" jeered Theodore. Chugging along the final mud track road, their new home was within reach. Number 13 Strendur was Martha's childhood home and would soon host the next generation of the family. It stood with perfect proportions, proudly, at the bottom of the road, overlooking the fjord. The exterior was stone at the bottom with black wooden cladding from the first floor, large white windows and, the crowning glory, a mass of moss green roof. The garden was overgrown with moss as a lawn instead of grass, and there was a wooden bench looking out to the fjord. As Theodore battled with opening the front door, Martha lovingly scooped up Tom from the rear car seat. With renewed enthusiasm, Savannah stuck close to her father as they burst through the ancient, warped and creaking wooden door into the cold hallway. The owner of the wind farm company, Mr Froodroy, had kindly arranged for some of their furniture to be transported ahead of their arrival, and Savannah felt a warm familiar comfort in her chest as she saw the kitchen table and usual paraphernalia, albeit in a new location. Martha scuttled up the stairway carrying Tom, quietly blowing them goodnight kisses before heading into the only available bed. The rest of the furniture would be delivered by the removal man with halitosis in the morning.

Theodore turned abruptly to face Savannah. "Let's explore," he smiled mischievously. "I haven't seen this place since I visited your grandparents, all those years ago." There was a cosy lounge room with a fireplace that Theodore promptly lit, opposite which was another room that Theodore decided would be a study. Walking down the small wooden-floored hallway led them into a large kitchen with a huge Aga cooker. Separate from the house in the back garden was a large grass-roofed outbuilding. They walked through the house into the back garden to inspect the new laboratory.

"The lab of my dreams," Theodore said, looking at it as if it were a newborn child. "That big house there, I think belongs to my new boss, Mr Froodroy," he added, pointing to a neighbouring structure. Savannah looked next door and saw a beautiful yet humble house. It was not grand or ostentatious, but elegantly refined and homely, with a grass roof the Vikings would have pillaged for. It had tenderly tweaked neat edges and was cut evenly throughout the vast top.

"Are you disappointed?" Theodore observed his daughter looking enviously at the Froodroy house.

"No, no, not at all," she replied, turning around and looking at the back of their new home. "I think our house is… what is that?" she said, flummoxed. Her father beamed smugly at Savannah's bemusement. She tentatively walked towards a glass structure attached to the study area of their new home. To all intents and purposes, it looked like an orangery, but how all the glass survived the ferocious Faroese weather was anyone's guess. "It can't be?" Savannah's forehead puckered as she looked to her father for answers.

"As you know," Theodore raised his hands in the air, giving Savannah a wink, "this whole place used to belong to Grandma and Grandad, and I'm sure Ma has told you how much Grandma loved plants. You know she was a botanist. Evidently, the only way Grandad could persuade Grandma to stay in the Faroe Islands was if he figured out a way for her to grow her favourite plants here. Being an inventor, he built her this. Steel spanning down thirty metres, no less, to hold it all in place. Reinforced glass with hand-welded metalwork and a wind-powered irrigation system. It's been empty for over twelve years now, so it needs a little work." He held out his hand towards the magnificent structure, dangling a key. The ornate metal doors had the most beautiful designs with a heart-shaped pair of handles to the double doors, matching the heart-shaped key. She delicately twisted the key and the door popped open. In the dim light of a glowing wood burner, Savannah saw movement. Sat on a rug next to the log burner, with one ear up and one down, was a black and white collie dog, wagging his tail gently.

"Here are your surprises," Theodore continued. "Here is your very own orangery; the only catch is Tricky here. This is Tricver, who I've always called Tricky. He's Grandma's dog. Whenever I used to visit your mother, after we first met in London, Tricky would always greet me with a wagging tail. God only knows how he's still alive." Savannah's lifelong dreams had been realised on one of the worst days of her life. Tricver slowly got to his feet, stretching his back legs and wagging his tail as he nuzzled into Savannah's neck and put two paws on her shoulders. A beautiful blue collar and a name tag gave her all she needed to know. It read, *I am Tricver. If found by the Fjord, please return to the Froodroy family.*

"He comes with the orangery. He won't leave the house, you see. The Froodroys looked after him after Grandma and Grandad went, but he kept escaping their house next door and coming back here. They didn't want to have him put to sleep, so they have just kept him here and bring him food and keep the log burner going for him every day, until now that is. Tricver now belongs to us, well, you, actually. If you want the orangery, you have to look after him. Deal?"

"Yes, Pa, yes!" Savannah immediately accepted, clapping her hands together.

"You stay and get acquainted with Tricver. He will no doubt be pleased of the company. I'll find a pan and boil up some water to make tea," Theodore grinned, meandering through the orangery to the study.

Savannah settled down next to the glowing log burner and sat with Tricver, who began licking her face as she sat on the sheepskin rug. The large orangery with a round central ceiling lantern had a small log burner to help keep it warm. It was easily as big as the rest of the house, with empty oak shelves and empty ground beds waiting for plants. Savannah's rollercoaster of a day had left her exhausted but with a nervous energy she could not shake off. Savannah had tried desperately to put the ferry incident out of her mind since arriving on the island, but now the excitement had worn off, she was left feeling shaken. Despite her injuries, the memory of the eerie screeching sound was indelibly tattooed on her brain, yet the fear she felt commanded her fascination. If ever evil had a voice, she was in no doubt that she had been in the front row of its performance.

"Here we go, love, I even found the milk and sugar; your ma packed it ready in her handbag," Theodore said. He did nothing by halves, serving the tea from a teapot, albeit into old enamel mugs he had found on the potting table. "Before you ask, Savannah, the answer to your question is no." Savannah hadn't asked him anything, but he continued. "I don't know what on earth happened on that ferry, but it wasn't a natural occurrence; it wasn't even a natural freak accident. Mother Nature had no part in that event."

Theodore engulfed Savannah in a huge hug, helping to ease her distress. As he did so, the necklace Mai had been so interested in dangled around her neck and became visible from her cardigan neckline. Tricver lunged for it, barking and scratching at Savannah's neck.

"Get off, Tricky!" Her father rescued the necklace from being assaulted by Tricver and removed it from Savannah's neck for closer inspection. "This old thing! Where on earth did you find it? Your mother said she had given it away! I remember your grandmother used to wear it, although it didn't look this bedraggled back then. Tut, tut, you can't leave it in this state. You have to look after jewellery, Savannah. You can't keep wearing it in this state," Theodore nagged, unhooking the chain and putting it back around her neck. "Remind me tomorrow and I will teach you how to clean it," he added with a furrowed forehead.

"Thanks, Pa." Savannah knew he was right; she would definitely have to remind him.

- ▾ -

Savannah woke up to the glorious sound of rain pattering against the glass orangery roof, quickly followed by a cockney accent yelling, "Oi, Oi! Anybody home?" It was the now familiar removal man, tapping irritatingly on the beautiful smooth glass doors.

"Round the front, Terrence," Theodore hollered, who was clearly up and preparing his laboratory boxes. She got up and strolled into the house, and seeing the usual family occurrences comforted her. Thirteen Strendur already felt like home but with a greatly improved view, which she had been unable to appreciate in the dim light last night. The fjord was just 30 metres from the front of their home. Keen to explore her new surroundings, Savannah took a walk through the village. The fjord was always in sight, its crystal-clear water bounding wave over wave in an almost automated manner. She stopped at the church and, balanced on tiptoe, she peered in through the window. It was much smaller than the churches she had seen in England. It had three rows of seats on either side of the aisle and was neat and tidy with a small bunch of blue iris flowers on the alter. Her eyes were drawn to the ceiling of the church, which had wooden carvings of gruesome creatures that were surrounded by angels with extraordinarily large and beautiful blue wings, engulfing the enemies. As her eyes wandered to the centre of the church, she almost jumped backwards as a pair of iris-blue eyes appeared at the window. She wasn't startled for long, since the eyes seemed friendly and inquisitive and the person had thick blond bushy eyebrows, which were wiggling up and down in a caterpillar motion, making Savannah snort with laughter. Savannah pressed her nose up hard to the window, squashing her nostrils, which caused a smear across the glass. Gradually, more of the face behind the glass began to appear and soon she saw the person's mouth crease upwards, until she found herself returning a smile to a complete stranger. The face ducked down out of sight, and after a gentle waft of the solid oak church door, a short, chubby boy stood in the archway.

"You're Savannah Wood, aren't you?" the boy bleated as he timidly shuffled towards her. "I'm Richard Froodroy, but most people call me Rich."

Savannah nodded, blushing as she realised this boy who appeared to be the same age as her had seen the inside of her nostrils before she had even introduced herself. "I know who you are because my pa is Mr Froodroy. He owns Froowind; your pa is going to be working with us."

"Ah, that explains it," she replied politely.

"I met your pa when he visited us about a month ago," Rich smiled. "He's a genius, isn't he?" Savannah was unconvinced by her father's newly inherited genius status but smiled all the same. "Pa is so excited about the work he's going to be doing. It's super high tech, you know," Rich added.

Their chat was interrupted by Theodore strolling towards them, already shouting, "Good morning, young Froodroy," extending his palm and shaking Rich's hand, an altogether more gracious and customary introduction than the inside of nostrils.

- ▼ -

The Wood household scented the surrounding area with a freshly baked cake emanating from its oven. Theodore, Tom and Rich stood close to the range oven door for warmth and possibly the anticipation of a slice of warm, sweet sponge cake. There was a loud thud at the door and in strolled a short lady with brown hair, a tall and muscular man with dark hair in a slicked back hairstyle and two children Savannah's age. They introduced themselves as Dana, Jan, and their twins, Ava and Frank, who would be in Savannah's new class at school. The man was Jan Johannsen, the owner of a large offshore oil company, who lived with his family in the biggest house on the island. Directly next door to the Wood family were the Froodroys. The cake was tentatively transported from oven to table, and the kitchen began to swell with introductions, laughter, stories and a very messy crumbed floor, swiftly hoovered up by Tricver and Tornado. The Woods were welcomed by their neighbours; however, some locals proved to be more elusive.

- ▼ -

Summer had passed in their new home, and in between introductions to local villagers and unpacking her bedroom contents carefully into her new bedroom and orangery, Savannah was surprised to realise she hadn't even thought about her new school, which she started in a few days' time. Rich Froodroy was in her new class, along with the twins Ava and Frank, who were totally different to each other in personality and looks. The island had become home very quickly, and Savannah felt confident travelling around the island by bicycle on her own, something she would never have done before the move. She packed herself a picnic and clumsily mounted her old bicycle, throwing her picnic in the bike's front wicker basket. Tricver jumped up at the orangery door and slumped his head miserably against the glass.

"Do you want to come, Tricky?" She questioned the dog as if expecting a response. As he wagged his tail and cocked his head sideways, Savannah opened the door and called him to heel. She and Tricver stopped outside the Froodroy house next door and took a moment to admire their beautiful grass roof. One of the upstairs windows flew open and Rich appeared.

"He's not dead yet, then?" Rich gestured to Tricver. "Silly thing just wouldn't leave that house of yours. We gave him the life of a king, but he still thought he was better off in that glass house!" Rich wrinkled his nose indignantly. Tricver sat cooperatively next to the bike but peered around the rooftop, ignoring Rich but apparently looking for something. "Yeah, that's right, you mangy mutt. Ignore me and look for Elvis. Stay there, Savannah. I'm coming down," Rich hollered.

"He'll be waiting a long time, Rich. Elvis officially left the building, many years ago," Savannah giggled.

Rich jogged along the front path towards Savannah, swaggering his hips and snickering, "Not Elvis, the king of rock and roll. *That* Elvis," pointing his index finger at the roof. Rich repositioned his hands around his mouth into the shape of a megaphone and yelled, "Elvis!" Trotting on top of the rooftop was a goat. A dishevelled-looking specimen with beady eyes and long horns with tufts of dreadlocked hair that encroached on his visibility nearly covering his eyes. "Savannah, meet Elvis, groundsman extraordinaire," he introduced. Tricver wagged his tail and barked joyfully at Elvis, who promptly turned his large matted backside to him and trotted off audaciously along the rooftop to the back of the house. Rich grabbed his bike. "Where are we going, then?"

"I'm going for a picnic." Savannah raised her eyebrows.

"Well, I hope you packed enough for me, too," Rich smiled. He swung one of his dumpy legs over the tatty hand-me-down bike, which appeared to have seen better days, and together they set off, Rich's back wheel squeaking in complaint as he peddled. They rode through the village, past the school, past the church and around the huge rhubarb field. They peddled along the shoreline of the fjord, admiring Toftir, the village opposite.

"Toftir cheats." Rich pointed over to Toftir and made rude hand gestures in their direction.

"Rich, what on earth are you talking about?"

"Every year, Strendur have a rowing race against Toftir," Rich explained. "Us Strendur rowers, we are all bigger, smarter, have more practice sessions. Mr Johnson does our rowing strategy."

Savannah burst out laughing at Rich's apparent frustration, snickering into her hand uncontrollably. "Savannah!" Rich exclaimed through flared nostrils. "They are cheats. Strendur haven't won for fourteen years." He slammed his fists onto his handlebars, which tinkled in cruel irony from the bicycle bell.

"Okay, okay." Savannah held her arms up in the

air, surrendering to further debate. "Maybe at the next race you'll beat them, hey?" She nibbled on her bottom lip, feeling slightly ashamed for goading him.

"Next year, Sven and the rest of you Toftir lot, Strendur will run supreme!" Rich hurtled his voice across the fjord, shaking his fists and flexing his muscles in a mocking manner towards the picturesque town of Toftir, accompanied by Tricver barking in approval. They continued on their bike ride, putting Toftir to the back of their minds and finally stopped peddling at the mouth of the sea.

"Picnic time," Rich panted. They got off their bikes and walked through a large field filled with tall white flowers. They unceremoniously threw down their bikes and seated themselves in the middle of the swathe of flora. They greedily tucked into their jam sandwiches and slurped homemade rhubarb fizz from the thermos flask. They lay in haphazard contentment on the thick carpet of flowers, with Tricver sat patiently by their side waiting for scraps. The ambrosial rhubarb fizz was a little warm but proved thirst-quenching, and the high sugar content gave Savannah a much-needed energy boost after the long cycle ride. On the other side of the field, a fair distance away, tucked behind masses of blackberry bushes, was a cottage. The most beautiful traditional Faroese cottage, covered in white flowers with a puffin circling the roof as if playing in the wind.

Rich observed the direction of Savannah's gaze.

"That's the house of the doomed widow," he declared benevolently, rolling onto his front with his head facing towards the cottage, still chewing a mouthful of sandwich. Savannah caught his contagious laugh and also rolled over so the pair of them were both peering towards the dwelling. Rich crooked his neck towards Savannah's and whispered, "She's a witch, apparently." Rich kept talking but moved his arms so that his head could rest on his knuckles with his elbows on the ground. "Ava told me that a long time ago, before we were even born, this lady, the doomed widow, was married to Sid Rawling. Most people called him Sid the Sailor because he owned the biggest and most successful fishing boat on the islands. One particular year, the weather had been brutal and, on a November day, he went out to sea and got caught in a bad-tempered storm. If you look at the front of the house you can see a window looking straight out to sea." Savannah moved her neck away from Rich and glanced towards the front of the cottage. She noticed the window, its frame clothed in the same delicate flowers. Indeed, it boasted a perfect panoramic sea view. Shifting her eyes to the roof, she saw it was lush and neatly trimmed with the same flowers from the window frame lining the roof and doors.

Rich nudged Savannah's elbow, making her posture wobble. "As I was saying, the doomed widow looked out to sea where she could see her husband's boat tossing and turning dangerously in the waves.

Then came an almighty explosion. A tsunami-sized wave swallowed up Sid's boat, throwing fish, whales and an ocean of water out of the sea, over her and the neighbouring homes. She saw the whole thing, but somehow, she and her house survived, when all the other houses were completely destroyed and washed away. Several people were lost, including Sid, whose body was washed out to sea never to be found. That's why no one else will live here."

Savannah directed her soft gaze back to Rich. "Poor woman, it's not her fault, though. Why call her the doomed widow?"

"Savannah, no one caught in the explosion survived apart from her. People in Strendur think losing her husband made her go mad. The whales and fish were all dead when they were found; nothing the tsunami hit survived, nothing except her and that damned house." He wagged his finger to the cottage accusingly. "Rumour has it she's a witch who cast a spell to save herself and now she is doomed for surviving," he ranted, while taking a sip of rhubarb fizz from the flask. The clouds had shifted since they first lay their heads down in the field, and the sky was quickly changing colour from blue to the grey shadow of flint. A soft drizzle of rain began to coat Savannah's cropped, messy hair with a fine mist. They had been too busy gossiping about the doomed widow to take notice of the change in weather. Rain trickled down over Savannah's eyebrows, forcing her to rise from the wet blanket of flowers to pack away the remnants of the picnic.

"Come on, Rich, you can help, too, instead of guzzling the last of the rhubarb fizz," Savannah pestered over the quickening howl of wind, placing the flask into her bicycle basket. On doing this, her gaze returned back to the cottage in the distance and she noticed a lady coming out of its side door. She intuitively stopped and leaned forward, scrunching her eyes in an attempt to improve her vision.

"Rich, is that her? Is that the doomed widow?"

Rich looked over and scarpered around the rest of the picnic debris, throwing it hard into the basket and dragging his own bike from among the tangled flowers. "Just get on, Savannah, grab Tricky and get on your bike, quick!"

There wasn't enough time; the old woman was heading straight for them. She glided in a stealth-like motion across the field. The pretty white flowers parted as she slid towards them and, within a couple of seconds, they were face-to-face.

"Miss Wood, I presume? We've been waiting for you."

CHAPTER 3

THE DOOMED WIDOW

Savannah and Rich were frozen to the spot. Rich had one leg on and one off his rusty bicycle, so he slowly swung his mid-air leg to the ground, being careful not to take his eyes off the old woman in front of him. She wore a long velvet navy hooded cape, with flyaway grey hair tucked into the hood. Her pale complexion made her majestic blue eyes twinkle.

"We knew you were coming long before you arrived, Savannah. My name is Doreen and it is a real pleasure to meet you, my dear. I see you have met Tricver." The doomed widow smiled and held out her hand to Savannah, who shook it and returned the smile, without hesitation. Doreen nodded behind her and much to Savannah's surprise, she saw Mai walking towards them from the house.

"Are you going to put a spell on us?" Rich croaked. Doreen laughed softly, breaking her serious composure into a friendly smile. Mai reached them and warmly greeted Savannah before answering Rich's concern.

"I'm very pleased to introduce you to Doreen, Savannah." Mai smiled at Savannah and turned on her heels to Rich, answering, "Mr Froodroy, we are here to help and protect you. Will you please both come into Doreen's home for a cup of tea and we will tell you more?" Savannah accepted the invitation immediately and took hold of Mai's outstretched arm and linked it with her own, beginning to walk towards the cottage.

"Hold on, hold on." Rich stepped back in alarm. "How do you know my name?" He eyed Doreen with scrutiny. His chest fell as he looked to Savannah, who was already making her way across the field towards the cottage with Mai. With no other option, he ran to catch her up and scuttled alongside her, reluctantly clutching Savannah's spare arm, which she gave a little nudge to as they walked.

Inside the cottage was a welcoming botanical aroma. The kitchen was small with a round wooden table in the centre of the room, positioned under a skylight window, something Savannah hadn't considered possible with a grass roof.

"This is Richard Froodroy, but he prefers to be called Rich," Savannah introduced.

"So, where's your cauldron then?" Rich questioned Doreen cheekily. Savannah glared at him, but her scowl went unnoticed by her now belligerent companion.

Mai sat herself down on a worn brown leather chair as Doreen busied herself making tea. "It is true, people like myself and Mai are sometimes referred to as witches, but times have moved on, Mr Froodroy. We don't use cauldrons and we rarely cast spells on children," Doreen said, winking at Savannah.

"We also don't wear pointy hats or have black cats," Mai retorted to Rich, raising her eyebrows. Savannah smiled heartily at the ladies' good humour.

"Come and sit, tea is ready." Doreen gestured towards the table.

"Mmm, peppermint." Savannah exhaled as she blew on the surface of the steaming liquid in her fine bone china cup, to cool it down, before indulging in a tentative sip. As she did so, a large plant pot caught her attention on the windowsill, accompanied by several other pots of well-maintained herbs. "Doreen, I don't mean to be rude, but did you know that some people refer to you as the doomed widow?" Savannah asked cautiously. With this remark, Savannah noticed Mai move her gaze out of the front sea view window, the one that Rich had shown her during the picnic.

"I suppose it is only fair I should tell you why I earned such a reputation with some locals," Doreen replied thoughtfully.

"No, Doreen," Mai said firmly, getting to her feet. "Now is not the right time."

"Mai, these children have trusted us enough to come into my home and give us a chance, despite my hideous reputation. We are not blessed with the gift of time. Just look at the Scrabster ferry saga." The unlikely crowd sat huddled around the table, Savannah's and Rich's eyes wide with intrigue as Doreen prepared to recount her story of how she became known as the doomed widow. She cleared her throat and began...

"This is more than my recollection of events of the fateful night I lost my husband of twenty years, my darling Sid. Listen, for what I am about to tell you are facts of the Faroes that only a select number of patrons know. Over time, these facts have turned into whispered fables long forgotten by local people, but be warned – with this knowledge comes great risk and moral obligation." Savannah and Rich nodded in response.

"In the middle of the Norwegian Sea there is an underwater volcano, just one nautical mile from the coast of Strendur, which over the centuries has been given the name the 'Hellson'. The Hellson underwater volcano harbours a secret, evil, underwater world, miles wide, created and consumed by gas and greed."

"But how come it's not on maps?" Savannah questioned.

"Hundreds of years ago, Vikings were some of the first inhabitants to settle on these islands. However, they were not the first to discover them. Long before the Vikings discovered these islands, the Faroe Islands already provided an idyllic home to several farming families. However, despite their mild and gentle way of life, these local people maintained a secret: that out in the fjord was the Hellson, the cruel underwater world that had already claimed the lives of unsuspecting local sea folk. They believed the island they adored would provide their community with an answer to this problem. This answer came in the form of sapphire stone, naturally occurring in the land here. With experimentation, the locals found a way to use sapphires to prevent the Hellson exploding gas and trapping people. They discovered that sapphires soak up the Hellson's gas like a sponge, trapping it and containing it. So, they set about making a sapphire sea fortress. A simple boat containing beautiful sapphires, which they anchored directly above the Hellson to clean the expelled Hellson gas and prevent further entrapment of humans. The locals felt sure their prayers had been answered and the sapphire sea fortress worked well for several decades, until Ragnar and his men came sailing by. The Vikings stumbled across these islands by luck. This particular group of Vikings were led by Ragnar Wolff, an infamously brutal warrior, feared by all and fuelled by greed. In search of new lands to conquer, they rowed here, in between Strendur and Toftir to our fjord connecting to the Norwegian Sea, in order to murder and enslave the Faroe Islands' inhabitants and take the islands as their own. Ragnar Wolff's greedy eyes instantly spotted the glistening sapphire gems bobbing invitingly in the crystal-clear water and he set about removing them from the sapphire sea fortress by axe, splintering the boat and unsettling the gas below. On removing these gems, he destabilised the Hellson's gas below, causing an almighty explosion, catapulting the whole Viking longboat down into the Hellson underwater world, never to be seen again. The villagers watched the event unfold, knowing the pure greed of the Vikings entering into the Hellson would only feed the destruction and the savage, murderous cycle further. And so, the Sapphire Society was born. Although the community had been saved from Ragnar Wolff, the Hellson had gained an enormous amount of gas producing strength from the greedy Vikings it had entrapped. The locals could no longer set sapphire defences in the sea, for other Vikings and explorers would only steal them, so they developed a highly trained group of local villagers who would chase and cleanse the expelled gas and deal with any Hellson events, so as to maintain balance and prevent the Hellson taking over. Hellson gas is absorbed by sapphires, which is why their sea fortress had them on board, but it is not just sapphires that are required for the gas-removing process. Once the sapphires are full of gas, they begin to lose their ability to soak up foul smog, and lose their shine and splendour. It takes a meticulous individual specialist blend of local herbs to filter the gas and carefully release the cleansed molecules from the gem, safely into the atmosphere. Patrons of the Sapphire Society take on one of two roles. The first role is of a 'shiner'. These are hedge witch members who have the plant knowledge and intuition to make the recipe for the sapphire-cleansing process, like myself, and Mai is an apprentice. The second role is of a 'chaser'. These brave society members attack and soak up Hellson gas, using sapphires, disarming the Hellson and neutralising the surrounding air to prevent the Hellson exploding and trapping more victims."

"What do you mean, entrapment?" Savannah asked, finally intervening.

"The leaking gas will attach itself to people passing over the Hellson," Doreen reiterated. "You cannot see the Hellson, so people rowing over, or on ships or planes, have no idea it is there. When a human passes over the Hellson, it secretes a vast black gas cloud and poisons the person to unconsciousness, until the unsuspecting person is suctioned down into the Hellson's entrance," Doreen explained.

"Well, what then? What happens to these people dragged down into the Hellson?" Rich asked.

"The underwater world has turned into a strange community of trapped victims. The gas intoxicates their brains. Nourished only by the noxious gas, the trapped victims remember nothing of their life above the Hellson, surviving below water in a vicious cycle. The more people it entraps, the more gas is released, in turn entrapping more people by an ever-widening gas perimeter," Doreen explained.

"So, Doreen, when I was on board the Scrabster ferry, something happened, something strange," Savannah said.

"My dear, it was indeed the Hellson erupting. It was no coincidence that Mai was on board. Like I said, we knew you were coming, and we knew there would likely be repercussions for someone with your heritage venturing so close to the Hellson boundary. We had Sapphire Society members protecting you every step of your journey. What we didn't anticipate was you wearing that," Doreen said, pointing to Savannah's necklace. "What do you know of this necklace?" Doreen asked.

"What do you mean, my heritage? All I know is what I told Mai on the ferry. It was my grandmother's, she gave it to my mother, but she didn't like it so she gave it to me," Savannah replied.

"Savannah, your grandmother was of paramount importance to the Faroe Islands' Sapphire Society and to the international bureau. All over the world there are societies like ours, battling against underwater volcanoes of greed. The human race is at a crossroads. In every one of us there is a darkness and a light. No one is all good or all evil, but as individuals, we have the choice which side wins. Your grandmother dedicated her life to good. She chose to feed the light in her soul and encouraged and assisted others to do the same. So much so, she was awarded the sapphire of light, which is what you are wearing now. This is an international bureau award for outstanding bravery and commitment to our cause. Our battles against the Hellson are becoming more troublesome. The bubbles of escaping gas are making our waters increasingly turbulent, and the perimeter of noxious gas is widening at an alarming rate."

"So, if it was the Hellson that caused the trouble on the ferry crossing, there is something I need you to explain," said Savannah. "When I was on the deck, holding on to the door, I saw a large mass of black fog, which I guess must have been escaped Hellson gas?"

"Yes, that was Hellson gas, trying to suffocate and intoxicate you in order to make you unconscious so that you would fall in the water," said Mai.

"But that noise, what was that awful ear-twisting, disturbing noise?" Savannah questioned.

"I know the very sound of which you speak, for it still haunts my own nightmares. That noise is the cry of trapped souls below in the underwater world. Humans are trapped in by the gas, but soon the noxious gas poisons their brains and mutates them into green-eyed beings, which we call 'the muted'. The gas does not trick the disturbed souls, like the body. The bodies of these poor trapped people are poisoned, unaware of their demise, but their souls aren't as easily fooled. The souls are crying out for help every time there is an explosion, and they are getting louder with increased frequency," explained Doreen, solemnly.

Savannah looked down to the necklace lying bedraggled and lacklustre in the palm of her hand. "I only put it on because it used to belong to Grandma. It was supposed to be a pretty sentimental heirloom, not a container for stinking old gas," Savannah said, fighting back tears. Doreen walked over to Savannah, kneeled at her chair and held out her hand, gesturing for Savannah to give it to her. Doreen took the necklace and walked over to her windowsill, picking herbs with her spare hand.

"Blimey, Savannah, do you think she's going to give it back?" Rich muttered under his breath.

"I'm not sure I want it back," Savannah whispered.

Mai held out her arms and gently ushered the children to the window, so they could see what Doreen was doing. Doreen had a wicker trug cradled in her left arm and she was picking some of the white flowers from the field where Savannah and Rich had eaten their picnic. She walked over to a tree at the field's entrance, carefully selected a leaf and also put that into the trug.

"You have to admit, Savannah," Rich said, whispering into her ear, "with the dark blue cloak, serious nature and odd habits, she really does look like a witch."

"She wears dark clothing because she is still grieving for her husband, Mr Froodroy," Mai replied in a surprisingly quiet tone, considering Rich's insensitive statement.

Doreen spent a short while walking in and around the house, beach and fields, foraging for whole plants, leaves, stems and flowers. She returned through the kitchen door, adding some of the white flowers that covered the cottage into the now large collection of different plants over spilling from the trug. She tipped the contents of the trug onto the oak table and the children watched in awe as she prepared the plants. Some she lay under the skylight on the kitchen table, where the sun would reach them. Others she bashed ferociously with a large wooden mallet. The petals of some purple flowers were ground into a paste with a pestle and mortar, while the white cottage flowers that Doreen called angelica were made into a decoction using hot water. Finally, Doreen took the ingredients and put them all into a small bowl, placing Savannah's necklace into the mixture.

"In an hour, your sapphire will have its glow back. We must not move it or the escaping gas will cause turbulence on the island," Doreen instructed.

"Thank you," Savannah smiled.

"Wow, have we just witnessed sapphire-cleansing?" Rich asked.

"Yes, Rich, you certainly have, and not a black cat or broomstick in sight," Mai jested. The four reunited around the kitchen table and watched the cleansing process at work. The dull sapphire slowly began to gleam, with the toxic gas being removed. Doreen opened the skylight above the table and Savannah watched in awe as a small dark cloud emerged from the plant mixture. It revolved with the same action as a tornado, but in slow motion.

"So why are you called the doomed widow?" Rich asked Doreen thoughtfully, with newfound admiration.

"My husband cannot rest yet, stuck in that underwater hell. As Savannah heard, his and many others' souls are crying out for help. He cannot rest, so nor shall I. He was captured twenty years ago and I made a vow I would not leave our home and I would not rest until either he is back or I have cured these islands of this curse," Doreen replied.

"Surely this is just a natural phenomenon, a hiccup of mother nature?" Savannah questioned, missing no detail of what Doreen had said.

"Mai here joined us as a trainee apprentice from Utsira, a tiny little Norwegian island where underwater volcanoes are even becoming a problem there in such a remote place. This, my dear, however, is a discussion for another time. Your mother will be worried. Take your necklace, along with a bunch of angelica, and go home. Here, Rich, this is a gift from me," said Doreen. She handed him a small, perfectly spherical shiny blue sapphire.

"A sapphire!" Rich exclaimed.

"Yes, take it; you will need it as an entry requirement for the next Sapphire Society meeting. I want you to chaperone Savannah. Now go, our next meeting is tomorrow evening at the church at 7pm. Don't be late, and remember, you must have a sapphire on your person, easily visible, to be allowed in," Doreen said as they walked outside.

Savannah and Rich mounted their bikes and cycled home quickly to avoid repercussions from their parents. "I can't take it all in," Rich shouted over the wind and in between panting breaths as he pedalled. "How many people are in this society, do you think? I've lived here my whole life and I never knew anything about sapphires, let alone the Hellson." He pointed out to the fjord, making his bike wobble unsteadily.

"I don't know. I guess we'll find out tomorrow," said Savannah. "I'll meet you at the side of the church, under the big window at five to seven."

"The window where I first saw the inside of your nostrils?" Rich joked. Savannah didn't respond. She blushed but reached home before Rich noticed her embarrassment.

CHAPTER 4

TRAINSPOTTING

Rich waited outside the church window ten minutes earlier than they had arranged. He had spent the day finding ingenious ways of displaying his sapphire. After first attaching it to his glasses then sewing it onto a tie, he settled for borrowing his father's old trilby hat and sewing it onto the side artistically. Not many people would notice the small stone, but those who needed to would see it revealed in its full glory, proudly on display.

Savannah made her way along the sea bridge, plucking and eating ripe, juicy blackberries as she walked towards the church. Her own day had been spent looking after Tom while her parents went to visit friends on the other side of the fjord. Time spent with Tom was always fun and made her feel useful.

"Nice hat," Savannah said, noticing the new ensemble instantly.

Rich beamed. "Ready, Miss Wood?" he asked, holding out his arm for Savannah, like in old black and white films.

"I think so." She swallowed, pointing to her now gleaming sapphire necklace draped around her neck. The pair walked up to the door but quickly found themselves feeling a little crestfallen. There was a poster on the church door, which read, *Trainspotting with the church. Every Tuesday at 7 pm.*

"What?" Rich cried, dropping Savannah's arm. "It's Tuesday today! We're not here to learn about locomotives." But suddenly Mai appeared behind them.

"Just tilt your sapphire to the door knocker," Mai whispered covertly, "and the door will open." Rich tipped his hat towards the door, and as Mai had said, the door creaked open.

"Did you just hear a growl?" Rich asked Savannah quietly as they shuffled through the doorway. Savannah didn't respond. The church had only a few people present, sitting separately on pews. All eyes followed the pair as Rich and Savannah took their seats next to Doreen, who was sat near the back.

"Are we in the right place? Only, the poster on the door said that tonight is the trainspotting group," Rich questioned Doreen immediately on being seated. Doreen and Mai chuckled mischievously.

"We have to have a guise for the Sapphire Society, so non-members don't become suspicious or concerned. We used to be the knitting club until one Tuesday night, Mrs Nillson at number 73 decided to come along." As Doreen relayed the details of the incident, Mai was crying uncontrollably with laughter and described how the whole group had to knit for twelve weeks every Tuesday night, just to make sure Mrs Nillson didn't become suspicious of the real agenda.

"After a non-member accidently joined the group, it was decided we should make the group something nobody in the village would be interested in," said Doreen.

"Still waiting for the chairman?" Mai enquired of Doreen.

"Yes, I informed him of our new members, so he said he would be a little delayed," Doreen whispered in response.

"Actually, trainspotting is becoming quite popular, despite our islands not having a rail system," Rich piped up. "My pa is an avid anorak; he travels all over the world to view trains." Mai and Doreen gave Rich a weak smile, and without needing further introduction, the chairman of the Sapphire Society entered the church. Rich and Savannah gasped in unison when they saw who it was. The small group of people rose from their seats and the room fell silent. Savannah beamed as the chairman walked towards her.

"Pa?" Rich shouted out, finally able to find his voice. Mr Froodroy gave a nod to the rest of the members, and they were all seated, apart from Rich and Savannah, who were too stunned to notice what was going on around them.

"I am pleased to see you are joining us, Richard. Doreen tells me she and Mai have filled you in on some of our islands' issues," said Mr Froodroy.

"Are you really the chairman, Pa? I thought you went out on Tuesday nights to trainspot," Rich said shakily. Sniggers ensued from society members at hearing Rich's comment.

"Yes, son. I really am the chairman, and before me it was your grandfather. We are not here to learn about our non-existent railway network, but we are here legitimately to do good work," said Mr Froodroy, a remark at which members of the group cheered. "Welcome, son, and welcome, Savannah; we have long been awaiting both of you. In fact, you are the first new members since Mai joined us two years ago." Rich gave his father a hug and sat down proudly. Mr Froodroy wore a long navy blue gown with a hood which dangled down his back, and a flower in his buttonhole. With closer inspection, Savannah noticed it wasn't a real flower and the centre was a beautifully spherical sapphire, much like the stone Doreen had given to Rich. Mr Froodroy slid almost motionlessly past their pew and to the front of the church.

"How did he do that?" Savannah whispered to Rich.

"*How did he do that?*" bellowed Mr Froodroy loudly to Savannah in a jovial tone. Savannah's face burnt instantly crimson. She thought she had whispered quietly but hadn't taken into account the acoustics of the small church. "That and many more questions will be answered this evening. Tonight, my gems, we will welcome my dear son and the much-anticipated Savannah Wood into our little community." Raucous applause and shouts of welcome echoed through the church. "Firstly, I would like everyone to introduce themselves and describe to our new apprentices who they are and what they do. After which, we will have some of my good wife's rhubarb fizz and I will answer any of the new members' questions." He stepped down from the pulpit and gestured to a lady in the front row to stand forward. The lady now standing in the pulpit was petite and plump, with wild ginger hair and spectacles. She too wore a navy blue robe, which Savannah then noticed all members except Mai were wearing.

"Hello, Richard. Nice to meet you, Savannah. I am Delia Tuni. I have been a society member for twenty-seven years and my role in our little society is as a chaser." Delia had sapphire spectacles, which were rather outrageous but suited her, in a funny sort of way. "I am also your new teacher, so in school, you will refer to me as Mrs Tuni please."

Rich rolled his eyes, whispering, "No way, Mrs Tuni, a chaser?"

Delia continued, "Doreen, would you stand up next, please? Doreen is our chief shiner and also our deputy chairman. Doreen is also known frequently in these islands as the *doomed widow*." Delia boomed her voice for the last part in a humorous tone, making her audience laugh riotously. Doreen glided the short distance to the pulpit and received a ripple of applause from the other members.

"I am very pleased to see you all here safe and well this evening; I understand it has been testing times for the chasers among us." Doreen continued to describe to the society members how she introduced herself to Rich and Savannah. Savannah couldn't help but notice the calmness and awe that her persona commanded. Members leaned forward to listen intently to her quiet tone of voice and awarded her raucous applause when she graciously finished speaking.

The next member to introduce himself was Terrence Ruff. He was a short, stocky man with a shaved head. Savannah recognised him but couldn't place where from. He spoke in a gruff cockney accent and wore a sapphire stud earring in his right ear.

"'Ello again, Savannah, Rich. As you may remember, I am Terrence Ruff, but most people 'ere call me Truffy. I am a chaser, but I also work as a removal man," he said.

"That's it! Terrence was our removal man," Savannah whispered to Rich.

"I apologise for the bad breath. It was Mai's brilliant suggestion," he continued. "She made me eat a special type of Norwegian seaweed to give me such bad breath, you wouldn't want to come near me, so I could get on with the job of *chasing the 'ellson*." He jeered, throwing his fists in the air, much to the amusement of the small crowd.

Mai was the final member of the group to stand forward. She sauntered to the pulpit, her long, silky hair bouncing in time with her footsteps.

"As you both know, my role is as an apprentice sapphire-cleanser, or shiner, as we prefer to be called. I would very gladly assist you both with anything that you need," Mai concluded.

"Now we are all introduced, I would like to ask some of our long-standing members to put themselves forward for mentoring our new gems," said Mr Froodroy. "Our present count is as follows. We have two shiners; Doreen and apprentice, Mai, and three chasers; myself, Truffy and Delia. There is no rush for either of you to decide your chosen path."

"Chaser!" shouted Rich.

Mr Froodroy chuckled at his son's interruption. "Yes, I thought you would be best suited for that role," he said.

Truffy stood up from his pew, straightened his cloak and said, "Mr Froodroy, I wonder if you would consider meself as young Rich's mentor? I've chased both 'ere in the Faroes and all over Blighty for the diamonds, totting up twenty years' worth of chasin'. I would be honoured to train young Rich in the realms of chasing," Truffy said, doing a little bow after he spoke.

"Oh, bravo, Truffy. All in favour, say 'aye'." said Mr Froodroy.

A unanimous chorus of 'aye' bellowed from the pews, and Truffy stuck his thumb up to Rich, who grinned in response.

"Which leaves Savannah," Mr Froodroy smiled, tilting his head to one side, as if her answer was written somewhere on her head. Savannah inhaled deeply. She felt sure she wanted to be a shiner, but her determination on the ferry just a month ago spurred her on that she could maybe rise to the challenge of chasing.

"Mr Chairman, if I may interject. I think we must consider Savannah's complicated family history," Delia speculated.

"Yes, yes, Delia." Mr Froodroy flapped his hands dismissively. "But that is for far-in-the-future contemplation."

"But Mr Chairman, we cannot rule these things out. Her grandmother——" Delia was swiftly interrupted by Mr Froodroy, who put his hand up in a halt gesture and stood up sharply, causing a loud screech as his chair scratched the floor.

"My dear Savannah, where do you think your skills lie? What are your thoughts?" Mr Froodroy twiddled his sapphire flower between his thumb and forefinger as he spoke directly to her.

"Since I was young, I have always wanted to be a hedge witch," Savannah said slowly. "I want to make people better with plants, but my skills in this are pretty non-existent, Mr Chairman."

Delia huffed but Mai and Doreen responded with a smile. "Wonderful, wonderful. Doreen? As chief shiner and deputy chair, I presume you would take on Savannah's mentoring?" Doreen smiled but upon opening her mouth was quickly interrupted by Mai.

"Actually, Doreen, Mr Chairman, I know it is rather against the president's wishes, but I wondered if I might take on Savannah's mentoring?" she asked, her long brown eyelashes fluttering.

"That is against the rules, Mai. As you know, a new recruit must be trained by a fully cloaked, long-standing Sapphire member, and although you have reputedly done good work in Utsira, you still have your own exams to pass and have only been a trainee member with the Sapphires for two years," replied Mr Froodroy. Mai looked to the floor, and Doreen rested her hand on her shoulder.

"Mr Chairman," Truffy said, standing up. "I believe I may 'ave a solution for my Mai – I mean, our Mai. She has been telling me for an age about wanting to train young Savs, so what about a job share? Doreen can keep an eye on 'er, but Mai can help with her training."

Mr Froodroy looked at Doreen, rubbing the flower in his buttonhole carefully, pacing up and down the church aisle before responding. "Savannah, congratulations. You have two mentors." Mai and Doreen both looked at Savannah with smiles.

"I can't wait to get started," said Mai.

"Well, my gems. What an evening! We have two new apprentices. I will have to inform our international president at the bureau," announced Mr Froodroy. Savannah's and Rich's baffled faces were immediately spotted by the chairman, who Savannah could already tell missed nothing. "Savannah, Rich," Mr Froodroy spread his arms out wide and continued, "it is not just the Sapphire Society fighting the Hellson. All around the globe are little societies like ours battling against the consequences of human greed. Every ocean, even some stretches of rivers and fjords, have their own debilitating underwater volcanoes trying to wreak havoc on mankind, causing the same problems as our own Hellson in the fjord here. There is the Diamond Society in England fighting the trojan beneath the Thames, the Ruby Society in South Africa, the Slate Society in Wales, the American Onyxes, to mention a few. There's a map showing all of our societies, which I will ensure you get a copy of, Savannah. All of our little societies are governed by the bureau, the best the world has to offer in aqua defence. Our president of the bureau, Nanuq Samossen, has been expecting our news. I will contact him at the earliest opportunity. Now, Truffy, Delia, I am gasping for some fizz. Can your chasing results wait until next time? We have such a joyous occasion, it seems a shame to spoil it with reality," said Mr Froodroy. Delia and Truffy reluctantly nodded to each other and Truffy whispered something into Delia's ear, to which she nodded again.

"My gems, I can see Doreen is ahead of me as usual and has prepared refreshments at the back of the church, so I will conclude today's meeting without further ado." With this remark, all society members, except for Rich and Savannah, put their hands by their sides and raised their feet at least two inches from the ground.

"Fear not, Richie boy, I'll teach you this, all right. You'll be the best gas glider this island has known by the time I've finished your training," shouted Truffy across the church.

After drinks, Savannah and Rich headed out of the church but Truffy grabbed Rich by the shoulders.

"Right, mate, tomorrow after school, you come to the removal depot and bring your rock," he said.

"My rock?" Rich replied.

"Well, yeah." Truffy pointed to the sapphire on his hat. "You ain't gonna get very far without it now, are ya?" he laughed, tapping Rich on the back. Truffy then reached over and linked arms with Mai.

"Come on, me lovely mentor, I'll walk you home." Truffy bowed his head a little as he softly addressed Mai.

Mai returned his smile. "Thank you for persuading the chairman to give me a chance, Truffy." Mai smiled coyly at Truffy and linked tightly with his arm. "Goodnight, Savannah. I'm so pleased the chairman has let me teach you. Meet me at Doreen's tomorrow after school and we'll go from there," she said, her long brown hair catching the wind as she and Truffy walked off arm in arm. Savannah and Rich mounted their bikes.

"Do you think your ma knows about all of this?" asked Savannah as they gently peddled home.

"Well, I'd imagine so. There's no secrets in my house," Rich replied. Savannah giggled but chose not to point out the large secret that had been kept from him.

"What about your ma? Do you think she knows about the necklace and your grandma and the Sapphire Society?"

Savannah didn't respond but pondered the question long after she had said goodbye to Rich and tucked herself into bed. She couldn't decide on the answer.

CHAPTER 5

STRENDUR SCHOOL

Strendur school was located past the church and along Strendur Fjord, boasting good fjord views reaching over to Toftir, the village opposite. Savannah's walk to school took exactly nine minutes. From her home, number 13, she walked past the Froodroys', down past the main stretch of houses, past the church and the boat builders' yard, past Truffy's removal depot and over the sea bridge, which wasn't actually a bridge but a raised path that ran directly along the edge of the fjord all the way to school. As she walked, she took in the beauty of the island. The water of the fjord was gently lapping at the sea bridge, and she noticed four rowing boats heading towards the school from Toftir. She continued walking, dodging the water, which threatened to drench her shoes and lapped around her feet. With dry shoes and an equally dry mouth, Savannah reached the door.

The school building was totally different in appearance to the rest of the buildings on the island. It was more like a castle constructed out of flint, with a moss roof and floor-to-ceiling arched windows with gargoyles sitting on top of every one. It was also the tallest building on the whole of the Faroe Islands, not just Eysturoy. It had a regal round tower nearly touching the clouds, the crown of which was a lighthouse; its jewel, a glistening brass bell. The whole building looked like it was sat on a cloud of moss. In fact, parts of the building looked like moss had almost taken over. Savannah struggled to push the huge front door open and on seeing inside was surprised to see a grand-looking entrance hall, with not one but two staircases. A grand oak staircase took centre stage in the middle of the hall and a small spiral metal staircase, almost hidden from view, was tucked in the back corner.

"We're in here." Savannah heard a voice from the room to her right but became aware of a group of people behind her. A group of children carrying oars and school backpacks smiled and said good morning as they walked around her into various different classrooms. Savannah gingerly entered her classroom and immediately saw Ava and Frank, the oil baron's children, sitting on desks at the back of the room.

"It's so nice to have a new face in the class." Ava stood up. Frank looked at her, expressionless. "Your desk is here, between me and Rich," she added, pointing to a wooden flip-top lid desk.

"Good morning, class, and what a beautiful day it is! Are we all present and correct? The time is 08.19, so I expect you all to be correctly positioned with your outdoor wear hanging in the hallway, which includes wet oars, Sven," announced Delia, looking directly at one of the boys from the large group who came into the class behind her.

"They are from Toftir; they row here every morning," Ava said about the group of children behind them and pointed out of the window to their boats tied up in the fjord.

"As you can see, we are very pleased to welcome our new student, Savannah Wood. For Savannah's benefit, I will quickly run through our school's schedule. School begins at 08.20 and finishes at 15.30. The sea bell shall be rung at these times." On cue, the bell sounded loudly, making the class jump. "Yes, yes, there it is. It is exceptionally loud, and after twenty years of teaching here, it still surprises me every time."

Rich arrived, thundering through the door, with his coat half on and very red-faced, just as the last chime of the bell struck, dropping his flask and books as he skidded to his desk.

"Master Froodroy, I see our little end-of-term chat regarding punctuality has been long-forgotten during your holidays." Rich looked at Savannah, grimacing. The first lesson of the day was English literature. Savannah remained attentive but occasionally diverted her focus to her new classmates. The rowers from Toftir seemed friendly but kept to themselves. Freya sat behind her and Rich, proving herself to be especially studious, with long locks of golden-brown hair which she twirled around her finger as she read. Ava seemed to be very bright but calm and reserved, with a slight mischievous streak, which Rich generally tried to bring out by engaging her in anything he deemed they could plausibly get away with.

At lunchtime, the class moved into the dining room. The chalkboard menu on the wall read, *Fish pie and rhubarb crumble for pudding.*

"Ah, delicious," Savannah said breezily. The rest of the class groaned, slumping forward onto their desks.

"The first time you taste it, it's good. Maybe even the second, third and fourth time, but this is our lunch every single day," explained Frank.

"It's all stupid Mr Johnson can cook and, quite honestly, it's just not good enough," shouted Sven, standing up and pushing his chair back with a squeak. The room fell silent.

Bursting through the door came a decrepit elderly man, wielding a wooden spoon. "Is that so, you ungrateful, nasty little piece of detritus?"

Rich leaned over to Savannah and whispered, "Meet Mr Johnson." He smirked and folded his arms as he began to rest back into his seat.

"Mr Johnson, I, er, wasn't being, er…" Sven leant back, stuttering.

"During the war, I cooked for 452 troops every day, three times a day. None of them ever complained! In fact, they were grateful." Mr Johnson waved the wooden spoon with ever-increasing closeness to Sven's face. "The squadron said please and thank you and can I have more, please? You lot don't know you're bloody born!" he snarled.

"Mr Johnson, language, please! Now, what appears to be the kerfuffle?" Delia calmly interrupted his rant, much to the apparent relief of Sven who was still eyeing the wooden spoon near his face. Delia led Mr Johnson out of the classroom to the courtyard outside, where the children could hear muffled voices and soon smelt a large waft of pipe tobacco.

"Oi, Sven. Why do you have to be so rude all the time?" asked Frank.

"Me? Rude? I was just telling the truth. The silly old twerp, he shouldn't even be here," shouted Sven, storming out of the dining room.

"What did he mean by that? He shouldn't be here?" Savannah asked her classmates. The class looked down at the table. No one spoke or answered Savannah's question. Even Rich pretended to be distracted by something outside.

"As boring as it can be, Sven hasn't eaten his rhubarb crumble. I think I'll help him by finishing it off," Rich diverted. Ava and Freya chuckled as they watched the leftovers of Sven's lunch quickly disappear.

The rest of the school day passed without further excitement or explanation of the lunchtime incident. "I love this walk home. I don't think I'll ever get bored of it," Savannah said, once they had left school for the day.

"Bye!" Rich shouted to the group rowing across the fjord to Toftir. "They are still cheats at rowing, though," he quietly confided to Savannah. "Ooh, look, a seal!" Rich pointed to near the Toftir rowing boat. "Is that how you lot win the race; you get the seal to push you along?" Rich jibed at Sven and his friends.

"You're a bad loser, Froodroy. You lose because your knitted scarf gets caught in your oar," Sven laughed.

"He seems... interesting." Savannah raised her eyebrows.

"Who, Sven? Yeah, he's great," he said sarcastically with a grumpy face. "If you don't mind the sporty blond hair and good-looking curse he has," Rich said, lightening the tone of conversation.

"Well, he and Frank both seem grumpy to me," Savannah said.

"Sven is a pain, but Frank is usually okay, although he has been a bit out of sorts recently," Rich replied, pulling a grumpy face as he said it, making Savannah laugh.

"What did Sven mean when he said Mr Johnson shouldn't be here?" Savannah asked.

Rich paused thoughtfully before replying. "Well, Mr Johnson came to the Faroe Islands during the Second World War, when he met his wife, Helga, a local girl. Shortly after they married, Helga Johnson disappeared. The British army wanted him to return to England, but he wouldn't leave without Helga and wanted to stay here in case she ever decided to come back to him. The army called him a deserter. The local people in Strendur think he bumped her off. Some people say he has no right to be here because Helga has gone, but he's made this island his home and has been here a very long time. He never did remarry," Rich explained.

"There are rather a lot of sad love stories on this island, aren't there? How did she disappear?" Savannah asked.

"Well, if we knew that, she wouldn't be missing, would she!" Rich replied cheekily. Before Savannah was able to respond with an equally cheeky comeback, a huge wave reached over the section of the sea bridge where Ava and Frank were walking ahead of them, drenching Frank completely but just missing his sister.

"What the shmuggles was that?" roared Frank, looking angrier than Savannah could have imagined possible.

"That was water, I think," whispered Rich in Savannah's ear, making her laugh uncontrollably.

The crowd rowing back to Toftir cheered and shouted, "Do you want a towel, Frank?"

The wave had narrowly missed Ava, who was walking a few steps behind. "I can't wait to tell Ma about this, Frank," she said, giggling.

"Well, as much as I would love to continue laughing at grumpy Frank's expense, I'm going to see Doreen now. I bet she'll be able to tell me all about Mr Johnson's wife," Savannah said.

"Yeah, well, I'm off to Truffy's. He's going to make me the best gas glider on the island, whatever one of those is," said Rich.

Savannah said goodbye and continued in the opposite direction to Rich, towards Doreen's cottage. It was quite a long walk from school. She had to walk along the whole length of the sea bridge and across a stretch of rubble coastline, up a driftwood staircase and across the angelica field of white flowers. The pretty blooms on the angelica plant were beginning to wilt as summer faded and autumn came into season. Savannah saw the dazzling floral roof glisten in the afternoon light and watched smoke puffing comfortingly out of the chimney. She felt a warm breeze behind her and, on turning her head, noticed Doreen gliding alongside her.

"Eooh, Doreen! You scared me!" Savannah yelped, jumping back and laughing at the same time.

Doreen's eyes twinkled mischievously and while linking Savannah's arm, she raised her left arm palm-side down, and Savannah felt her feet and body rise up from the ground in a smooth but forceful motion, the wilting angelicas bending around her toes, so that she wasn't even touching them. They glided gracefully through the fields and stopped at the front door, where, for the second time, she noticed a puffin.

"I thought you should sample some of the Sapphire Society benefits, since you have already encountered so many society responsibilities. Oh, and that's my puffin, Petunia," Doreen added, gesturing to the puffin and opening the front door. Doreen's cottage was a quiet hive of activity. The kettle was bubbling on the fire and there was a gas formation above the kitchen table, which was gently dispersing through the open skylight in the roof above the table. "I'm not sure where Mai has got to, but I'm sure she won't be long. In the meantime, I'll show you something I shined earlier. These are Delia's sapphire shield glasses," she said, holding up the pot that held the spectacles. "They were full of fog and gas when she gave them to me this morning, but now they're nearly as good as new. Have you got your sapphire shield on you, my dear?" asked Doreen.

"Sapphire shield?" Savannah raised an eyebrow. Doreen pointed at her necklace. "Oh, I see, my necklace. Yes, I see what you mean. I suppose they are shields, aren't they?" Savannah pondered.

"You can get closer as long as you have your sapphire on you. Rule number one of shining, Savannah: always be a safe shiner. If you get sucked into the Hellson, it could be decades before we can replace you, so shining safety is paramount."

Savannah nodded but was more concerned about getting stuck in the Hellson than how the Sapphire Society would replace her. They both leaned in closer to the pot containing Delia's murky blue framed glasses, watching the gas gently and occasionally aggressively exit from the stone. Mesmerised, Savannah sat with a cup of tea, watching the gas's reluctant dance to exit the sapphire glasses. Doreen began to chuckle, looking directly over Savannah's shoulder. Savannah turned around to find several potted plants crowded around the base of the chair. She knew Doreen hadn't moved them there; she had been with her the entire time.

"Keep watching; more are on their way," Doreen said. She was right; the large potted lavender slid gently off the windowsill and started to shimmy towards the table.

"How is this possible?" Savannah asked, flabbergasted. Another pot, a black Mitcham peppermint plant, also started moving towards her, albeit less gracefully, in a crab-like motion, the bottom of the pot rotating each side at a time to edge a tiny bit closer with each shunt.

"One of the joys of being a shiner is that plants seem to intuitively want to be around you. They can move, if they trust their audience, but can also communicate very effectively with each other and with certain people, too," Doreen explained. Savannah's attention had moved to the plants instead of the gas. She noticed her favourite plant still on the windowsill.

"What is your favourite plant, Savannah?" Savannah pointed to the aloe vera. "You will find aloe vera at the centre of your shining recipe," Doreen said.

"But aren't you going to teach me the shining recipe for sapphire-cleansing?" asked Savannah.

"Oh no, no, no. Each shiner has their own unique characteristics, their own strengths and flaws, which all need balancing in their concoction," she explained. "Therefore, each shiner must make their own elixir, from past experience, research, learning from mentors and most importantly, based on what they feel is the right combination for the specific gem that is being cleansed," Doreen explained.

Savannah felt slightly crestfallen. She had hoped to prove herself useful to the Sapphire Society quickly but now realised she had lots to learn before she could really help defend the island against the Hellson.

"Don't feel disheartened," Doreen smiled. "Plants have an intuitive power to know what is right in this world, and I believe you do, too. As you can see, the aloe vera seems to share my opinion, because I've not seen this happen to anyone else before."

Doreen pointed to Savannah's feet. A huge aloe vera plant had appeared next to her leg, and more were coming her way, some moving in a very slow sloth-like motion, while some smaller ones were skidding quickly across the floor. Within a few minutes, Savannah was surrounded. The largest of the aloe vera crawled slowly up the table leg and positioned itself in front of her, wrapping its jelly-filled stalks around her wrist.

"Their wish is clear. You must take this home and nurture it like you would a child, for this is the beginning of your shining journey. You will find your recipe through the paths you choose and the innermost thoughts of your being. Listen, my dear, for your recipe will then unfold, often in the strangest of journeys," said Doreen.

"What's your main plant?" asked Savannah.

"Angelica, of course. I spent a year trying to clear it off my roof; it just returned. Then the field around me became filled, too. It was only when the bureau president, Nanuq Samossen, came to visit Sid and I many years ago and he pointed out the plant's overwhelming desire to be near me that I realised its significance. Angelica has defended me and my home and brought me back from despair when all hope was lost," Doreen said, pausing a moment in silence. "The aloe will help defend you and your home against the Hellson." A knock at the door interrupted them.

"Ahh, it must finally be Mai," Doreen said, but in fact it was Delia who entered, bellowing, "Hello, shiners!"

She sat herself down brusquely into the chair opposite Savannah. "I hope you enjoyed my teaching today, Savannah? Any tea going, Doreen?" Doreen smiled, getting up and putting the kettle onto the stove. "Did you see my specs, Savannah? They were the murkiest I have ever seen them. It was one hell of a chase. I caught a whole bubble, right there out in the sea near the school!" Delia pointed past the angelica field and into the fjord. "Cheeky gas leak made it all the way up to the school path; it could have been disastrous. It's great to have back-up in the school in case it happens again," said Delia, carefully examining her sparkling spectacles before positioning them back onto her face.

"Savannah is concentrating on shining at the moment, Delia," Doreen replied shrewdly.

"Yes, yes, I know," Delia replied, giving Savannah a wink.

CHAPTER 6

SECRETS REVEALED

"After-school club, Savannah?" Theodore looked at his watch as Savannah walked through the front door later than her parents expected. Savannah didn't reply but attempted to get herself and her new plant through the kitchen and into the orangery without drawing too much attention to Doreen's gift.

"Oh, that sounds nice, darling. Are you enjoying it?" added Martha as she put dinner onto the kitchen table.

"Yes, Ma, it's great," she said, walking as quickly as she could past Theodore but then finding herself face-to-face with Martha.

"I saw Mr Froodroy today, and he told me you and Rich went to the trainspotters' group last night. I had no idea that's where you were both going." She stood, holding a steaming hot plate of sausages and mash.

"Well, we, er…" Savannah fumbled to find words and felt her face flush red. "It's not really about being interested in trains, Ma, it's just nice to spend time with Rich, Mai and Doreen," Savannah finally stuttered, trying to lean past her mother and the hot plate of food to get her plant safely away. Tom was learning to feed himself and was happily sat at the table flicking food off his high chair and into the air, being promptly caught by Tornado, who sat impatiently by his side, catching every flying morsel.

"I thought that might be the case, so since you are spending so much time with Doreen and Mai, I thought it might be nice if they came for dinner one evening," said Martha.

"Don't forget, Martha, we have the Froodroys and Delia coming to dinner on Friday. Yes, I know, Martha. Why don't we get the other table out of the loft and invite Doreen and Mai too? If there's room in the heart, Martha, there's room in the home," Theodore announced, with his hands on his hips.

"What a good idea, darling." Martha cocked her head. Savannah eyed her mother with scrutiny, for she was almost certain this had been her mother's intention from the start, but she enjoyed letting her husband take the credit for it being his own idea.

"You can ask them at your next trainspotting meeting," Martha said to Savannah with a glint in her eye.

"So, Pa. How's your job going at the wind farm with Mr Froodroy?" Savannah quickly diverted the conversation away from herself and shoved the plant further behind her, hoping to block it from view.

"Marvellous, absolutely marvellous. Mr Froodroy is a real entrepreneur. He's asked me to work out some plans for sea turbines to be put in the fjord here," he replied.

"Turbines where?" Savannah replied, aghast at the thought of the Hellson in the fjord and how dangerous construction there could potentially be.

"Yes, I know, exciting isn't it?" Savannah found herself having to take a seat, for the worry of this suddenly seemed too much for her legs. Theodore continued, "Unfortunately, there's quite a lot of disapproval from the oil chap."

"Ava and Frank's pa?" Savannah questioned.

"Yes, Jan Johannsen, it seems, would rather continue his highly lucrative oil and gas drilling. He is contesting that he already owns that section of the fjord for drilling. I mean, honestly, he's a crazy man."

Savannah laughed nervously. Frank clearly got his personality from his father. She quickly excused herself under the guise of going to wash her hands before eating.

"What's that, Savannah?" her mother asked. Savannah turned around slowly, realising she could hide her new aloe no more. Again, her cheeks blushed strawberry red.

"It's an aloe, Ma. Er, Doreen gave it to me," she replied tentatively.

"Well, I never. Wonderful. Did she really? So, did she know it's your favourite plant or was it just a lovely coincidence?" Martha leant in closer to Savannah. She knew instantly her mother recognised something was going on. There was no hiding anything from her. Her mother was the quiet cogs of the family that kept everything working soundly, and that meant nothing escaped her attention. Meanwhile, her father was busy laying out the cutlery and Tom was still flicking food at Tornado. There was no plausible diversion to get out of answering her mother's question.

"Well, I told her my favourite plant was aloe vera, and it kind of wanted a new home, so…" Savannah croaked, shoving her spare hand in her pocket.

"Is that so?" replied Martha, looking Savannah squarely in the eyes. The tension couldn't be ignored.

"Do you mind, Ma?" Savannah asked her mother gently. Martha sighed a long exhale of breath, but she didn't reply. Instead, Martha put her finger to her mouth in a *shh* motion and gestured for her to follow her. Savannah picked up her new plant and followed Martha into the orangery, where she placed her hands firmly onto her daughter's shoulders.

"Show me the plant," Martha directed. Savannah held it out at arm's length for her mother to see. "Beautiful?" she questioned Savannah.

"Yes, I think so. Look at the—" Savannah began, but her mother flapped her hands in the air, as if wafting smoke.

"You really think so? I suppose it's your choice. Tut, tut, Savannah, that pot won't do," said Martha.

"What do you mean, the pot won't do? It fits perfectly," Savannah protested.

"Do you think so?" Martha raised an eyebrow.

Savannah snorted through her nostrils, feeling slightly irritated that her mother was questioning her judgement on such an obviously correct trivial matter. "Yes, Ma, I do," Savannah replied firmly.

"Okay, okay." Martha raised her hands in the air. "If you happen to change your mind, I have a more suitable pot." Martha maintained her firm stance while reaching down onto the bottom shelf, dragging a very large blue pot across the floor. "Here we are. This is a pot Grandma gave to me. Be careful with it, though, it's made from raw sapphire."

Savannah could hardly believe what was happening. Her mother took the aloe vera out of her hands and placed it onto the floor next to the huge sapphire pot. Taking Savannah's hand, she sat both of them down, cross-legged, onto the cold floor. "I knew nothing about the Sapphire Society until Grandma disappeared, when you were just a baby. Rich's grandfather visited me and your father in England, telling me my parents were gone. Your grandparents didn't die in the war, darling," Martha added.

Theodore leaned around the orangery door with Tom asleep on his shoulder. "Dinner's getting cold. I wondered where you were." Her father looked towards the floor as his wife and daughter sat with the sapphire pot in between them. "You finally gave her the pots, then?" He swallowed hard.

"You also know about Grandma and the Sapphire Society?" Savannah asked.

"We had a visit from Mr Froodroy senior, in England, just after Grandma and Grandad went missing, but we thought he was barking mad. We never dreamt any of it could possibly be true. We knew Grandma was green-fingered and had helped the island with her gardening skills, but that's all she ever told us. After the incident on the ferry over here, I wondered if there really could be an underwater evil world that Senior Froodroy spoke of, so as soon as I met Mr Froodroy, I confronted him. He confirmed his father was not mad and that the Sapphire Society is still going strong and was needed by the island more than ever. He also revealed that was the reason I was needed, not to be a member of the society, but to secure the fjord and invent a way to help disperse the hideous gas that keeps causing all these problems," Theodore said.

Savannah let all of this information sink in. Then, she remembered something. "Did you say pots, as in plural? Are there more of these?"

"More? There are hundreds of them. Your father wanted me to throw them out, but I couldn't part with something that was so important to Grandma. Grandad made them all from raw sapphires he managed to dig up on the island when he was trying to persuade her to marry him." Martha laughed. "I can almost picture her here now, in this very room, tending to her blue blooms, as she used to call them. A skill we now realise has been passed down the genes to you."

"If you really have got Grandma's way with plants, you're going to need all those extra pots before we know it. I'm taking Tom to bed, then I will get them out of the loft," said Theodore.

Savannah thought her parents would have disapproved of anything so potentially dangerous, but her mother's unwavering confidence in her shone through.

"Didn't you want to be a shiner for the Sapphire Society, Ma?" Savannah asked, curiously.

"Oh goodness, no, getting your hands dirty and fiddling around with potions isn't my cup of tea. I look after people, not plants, darling. My calling in life is rather different to yours and Grandma's." Martha smiled with pursed lips, closing the orangery door behind her.

Savannah smiled to herself. With Tricver at her side, she scooped up some fresh compost and tenderly repotted her new aloe vera into the heavy sapphire pot. Six months ago, she had struggled to find purpose in life, with no friends to speak of and feeling anxious just getting on the school bus. Now she was about to take on the fight of her life against the Hellson, yet she had never felt so happy. She snuggled with Tricver on the fluffy sheepskin rug in front of the wood burner in the dim light of the orangery and felt sheer contentment for the first time in her life. She couldn't imagine how life could get any better. The warmth she felt soothed and replenished her healing soul, removing the pain of past hurt and worry. Savannah felt an inner strength she never imagined possible. She was home, and she had never felt more prepared to face the greedy demons of the Hellson and beyond.

- ▼ -

Savannah awoke to the sensation of being tickled. Although her eyes were closed, the brightness of the rising sun streaming through the orangery glass made her aware it was morning.

"Tom, I'm asleep. Just give me five minutes," she slurred sleepily, knowing her little brother had obviously crawled on top of her to wake her up. The tickling continued, followed by laughter at the orangery doorway.

"All that excitement yesterday made you fall asleep with Tricver and Tornado on the rug instead of your bedroom," Theodore laughed.

"Yes, but can you tell Tom to stop? My alarm hasn't gone off yet," Savannah said, in the luscious state between slumber and waking.

"Martha, come and see this. I was right," her father called out.

"We're coming!" Savannah listened with her eyes still firmly shut, savouring her last few moments of slumber, listening to her mother walk across the noisy stone floor into the kitchen and tap across the orangery marble floor. "Hmm, just like Grandma," Ma said from the doorway. Tom chuckled and squealed. Then, Savannah realised that Tom's gurgling was not next to her head where she felt the tickling. Gingerly, she opened her eyes to see the orangery teeming with life. Tens of, maybe even a hundred, aloe vera plants of various sizes. The largest, which Doreen gave her yesterday, was leaning out of its new pot next to the wood burner and using its stalks to tickle under her chin.

"Oh, my goodness, what's happened?" Savannah shouted with a mixture of shock and delight. Tom couldn't contain his excitement a moment longer and, wriggling free of Martha's grip, he crawled across the floor, pointing and gurgling at the plants. One of the smaller aloe veras abseiled down the windowsill, where it had been nestling, and into Tom's hand, tickling him, too. Tom rolled around with shrieks of joy and was soon the centre of a large ring of observing plants. Savannah's own plants which had come from England with her remained in their set places but were bending and flexing their leaves and stems to capture the event.

"Is this what happened to Grandma?" Savannah quizzed her parents.

"Exactly. Grandma could grow anything, anywhere, with lightning speed, in these pots of hers," Martha chuckled.

"The rest of the pots are in the hallway. I got them out of the loft for you last night; I had a feeling something like this might happen," said Theodore, beaming.

Savannah got to her feet and tucked her cold toes into her slippers. The aloes had quietened down now and were huddled around the largest plant in the sapphire pot, as if awaiting instructions. "Now, big aloe, you stay here in the orangery. Medium aloes, I will find you pots and distribute you around the house. Little aloes, well, I haven't thought that far ahead yet." The little aloes hitchhiked in Savannah's dressing gown pocket and stayed with Savannah as she ate her breakfast in the kitchen. "Isn't it incredible? I can't believe how quickly they've grown!" Savannah said to her mother, while scoffing a boiled egg and guzzling orange juice.

"From what very little I know, the process will only occur with someone who has this innate skill.

You've been mad about plants since you were Tom's age. I never had this love of plants, so I assumed you wouldn't have the skills Grandma had, but I guess it just skipped a generation," her mother said, pouring tea from the teapot into her cup. The small aloes wriggled out of Savannah's pocket and sat themselves onto the table top, as if listening and taking note of the conversation.

"What do I do with these little ones? I can't leave them without soil and water, but the sapphire pots are too big."

"Darling, you are asking the wrong person. Maybe Doreen can help." Martha sipped at her tea. Savannah finished her breakfast and opened her dressing gown pockets wide, gesturing for the little aloes to jump in, which they did. Savannah chuckled to herself. She could almost imagine the plants shouting *'weeeeee!'* as they did so. Savannah quickly got dressed for school and hung her dressing gown on the back of her bedroom door with the little aloes safely nestled in the pockets. She would visit Doreen after school and ask her guidance; she would know what to do.

Straightening her school tie in the mirror, she noticed a flash of green behind her. The little aloes had sneaked into her school bag. Deciding they probably knew a better solution to their rehoming requirements than she did, she called out, "Okay, come with me, but don't get squashed under my history book," in a motherly tone.

She dashed into the orangery and sprinkled water over the new plants. "Bye, big aloe, see you tonight!" She felt a little embarrassed to be talking out loud to plants, but the big aloe waved its largest leaf in a sweeping motion, as if gesturing thank you. "You are welcome, and I think I'll call you 'Big Al' from now on."

"Rich is here," Martha hollered. Savannah ran out of the front door and greeted him at the front gate, waving goodbye to her family as they began their walk to school.

"Savannah, you are not going to believe what happened to me last night," he said.

"Same here, tell me your news first." Savannah rested her hand on his shoulder.

"It turns out Ma knows all about Pa's chairman responsibilities, but she's not interested in joining, something about not wanting to get into trouble. How weird is she?" He threw his hands up in the air with disbelief and continued. "Anyway, I visited Truffy at his yard and he taught me a bit of gas gliding—"

"What's gas gliding?" Savannah interrupted, wondering if that was what she did yesterday with Doreen in the angelica field.

"It's the weird gliding thing all the society members can do, where they use their sapphire shields to force positive emotion down on the ground, making you glide off the floor. That's why Doreen caught us so quickly when we were eating our picnic; her feet weren't even touching the floor," Rich explained. "Listen, after seeing Truffy, I went to bed as normal last night. I tucked myself into bed with my hot milk, then whoomph!" Rich gestured outrageously with his hands. "My sapphire trilby hat shot across the room onto the bed. There were lots of bumping noises around the house, which I presumed were due to the weather being especially stormy. I hung my hat back on my bedroom door, went back to bed, took a sip of milk, then whoomph, same again. Hot milk spilt everywhere and the hat had flown onto my head. I called out to Pa, but he was fully dressed with his society cloak and flower pin. He said there had been a significant Hellson event in the town, which he had to go and investigate. Ma didn't want me to go, but Pa won her round in the end. We got out of the front door and there it was in the middle of the fjord. Hellson bubbles of stinking gas everywhere, corroding and fizzing away at the edge of the fjord like acid. I reckon we lost at least a metre from the edge of the whole island last night."

Savannah cupped her hands to cover her mouth at the thought of it.

"Pa told me to cover my face with my hat, and the chasers did some pretty amazing stunts to collect the gas. You, Doreen and Mai are going to be busy shining over the next few days. I was really just observing; my sapphire only collected remnants of gas but it's looking cloudy already. What happened to you?" They had already walked past the Johannsens' house, past the church and had just reached the sea bridge as Savannah swung her satchel around to show Rich the little aloes. Savannah recalled the previous evening's and morning's events in great detail, the grand finale being her swinging her satchel flap open to reveal the sapling aloes inside. With this motion, one of the little aloes fell out of the bag onto the side of the sea bridge.

"Was that one of them?" Rich enquired, pointing down to the path. They both lay down on the sea bridge path to return the aloe to the satchel but found it had nestled itself under a thorn bush. Savannah cupped her hands together and tried to pick the sapling up, but it was stuck.

"Rich, help me. It's stuck and it won't move," Savannah cried.

"There's another one," Rich yelled. He was right; the little aloes were flying out of Savannah's satchel at an alarming rate. It was unintentional guerrilla gardening on a grand scale. "They just won't budge. They have rooted themselves to the spot," Rich said. Savannah tugged at her hair in despair. Rich heaved at one of the saplings but removed his hand with no sapling inside and received a large swat in the face from the thorn bush above. "Hey, that looked deliberate." He pointed at the thorn bush, which had slowly sheltered the aloes with its thorn-filled branches. The school bell began to ring.

"We're late, Delia will not be happy with me." Rich shuddered.

"What do I do? I don't know how a desert plant will survive the elements of a sea water path," Savannah cried.

"Savannah. Richard. I can see you. Now, hurry up!" roared Delia out of the classroom window. Savannah had no choice but to leave her tender saplings to fight the saltwater and wind until she could seek further advice from Doreen or Mai.

- ▼ -

The school day dragged on for what seemed like an eternity. Delia was visibly tired after being up half the night chasing, making her decidedly grumpy during classes. At the final bell, Savannah ran out of the school door into the autumnal sunshine with Rich following closely behind.

"I'll try and collect them, if you could run and ask Ma for some compost and pots," she shouted, running to the sea path. When they arrived at the sea bridge, Savannah's heavy heart lifted. The sapling aloes had grown ten times the size they were that morning and were dotted along the sea bridge with even spacing along the whole path. There she knelt down and sighed. "This must have been their intention all along," Savannah smiled.

"Yeah, I knew you were worrying too much." Rich winked. Delia was now walking along the path behind them.

"Ahh, so this is what caused all the commotion and your delay this morning," she said, smiling.

"I would have thought they'd have died or been washed out into the fjord, but it seems they rather like it here," Savannah replied.

"We need all the help we can muster," Delia proclaimed. The three of them were alone, strolling along the sea bridge, so they chatted freely about society business as they walked. "I presume Rich filled you in about our eventful evening last night," Delia said. Savannah was totally distracted by checking the aloes as she passed them, marvelling at how they had incorporated themselves into their new environment. "It's great to have new members to help us out with these conflicts. And now we have three apprentices," said Delia, clapping her hands together.

"Three?" queried Rich.

"Yes, Mai has some assessments still outstanding with the bureau before she can graduate and have the cloaking ceremony."

"Assessments?" Rich startled.

"Yes, Richard. You don't just become a society member by showing up to meetings. It takes training and the successful completion of assessments before you earn your cloak."

"Pa didn't tell me that," Rich scoffed.

"I hadn't really thought about the process. How long does it take?" Savannah asked.

"Well, shining and chasing are different. With the right training and hard work, Richard could be cloaked within a couple of years, assuming he turns up on time and he passes all his bureau exams." Delia raised her eyebrows. "Shining, on the other hand, can take considerably longer and from what I can tell, is a pretty arduous task. Mai's been training for a couple of years now. I know she has some exams next week, because I'm chaperoning her to the bureau," Delia said.

"That explains why she didn't turn up to Doreen's for my training last night. She must be desperately studying," Savannah said.

"Is that Frank up ahead?" Rich interjected.

"He must have run all the way home, to be back here that quickly," added Delia. Frank was indeed power walking towards them.

"Hello, Frank," Delia said.

Frank stopped briefly, looking down at the path. "Hello, Mrs Tuni," he muttered.

"You must be a quick runner to get home and back this quickly. That training with Mr Johnson is doing you good," Delia laughed.

"Yes Miss," he mumbled, red-cheeked, before quickly walking back up the sea bridge. "Society business aside, are you any good at sports, Savannah?"

"No, no, I'm not," Savannah responded quickly.

"Well, we need a new substitute member of our Strendur rowing team, so I thought you might like to give it a try," said Delia.

"Brilliant idea; those Toftir lot keep beating our backsides," Rich added.

"That's settled then," said Delia.

"No, no, no," Savannah pleaded. "Didn't you hear me? Having me on the team would benefit no one!"

"It will be good for you," Delia said, ignoring her. "It will help you fit in with the local community and meet more friends. Plus, Mr Johnson is the coach, so resistance is futile, my dear."

"But, I'm no good at sport, just look at my last school report from England!" Savannah urged.

"You train in school, Friday mornings, so bring warm outerwear." Delia continued to ignore her pleas.

"Welcome to the team, Savannah," Rich laughed, raising his eyebrows. "I'm off to see Truffy. See you tomorrow."

Savannah felt her cheeks burn and her breaths become quick and shallow. Dread impaled on her insides causing her chest to feel like a huge bucket of vomit was inside her, waiting to spill out. She couldn't think of anything else for the rest of her walk home. Her new life in the Faroes had been going so well, until now, that is. She walked inside and gratefully accepted a steaming mug of tea and a slice of rhubarb upside down cake from her mother before going to her orangery to collect her thoughts. She sat on the sheepskin rug next to Tricver, stroking him for comfort as she sipped her hot tea.

"All well with the little aloes, darling?" Martha enquired as she proceeded to perch on the old winged-back leather armchair next to the wood burner. Savannah explained what had happened on the sea bridge.

"So why the long face? The aloes are safe, you like this school, don't you?" Martha asked, with tilted head.

"Yes, I mean, I was liking it. Delia has just asked me to join the rowing team. A sports club! I tried to say no, but she wouldn't have it. I start training on Friday," Savannah said solemnly. Her mother got off the chair and sat beside Savannah on the rug.

"Oh, I see." Martha began stroking Savannah's hair as she spoke. "Do you want me to speak to her? I can say something."

"No, no. It will be fine. I will be fine," Savannah replied.

"This school is different to Margale High; the people are different."

"Ma! I know, I just told you I'll be fine. I will be fine," Savannah snapped, pushing her mother's hand away.

"I'm here if you need me," Martha said as she got up off the rug and made her way back into the kitchen, ignoring her daughter's outburst.

CHAPTER 7

THE HOBGOBLIN

Savannah huddled at the edge of Strendur Lake. It was named Waterfall Mile because of its impressive tumbling waterfall and lake spanning a mile across. The wind blew with such force across the open landscape, even Savannah's cropped hair was windswept. The rest of the class were inside studying ancient Viking history, which she would have preferred to this.

"Right, everyone, we have a new recruit, which I'm hoping is going to bring us a bit of luck." Mr Johnson stood smoking his pipe and eyed Savannah critically. "So, what's your sports experience, Miss Wood?"

"None," Savannah replied abruptly.

"You must have played some sport," Mr Johnson snapped.

"I'm no good at sport, Mr Johnson. I did try and

explain that to Mrs Tuni." Savannah tried desperately to extract herself from her position.

"Well, neither are this lot. But try we must. In the army, we couldn't just give up, and nor can you. The Toftir rowing team have beaten us fourteen years on the trot. Fourteen bloody years, and February is our next race," Mr Johnson said in military fashion.

"Now I know why we race them in the lake and not the fjord – I never even thought to ask why before," Rich whispered to Savannah.

"Oh no! The Hellson was going to be my last excuse to Delia for not doing it," she whispered in reply.

"Froodroy, if you listened, we wouldn't be the losers that we are. So, stop the chit-chat and start warming up." Warming up included stretches, lunges and a mile-run around the field. They jogged on the spot, while listening to Mr Johnson. "Now, we are an eight-man crew—"

"Eight-person!" interjected Rich, tilting his head at the girls. Mr Johnson just rolled his eyes and carried on.

"This is referred to as a coxed eight, in which I will be the coxswain. That basically means I tell you what to do, and by Jove, you do it. The rowers, you lot, will face the stern, where I will sit and give said coaching and warn of any dangers up ahead. Each of you will have one oar, which you will hold with both hands, rowing either port or starboard."

The crew consisted of school students who lived in Strendur, most of whom were in older year groups.

Jorg was team captain. The other members were Frank, Rich, Freya, Ava, Oskar, Astrid and Victor. Savannah and Rich were the youngest in the crew.

"This is our boat, the *Hobgoblin*, made by Mr Nielson," said Mr Johnson.

"That's my dad. He is the best boat builder there is, so we know there's nothing wrong with our vessel," Jorg said, extending his hand to Savannah and shaking it. "I'm the captain. Now, training is every Friday morning at school, and Tuesday mornings at 6am. Pre-race, we train three or four times a week, but that's not until February," Jorg explained.

"Jorg, I hate to disappoint you, but sport just isn't my thing," Savannah said.

"No choice, I'm afraid. You're going to have to make it your thing, or you will let the whole team down. Rich and Freya only joined last year and they've picked it up quickly enough. The oar is attached to the boat, so there's no chance of being up the creek without a paddle. Just train hard and remember, team work is everything," said Jorg.

"Basics. Jorg, help Savannah into the boat," barked Mr Johnson. "Sit her behind Frank to counter the weight difference." Frank shot Mr Johnson a glare, which went totally unnoticed. "Mind you, Frank, I see you've lost a few pounds over the summer. Been working out, have we?"

"More like bad school food," Frank said under his breath.

After a steadying hand from Jorg, Savannah managed to get into the boat without too much bother. The lake was vast. She couldn't see the other side. Her cold hands seized the oar, but she managed to stay dry and keep her calm, thanks mostly to being distracted by Frank's grunting with every release.

"Not bad, Savannah, not bad at all," Mr Johnson said cheerfully as he helped her out of the boat.

- ▼ -

"Not bad!" Rich exclaimed. "He's never given me that much praise," Rich said to Savannah as they walked back to school.

"Oh, I won't be at trainspotting tonight." Savannah winked to Rich.

"Really, why?" he huffed.

"I don't really know, but apparently Doreen has organised something special for me and Mai at the cottage."

"No bother, just chasers tonight then. It could get rowdy at the church!" They giggled as they pushed through the school door.

- ▼ -

Doreen's cottage glowed like warm candlelight across the open fields. Winter was now setting in and the island was cloaked in darkness on most days. In England, this would have made Savannah feel low in mood, but the island felt more like it was in hibernation than hiding. Tricver trotted alongside her, clumsily crushing the frosted grass and wagging longer stems out of the way with his bushy tail. Now out of sight, Savannah did some gas-gliding practice. Ever since Rich had fully explained it to her, she had been eager to try when she was alone. She still kangarooed, jolting forward and stopping inexplicably without any sign of smoothness, much to her annoyance, since Rich had become quite adept at the skill. Doreen was uncharacteristically waiting at the front door of her cottage with her full-length sheepskin coat and wellington boots on when she finally arrived.

"No sapphire cape tonight, Doreen?" Savannah questioned as she jolted towards her.

"We will work on the gliding," Doreen laughed.

"Thanks," Savannah replied with a giggle.

"No, tonight is rather a special night that I wanted you and Mai to be part of," Doreen replied with a twinkle in her eye, passing Savannah a sumptuously soft sheepskin rug and an enamel mug with hot tea in. "Mai should have been here by now. Let's walk up; we can call her over when she arrives."

"Walk where? I thought we weren't going to the meeting tonight," Savannah said, juggling the rug and mug so as not to spill any tea.

"We're not. We need to go to the water's edge, although I don't know where Mai has got to again.

I think the bureau assessments are making her anxious." Doreen wrinkled her eyes as she peered across the fields.

They walked through the field. The white flowers she had admired so much on her and Rich's first picnic were long since gone now that the seasons had shifted forward. Out on the distant water there was a small flicker of light.

"Thank goodness," Doreen said. The flicker of light was far out to sea, way beyond the Hellson. "It will take a while for her to get here, so I will explain as we wait." As Savannah strained her eyes to look out over the fjord, she could see the tiny flicker slowly creeping closer to the shoreline where they stood.

"Has your mother ever told you about Selkies?" Savannah shook her head no. "Selkies are creatures that live as seals in the sea, but are able, once a year, to shed their skins and take up human form."

"But that's not possible. Why don't people know about this? How can this be?" Savannah felt her voice crack.

"Some of us do know. As a little girl, I knew the legend of the Selkies. I loved the story so much, I used to come to this very water's edge to feed them. Which is how I met Sid."

"So, Sid believed in them, too?" said Savannah.

"He had proof. Sid's father was also a sailor and had been acquainted with Selkies living far out in the ocean while he fished. For the most part, Selkies and humans have remained cooperative, but Sid's father made a mistake. He fell in love with a Selkie named Liv, who lives around here in the fjord. For several years he was content, meeting up with her on land once a year and feeding her the rest of the time in her seal form. She assisted his fishing pursuits and he protected her from starving in the winter. Until one year, he couldn't cope with the separation from Liv. He wanted to be with her all the time, so when the time came for her to return to life as a seal, he hid her sealskin so she could not return to her seal form. The Selkie community were furious, vowing never to take assistance from or give support to the local fishermen again," said Doreen.

"Why blame the whole of Strendur, when it was only Sid's father's fault?" asked Savannah.

"Men have been tricking Selkies for generations, and I suspect it still goes on, albeit well concealed. Liv did stay on land, and they married and had Sid, but she became flooded by darkness and felt trapped. One day, when Sid was just fifteen, she couldn't take human life anymore. She eventually stole back her skin and rejoined her Selkie family in the fjord."

"Poor Sid." Savannah shook her head. "Poor Liv, too."

"Sid met up with Liv every year, and honourably protected the seals and their environment, using his boat to discreetly feed them. He made contact with her whenever he could. When we married, he admitted his history and introduced me to Liv. I've been coming down to the shoreline to see her on the same night every year, even since Sid's disappearance. But last year, Liv didn't arrive, so I'm so relieved to see she's finally here."

Savannah looked out to the fjord. The small flickering light had come closer and as her gaze skipped across the water, Savannah saw the most mesmerising sight. She was expecting the Selkie to still be in the form of a seal, but instead she saw a lady, with sumptuous grey hair and wide, dark eyes, swimming effortlessly through the waves. In her hand, she held a fisherman's lantern, lit with a candle which flickered in the motion of the water. She looked younger than Savannah had anticipated, around her mother's age, and glided out of the water into Doreen's outstretched arms. Doreen wrapped the blanket she had brought around her.

"Liv, I've been so worried," Doreen said.

"You're right to be worried, my darling," the Selkie spoke. "All is not well. Who is this?" She directed her gaze aggressively to Savannah, snatching the hot tea from her hand and gulping the contents.

"This is Savannah Wood. She's a trainee Sapphire," Doreen explained.

"Shiner or chaser?" She looked at Savannah expectantly.

"Shiner," Savannah said quietly, handing Liv another cup of tea.

"Not just any shiner, Liv. This is Meinhild's granddaughter," Doreen smiled.

"My darling!" Liv cried, embracing Savannah. "My darling, darling child. It is an honour to meet you. Your grandmother was my dearest friend while living on the land. What happened to her was unforgiveable," anger once more colouring her face.

"Let's go inside! In this form, you need some warmth, Liv," Doreen said, distracting her.

"Yes, yes," she smiled again, regaining her composure. As the three of them walked into the cottage, Savannah noticed Liv hang up her sealskin near the door. It looked like a sodden pewter velvet onesie with speckled markings all over. They took rest near the fire; Liv placed her hand on Doreen's shoulder affectionately.

"Have you seen Sid?" asked Doreen.

"No. Like I told you, Doreen, all is not well in the fjord. The Hellson is a problem," Liv said.

"For us, too," Doreen replied forlornly.

"I used to be able to visit him," Liv explained. "Although he was confused, he at least knew who I was. I could fairly quickly remind him of his past on land, which helped keep his survival spirits up, and change his green eyes back to blue, but things have changed. Two years ago, a few weeks before lands night, a group of us went to visit the Hellson. It was bedlam. Ragnar has become stronger and greedier than ever. The Vikings won't be satisfied until Eysturoy is consumed. After they take over Eysturoy, they want to take the rest of the Faroes. They demanded our help, but we refused. Furious, Ragnar stole a young Selkie's skin, swearing to keep it until the island is destroyed. She hasn't been seen since. We spent two years searching, even up through the north to the pole. She's gone."

"Gone where, Liv?" Doreen said, startled.

"We don't know," she said, exasperated. "And we can't go to the Hellson again, it's just not safe. We are no longer allowed to enter the Hellson. I'm sorry, Doreen, but it's now been too long. When it last exploded, I went against the Selkie king's orders and snuck in through the under-seabed tunnel." Liv began to cry. "I tried with all my might, but I couldn't get Sid to remember me. Too much time had passed; the toxins in there are too strong. I tried to pull him out of the tunnel, to at least end his misery and release him to the sea, but he was too big and my seal limbs are not as dextrous as they are in this form." Her tears tumbled in despair down her porcelain white cheeks; the silence so engulfing, Savannah almost heard the teardrop thud as it hit the ground. "His soul screamed as I left, pleading for mercy. It's a sound I can never escape. His green eyes are not rectifiable. He's gone, Doreen."

Doreen clutched the arms of the chair. "What about the other Selkies with relatives and friends in there? They can't all have been abandoned?"

"We had no choice, Doreen. Ragnar's appetite for power is insatiable. The Selkie king won't risk the demise of our kind. We are the only herd left in the world. If it's not resolved soon, we have orders to move north, to the pole. There are no humans there, meaning no underwater volcanoes. We need to preserve our kind, Doreen, before we are wiped out entirely," Liv sobbed.

"So, no souls in the Hellson are intact? Not one?" Doreen asked solemnly.

"Only green eyes remain, those who have lost their souls," Liv repeated.

Savannah felt the sorrow in the room descend. Liv walked over to the door, with tears still dripping down her cheeks as she threw down the blanket and picked up her soggy velveteen skin, standing naked in the kitchen. "Anyway, you can't blame us, Doreen. It's not our job to maintain that fjord. That's Sapphire business, and what are they doing?" she rebuked. "I know you've lost your husband, but I've lost my only son, and I'm about to lose my home, too, because of the Sapphire Society's incompetence!"

"Liv, no. Don't leave like this, I'm begging you. We are doing all we can," Doreen said softly.

"It's not enough, Doreen. It's over!" she shouted as she walked naked through the freezing winds, wriggling into her sealskin on the shore and swimming back out to the deep.

CHAPTER 8

THE BUREAU

Savannah and Rich waited outside the school. Savannah had already been to rowing practice at Waterfall Mile Lake and was delighted to be going out for the day after Mr Froodroy offered her and Rich the opportunity to attend the bureau.

"What do you think it will be like? I wonder where it is," Rich said, wearing his sapphire trilby and donning an ill-fitting creased shirt. Truffy, Delia and Mai were collecting them from school.

"Oi, oi!" Truffy shouted, not from the removal van on the road, as they were expecting, but from a boat in the fjord.

"We're not rowing there?" Rich yapped. "Savannah and I have had enough of rowing already today!"

"Man up, me old china," Truffy laughed. The boat was not like any other Savannah had seen before. It was made of dark, almost black, wood and had the carved head of a woman with flowing hair at the front, and was adorned all over with sapphire-eyed seals.

"Isn't she beautiful?" Truffy said with dewy eyes and crossed arms. "Welcome, me gems, to the *Fortress*," he said.

"The *Fortress*? Do you mean this is *the* fortress?" Savannah asked, mouth agape.

"Ahh, so Doreen's been filling you in, I see. Yes, this is the one and only *Sapphire Fortress*. She's 'ad a bit of work done, like, after several bashings from blinkin' Ragnar, but she's good as new. More importantly, she's safe, thanks to the seals keeping watch, if you know what I mean." Truffy winked.

"So, the sapphires in the seal carvings should keep us safe over the water?" Rich looked unconvinced.

"Technically, we won't even be touching the water," Truffy said.

"Oh, come on, Truffy, you're having me on," Rich barked. "How can it not touch the water? It's a boat. You're not catching me out again!"

Truffy held his hands up in the air. "I swear on the beautiful Mai's life. 'Ave a look for yourself!"

Looking down at the boat, they were embarrassed to see he was right. The boat was effortlessly floating two inches above the water.

"We're not rowing there, mate, we're gliding," Truffy declared with a grin. "Now get in and you can help. It won't take long to get there," he said as he held out his hand to help them on board. The seating benches were also made out of unpolished sapphires and looked distinctly similar in texture to Savannah's plant pots at home.

"Hello, Savannah. Sorry I keep missing you at Doreen's," Mai said. "All these exams are getting the better of me." Savannah noticed she was looking unusually dishevelled. Her usually glossy, flowing hair was scraped into a ponytail and she had black circles under her eyes.

"We'll gas glide and leave Mai to do a bit of cramming, Truffy," said Delia, waving from the front of the boat. "We just need to teach them what to do."

"Righto," agreed Truffy. "Savs, you go on the left, Rich on the right. Put your sapphire in the 'and closest to the water and form a fist around it. Then, force all your positive thoughts down into the water." Rich instantly had a jet of bubbles next to him, like a jacuzzi. Savannah managed barely one bubble.

"No matter, no matter. Just keep concentrating, Savs. It will come with practice. I'm going to navigate."

"Not after last time, Truffy, we ended up in Bolivia!" Delia said, laughing.

"Oh, okay. Delia is navigating and steering then," he laughed self-deprecatingly.

"So where is the bureau?" Rich asked.

"Haven't I taught you anything?" said Truffy.

"Well, you haven't taught me that!" Rich rebuked.

"Oops, my mistake. Rich, I am taking you to the Bronx."

"In America?" Savannah asked.

"Well, yeah. How many other Bronxes do you know?" he quipped.

"In New York?" Savannah asked again, thinking that was surely impossible.

"Yes!" Truffy shouted indignantly.

"But that would take all week, and I haven't got any spare clothes. Not to mention school," Rich said.

"All week, my backside!" Truffy replied with his hands on his hips. "Never mind. Rich and Savs, Delia and I will take the lead on this one. You two just sit and watch the masters at work," Truffy smiled.

"That's more like it, Truffy. It's their first-time *Fortress* gliding, after all," Delia said. "Mai, you finish your revision and relax! You'll be fine."

"Thank you," Mai responded weakly.

"Ready, Delia?" Truffy asked.

"Ready, Truffy!" Truffy stood at the front of the *Sapphire Fortress* with his left hand in a fist forced down to the water and his right arm punching triumphantly in the air, shouting, "To the bureau!"

The *Sapphire Fortress* was propelled quickly out of the fjord, leaving no wake or spray behind them. Savannah wanted desperately to keep track of where they were and to see what she was passing, but the awe-inspiring speed made it impossible.

"We're just passing through the North Atlantic," Truffy said. "And in a few seconds, we'll 'it the New York rivers." They began to slow and, gradually, Savannah saw the Statue of Liberty on her left-hand side.

"We're now on the East River," Truffy shouted.

"This is the Hudson," said Delia. "Watch out for low-flying planes, Truffy. Do you remember when—"

"Yes, yes, Delia, I'm on it," Truffy interjected. The *Fortress* began to slow. They were now moving at a normal speed and Savannah could see her surroundings. The Yankee stadium, people walking along doing their shopping and chatting.

"'Ere we go," said Truffy. They passed under a massive bridge. It was not what Savannah was expecting. It was pitch-black, with no light at the end. She couldn't see anything, but she felt the *Fortress* steer left, then right, and then it made several other blind turns until they were back out into daylight, gliding out onto a small lake, where a huge man stood with a clipboard. He was tall and wide, with dark skin, a shaved head, and he wore a white suit with a black tie. He was dripping with diamonds. He had a huge diamond cross swathed around his neck and as he smiled, Savannah noticed he had a gold tooth with a diamond flashing a sparkle in the middle of it.

"'Ello, Billy. Still up for the game, then?" Truffy shook the man's hand.

"Nice to see you, Truffy," he replied. "Yep, my injuries have taken me off the field for a while, so I'm helping the bureau out in security. The rest of the diamonds are here, too. This devil of theirs under the Hudson is causing the American Onyxes a spot of bother, so us Diamonds have come over to help them sort it out. Mai, is that you hiding under the cover of *Facing your Fauna*?"

"Hello, Billy, yes, more exams today," Mai replied weakly.

"Come on then, I will walk you through to the exam room. Truffy, you'll be okay to park up, won't you? Oh, hang on," he said, peering at Savannah and Rich. "New recruits?" They both smiled in response. Rich stood up and shook Billy's hand.

"Nice to meet you, I'm Rich," he said.

"Rich Froodroy," added Truffy, jabbing Billy in the ribs with his elbows.

"Ahh, the boss's son," Billy said. "Very pleased to meet you, I know your dad well. And this young lady?"

"You won't believe us," Delia chipped in. Billy screwed up his eyes, one of which was totally bloodstained, to examine Savannah more closely.

"No, I've not met you before," said Billy.

"No, but you've read every blinkin' chasing book her grandma 'as ever written!" Truffy said as Billy stepped onto the boat.

"It can't be." Billy continued staring, now even more intently, at Savannah.

"Meet Savannah Wood, Meinhild's granddaughter, who we are pleased to say is joining the Sapphires," Delia said proudly. "Savannah, I am very pleased to introduce you to—"

"I know who you are," Savannah interjected. "You're Billy La-Vin, you play rugby for England!" Billy took Savannah's hand and shook it vigorously.

"Miss Wood, it's an honour. And yes, I play a little rugby when the Diamonds and the bureau give me some spare time. Meinhild taught me everything I know. Your family have saved me from being dragged down into the Trojan of the Thames no less than thirteen times. If you need anything, anything at all, please let me know," Billy said.

"All right, you mushy old fool," Truffy shouted jovially. "You can 'elp us by getting our Mai to her exam."

"Will do! Catch you Sapphires later. Oh, and the Laird just landed on the dome," Billy said, helping Mai off the fortress. "And he's got a shiny new helicopter!"

"Good luck, Mai!" Delia and Truffy both shouted as she slowly followed Billy.

- ▼ -

Following the river around the bend, Truffy threw a sapphire anchor into the water and they departed the vessel. All Savannah could see was a large brick wall with an archway smothered in climbing roses, not too far ahead of them. The close proximity of the water and the buildings reminded her of pictures she had seen of Venice.

"Welcome to the bureau," Delia said, her hand outstretched, gesturing for them to pass under the arch. When she did so, Savannah found herself standing at the entrance of a gargantuan Victorian glass building, so big she couldn't see where it ended. The entrance boasted double doors, the top of which seemed to go on past the clouds in the sky, and as they wafted open effortlessly, a tropical breeze warmed her cheeks. Savannah forced one foot in front of the other, although her mind was distracted by the implausible curiosities ahead of her. Indoor waterfalls, an immense lake and skyscrapers, all contained within the glass. The city that the glass structure inexplicably contained was crammed full of people, many of whom were openly gas gliding to and fro.

"This is incredible," Savannah stuttered.

"Your grandmother had the same look on her face when she first visited," a man with an unfamiliar accent said to Savannah, smiling. He was standing next to her, but with the distraction of seeing the bureau for the first time, his appearance had taken her by surprise. "Nice to meet you, Miss Wood, I'm the president of the bureau, Nanuq Samossen." Savannah shook Nanuq's hand, but words escaped her. The tall, dark-haired man was dressed in traditional Inuit attire, with several rows of gleaming emeralds around his neck. "I see you inherited Meinhild's medal of light."

"Yes, just a little while ago; I found it purely by luck." Savannah finally found her tongue. Nanuq laughed, making the emeralds around his neck jangle.

"From what the Sapphires tell me, you make your own luck, Miss Wood." Savannah didn't know whether that was a compliment or not but thanked him all the same. "So, is Mai going to pass this time?" He turned to Truffy and Delia, giving them strong embraces in turn.

"Of course she is!" Truffy replied swiftly.

"Hmm, we'll see, hey?" Nanuq smiled. "I'm afraid Scruffy is busy, Terrence, in Devil meetings, but Precious is free. She will do a tour for you. I warn you, Froodroy Junior, keep that hat of yours on. The darn starlings have migrated here again and they are making one hell of a mess." The Sapphires all quickly looked upwards and caught sight of the large flocks of birds chirping and pecking away happily, gas gliders swerving abruptly around them to avoid collision. "Speaking of hell, my lovely Delia, how is the Hellson?" Nanuq spoke directly to Delia.

"A pain in the jacksie," Truffy interjected.

"Yes, an inappropriate but accurate description, Truffy," Delia said. Then she turned to address the bureau president. "I have a meeting booked with you in an hour, to go over our long-term plans. Honestly,

I'm afraid it's just firefighting that we have been able to manage at the moment. But we can talk about that later."

"I understand." He folded his arms solemnly. "Ahh, here's Precious now." Walking towards them was a woman with thick afro hair that was cut short to her head. She wore letterbox red high-heeled stilettos, yet walked as if on air, skinny jeans and a crisp white shirt with ruby buttons and a ruby-encrusted choker.

"Delia, Truffy, so wonderful to see you," said Precious in a deep, gruff voice. "Delia, last time I saw you, you said you were going to get me some fizz," she said, with a coy grin.

"Here we go, Precious, two bottles of the finest rhubarb fizz, courtesy of Mrs Froodroy," Delia said, handing over two chinking bottles in a cotton bag.

"Thank you. They have it in the cafeteria, but it's just not the same as the Faroes' homegrown," Precious said, kissing Delia on the cheek and turning to Savannah and Rich. "It's my absolute favourite tipple. It's even worth braving the Faroese weather to collect it if you Sapphires aren't visiting the bureau. Nice to meet you. I'm Precious, a Ruby Society member. You could say I'm a precious ruby." She laughed at her own joke. Turning to Rich, she asked, "I presume you are Richard? We wondered how long it would be before you joined. Your father tells us all about you when we visit. How's the family? Have you still got Elvis and that strange dog?"

"I've never seen you visit," said Rich.

"No, your father thought it best you didn't meet society members until you joined, which he was certain you would. I'm glad to see he was right. Mind you, your father is always right. But don't tell him I said that " She laughed again.

"Anyway, Elvis is still about and as rude as ever, but we don't have the dog Tricver anymore; he belongs to Savannah now they've got the house," Rich replied, pointing in Savannah's direction.

"Aha! Now you, we never imagined would join us," Precious said to Savannah. "I'm very glad we were wrong. I never met Meinhild, but I wouldn't have passed my shining exams without her. Her books are fantastic, which, by the way, we have to collect from the library."

"I'm going to 'ave a look about for the laird. Billy said he's just landed," said Truffy.

"He has, he's got a lovely new—" Precious was interrupted mid-sentence.

"I know, I know. The jammy dodger has a new chopper. That's why I want to see him!" Truffy began jogging in the opposite direction and waved. "Rich, Savs, I'll see you later!"

"I'm going to leave you in Precious' very capable hands. She'll show you around and introduce you to a few society members," said Delia, walking towards one of the indoor skyscrapers.

"We'll glide, if you two don't mind. These shoes are fabulous, but a little pinchy on the toes,"

Precious said. Savannah looked down sheepishly at her own old mud-splattered trainers. Precious began gliding, with smoothness and grace, in the direction of a large stone building, with Rich steadily gliding behind. Savannah took a sapphire in her right hand and pushed down, but despite her best efforts, jolted sideways, knocking into another society member.

"Sorry," she yelled, with a look of distaste returned from the person she bumped into.

"Not mastered it yet?" Precious had spun around and was holding out her hand to help Savannah off the floor. Savannah shook her head. "Take your gem in your strongest hand, and fill yourself with strength and composure. Then, with all your might, release all those positive vibes through your right hand and make all those good feelings filter through your sapphire," Precious explained, resting her hand on Savannah's shoulder. Savannah knew she was going to jolt again. She followed Precious' instructions but only achieved a face-plant into the side of the wall, leaving a smear on the crystal-clear glass. Rich ran over and helped her up from the floor, closely followed by Precious.

"Don't worry, you'll get the hang of it soon enough. Anyway…" Precious leant into her handbag and pulled out a pair of flat shoes. "It's far more fashionable to wear flats mid-morning." She linked arms with Rich and Savannah and began walking into the expanse of the glass building. "Welcome to the library," Precious whispered. The candlelit underground labyrinth of tunnels housed row after row of books, which seemed to go on and on, far past Savannah's range of vision. Books were flying mid-air into people's hands at great speed. "Watch your heads." Precious pointed to the flying books. "The books are all bejewelled, so as long as you have a sapphire, you can gas glide the books to you as you need them. The librarian, Nigel, set it up. He says it was for society members' ease, but we joke that it's because he doesn't like leaving his desk." Precious sniggered.

"I heard that!" a wide-stomached man said behind a huge oak, leather-topped desk, on which his feet rested.

"Nigel, I didn't see you there." Precious turned around quickly. Making no attempt to move, the man, wearing a tight checked shirt and bottle green velvet bow tie glared in their direction. "Nigel, meet Savannah Wood and Rich Froodroy." Nigel's legs swiftly moved from the top of the desk, but the swivel chair his backside was firmly positioned on declined to follow suit, leaving the man tipped onto the floor like a dead fly, struggling to get up.

"Let me help you," said Rich, offering his hand to the grumbling man.

"Nigel, I've never seen you move that fast. Your poor posterior didn't know what to do." Precious laughed uncontrollably.

"Very funny," Nigel said irritably, dusting himself off. "Madam Savannah Wood, it is indeed a pleasure to meet your acquaintance." Nigel extended his hand to Savannah, who shook it in return. "Are you here to see your grandmother's books?" he asked, looking at her attentively.

"Er, no. Just to collect my beginner's guides," said Savannah.

"I'll get you the books, if you just let me look at it. I've never seen it up close before," said Nigel.

"He means the medal of light," Precious whispered, nudging Savannah.

"Yes, of course." Savannah took the necklace, now sparkling clean thanks to Doreen, and leaned forward, lifting it up for Nigel to see. Nigel took a magnifying glass out of his pocket and positioned the pendant between his thumb and forefinger. His eyes bulged as he carefully inspected it. "Thank you, Madam Wood," Nigel said, replacing the pendant back in place and returning the magnifying glass to his pocket. "There will never be another Meinhild. Her books are the most popular, even now. She's legendary with KAPOW," Nigel mused, much to Precious' amusement, who sniggered behind Savannah's back.

"Who are KAPOW?" Rich asked keenly.

"We, my friend, are an exclusive clan of committed society members of senior ilk."

"I see," said Rich, enthused.

"You mean librarians, Nigel. You're librarians." Precious rolled her eyes, causing Rich to appear immediately less impressed with Nigel's status.

"We don't expect the likes of shiners and chasers to understand," Nigel retorted, folding his arms indignantly. "KAPOW, for speed, the full title of which is Keeper and Protector of Words, an elite—" Nigel was cut off mid-sentence by Precious, who was pretending to yawn.

"Yeah, yeah, Nigel, we get it. You're a group of skilled individuals like no other. We understand. Now, can we get our books or what?" Precious' gruff voice had become even gravellier. Nigel positioned himself back in his swivel chair, holding out his right hand, which had a gold signet ring embellishing his little finger.

"*Society Handbook*, twice," Nigel shouted pompously. Two books came flying around the corner, the first hitting Precious on the back of the head, the second hitting her on the cheek.

"Nigel!" Precious shouted.

"My apologies," he smirked at Precious sarcastically.

Nigel held out his hand again. "*Chasing: The Shadow Guide, Gas Guzzling, Chasing: Running the Race for Humanity*." Three books came hurtling through the air, passersby dodging them with varying degrees of luck, until finally the books all landed in Nigel's hands. "Here we go, Mr Froodroy. A little light reading for you. Now, Madam Wood," Nigel said, directing his attention to her.

"Oh, please call me Savannah," she blushed.

"*A Shining Field Guide, Facing your Fauna, Purifying Plants*," Nigel summoned, again holding his hand up in the air. The books glided towards Nigel much more slowly, one of them flapping, another leaping from shelf to shelf, but all eventually landing on Nigel's outstretched hand. "These books are on loan to you," he began.

"What?" Precious interrupted. "Nigel, these books are theirs to keep; they do not have to return them," Precious began to rant.

"These are on loan. You may keep them while you are a Sapphire member. If you fail your training and fail to meet the grades, you need to give them back," Nigel repeated.

"These two won't fail," Precious retorted defensively.

"Thank you, Nigel," Savannah said, trying to ignore Precious' rudeness. They left, carrying their heavy books through the buildings.

"Now that's where you want to head," Precious said, pointing at a building that resembled a stately home with beautiful gardens. "That's the bureau university. Mai will be sat in there right now doing her exam. It's where the best of the best shiners and chasers are educated to develop their skills even further. Some of the university graduates end up working for the bureau directly. The current president of the bureau, Nanuq Samossen, went there. In fact, your father did, too, Rich," Precious informed them.

"Did you go there, Precious?" Savannah enquired.

"Nope. I'm more an academic of adventure. I'm afraid all the theory is a bit lost on me. I did well to pass my shining exams at all," Precious laughed self-deprecatingly.

"What's that next door, the other grand building?" Rich asked.

"Now there, you don't want to go. That's the bureau hospital. There I have been a few times," Precious grimaced.

"Oi, oi." Truffy waved from the distance through a sea of people, many of whom turned around, thinking he was yelling at them. "Savs, Rich, this is the Laird." The Laird was also smiling and waving in their direction, with red cheeks and a red nose. He wore a kilt and smelt rather strongly of whisky.

"Pleasure to meet you," the Laird said in a strong Scottish accent. "I'm Laird Stuart Douglas, chairman of the Scottish Pearls. Most of you Sapphire lot call me the Laird. You could say I'm a neighbour. Truffy said you might like a ride in my new helicopter to take in the city sights?"

"That would be brilliant, thank you," Savannah nodded. Rich buzzed with excitement at the prospect.

"It's parked up with Billy, let's go!"

The helicopter dwarfed the sea *Fortress*, its huge shiny cream-coloured glinting body adorned with a treasure chest of jewels which looked every inch regal.

"Come on, Billy," the Laird shouted. Billy, Savannah, Rich, Truffy and Precious all got strapped in.

"No gliding this time, Truffy, we are going with petrol power. All the locals where I live think I'm really flash with a pearl-and gem-encrusted chopper; little do they know what it's really for. I've got all gems covered on here so I can fly over anything," said the Laird via the headphones they all wore in the helicopter so they could communicate despite the loud noise of the machine.

"You still are flash, mate. This is brilliant," Truffy replied.

"I promised President Samossen I'd take you Sapphires over the Devil so you can see what it's up to. The Diamonds are there now, Billy. Scruffy's having a bad time of it." The helicopter swung over the Hudson, but the Devil needed no introduction. A spewing fountain, with thick gas emanating out of the top, awaited them below.

"I can't get too close, not while it's this out of control, but you get the idea. This is America's version of your Hellson."

"Oi, oi, there's me brother, Scruffy," shouted Truffy, forgetting to use his helicopter headset.

"Who's that he's fighting?" asked Rich. Down below, a short man could be seen in a boat, being punched by a larger man.

"What a liberty! We have to do something," shouted Truffy, unbuckling his seat belt and getting as close to the window as he could. Gangs of people were fighting in the fast-flowing river, the thick fog suddenly covering their vision, just like it had on the Scrabster ferry.

"It's exploded. The Devil of the Hudson has exploded," Billy bellowed. Truffy was trying to open the helicopter side door, but the Laird locked it.

"No, Truffy, we will get back to the bureau and collect more chasers. We can't throw you over here! You won't make the fall," said the Laird. He turned the helicopter back towards the bureau roof.

"What's happening, Truffy?" Savannah asked, panicked.

"The Devil has erupted, Savs. The muted are coming out," he replied as the helicopter swung back onto the bureau roof.

"But why is that bad?" Savannah shouted over the thwacking noise of the rotor blades.

"The people who went in have changed." He was now running towards the lake. "The people that come out are mutated. They can never return to being human. Did you see their fluorescent green eyes? You've heard of the eyes before, I presume. But maybe you don't know what it means. Green eyes mean they're toxic, they've mutated into what's been holding them. Once people's eyes turn green, their only thought is to entrap more people and drag them down into the underwater volcano, and if we don't get them back in, there'll be no stopping them."

Delia was waiting in a large group of people on a ferry at the edge of the lake, where emotions were clearly running high. Society members were jeering and banging their gems on the side of the vessel. "Get in, Truffy, Laird, Precious. We totally outnumber them," Delia yelled with determination piercing through her eyes.

The large ferry was holding around 200 people, all clad with bright shining gems of varying colours. Truffy jumped defiantly on board the ferry, swinging his dumpy legs over the metal railing as it pulled out of the bureau lake into the tunnel. "Go and collect Mai. Billy will take you both home on the *Fortress*," he called out over his shoulder as the ferry sped into the distance.

CHAPTER 9

THE SAPPHIRES' HOLIDAY WITH THE DEVIL

Strendur village square was decorated for Christmas with holly, ivy and mini fisherman's lanterns lighting the streets and homes. The last few weeks at school had been particularly strange. A stand-in teacher had taken over from Delia, who was away in the Bronx, chasing against New York's underwater volcano, the Devil of the Hudson, under the guise of visiting sick relatives abroad. All fully cloaked Sapphire members were there too, leaving only Savannah, Rich and Mai to worry about their friends' safety.

"I feel so helpless," Savannah sighed to Mai, hugging her knees while sitting on the sheepskin rug in the orangery.

"There's nothing we can do," Mai said, rubbing her eyes.

"Can you give me some lessons? Since you've finished your exams. At least then we'd be doing something, rather than nothing," Savannah asked.

"Okay, but I will need to collect my books from home." Mai exhaled a long, slow breath. They strolled along the snow-covered path; the cold weather made Savannah's fingers seize up. She had never been to Mai's cottage but had imagined it differently in her mind than the reality of seeing it.

"Sorry about the mess, I've been so busy…" Mai hesitated as she opened the door. The fire in the hearth had gone out and the room was cold and carried a faint hint of damp. In the darkest corner, at the back of the room, Savannah noticed a large mixing bowl, spoon and trug. There were two wooden chairs next to the fireplace, on a brown fur rug, so Savannah sat down and opened her textbook.

"*A Shining Field Guide*, written and researched by Meinhild Simonsen." Savannah smiled, sitting back in the chair. Mai positioned herself in the opposite chair, but her attention was out to the fjord. "Is that where you do your shining?" Savannah said, pointing to the table and bowl.

"It's where I try," Mai said, wrinkling her nose.

"Are you okay, Mai? Are you worried about him?"

Mai shuffled on her chair and replied solemnly, "I always have to worry about him."

"He will be back at the depot before we know it, shouting 'Oi, oi!'" Savannah smiled, trying her best to cheer Mai up.

"Truffy? Yes, yes, he'll be back soon." Mai snapped shut her own copy of *A Shining Field Guide*. "It's cold in here, let's go out and find some plants," she said brightly. They wandered over the fields near the boatyard to a rare glimmer of colour in the freezing weather. "*Calluna vulgaris*," Mai said, bending down to a tiny flowering yellow plant.

"This is what you need for your base shining recipe," Mai said, pointing to the yellow flower.

Savannah bent down and plucked the flower, putting a few stems into her trug. In the distance, she could see the fishing boats unloading their day's catch. "That's Frank," Savannah said, waving over to him as he clambered on board the boat, holding a large net.

"Do you mind if we go over quickly, Mai? Frank missed school today; I had better check he's okay," Savannah asked.

"No, no, I don't want to get wet. You go, I need to get on now anyway, Savannah. I'm a bit busy really," she replied. Savannah took her trug and walked down to the boatyard but turned and watched as Mai walked swiftly back to her cottage.

"Frank!" she shouted. He looked up, his yellow fishing overalls covered in fish guts and blood. "Hi, you weren't at school today. Are you not feeling well?" Frank looked at Savannah but did not respond.

"Go on, Franky, if it's all off and gutted, you can go home," shouted an elderly man from the shore. Frank stomped towards her, splattering fish blood from his overalls as he walked.

"What are you doing with that? Picking flowers for your mum?" Frank asked sarcastically, pointing to Savannah's trug.

"Oh, just bored," Savannah lied. "Anyway, I just wondered if you were going to be well enough for rowing practice this week."

"I'm not sure if I can make it," Frank said, looking down at his feet. They walked in silence back through Strendur village square, to Frank's house.

"Bye then, I hope you feel better soon," Savannah said.

"Thanks," Frank smiled as he walked through his gate.

- ▼ -

"He smiled?" Rich scoffed when Savannah told him the story at rowing practice.

"Yes, I know it was strange. I've never seen him smile before," Savannah giggled as she swept her long legs over the side of the rowing boat.

"Oi, where are Frank and Ava? They can't keep missing practice!" Mr Johnson shouted.

"They are both ill. They haven't been at school, either," Jorg responded. "Savannah, you're going to have to go and talk to Frank and tell him they can't keep missing practice. Mr Johnson doesn't like him anyway; he doesn't need more of a reason to get him off the team," Jorg whispered to Savannah.

"Why her? You're the captain, you should do it," Rich responded defensively.

"I've tried. He won't open the door or talk to me. You said yourself, just now, that he smiled at you the other day; that's more than most of us lot get. Just tell him he and Ava need to turn up, will you?" Jorg insisted.

The rowing sessions had become surprisingly enjoyable, despite the freezing weather. Savannah had improved at the techniques and even found herself getting praise from Mr Johnson, a rare treat, indeed.

"Well done, everyone. Everyone who bothered to turn up, that is. Jorg, you need to speak to Frank and Ava over the holidays and get them to turn up to practices, or you can tell them from me, they are both off the team," Mr Johnson said from behind his thick woollen scarf.

Savannah and Rich trudged back home. The Christmas holidays had begun and they were still missing their fellow society members. "That just shows you how miserable the Johannsen household is." Rich pointed to Ava and Frank's home on top of the hill. "They've got the most money and the biggest house, but they can't even find a bit of joy to put

Christmas decorations up." The large home stood alone on top of the hill. Its metal roof looked dull, even in the bright light of the overhead sun.

"Is that Mr Johannsen?" Savannah asked, pointing at a middle-aged man sat on a wooden bench in the front garden.

"Yes, it's rare to see him," Rich said, surprised. "He's usually away in another country on business."

"Come on then, let's go and talk to Frank now," said Savannah. "He's less likely to shout at us if his father's there. It might even embarrass him into coming to rowing practice." She grabbed Rich's arm as they walked through the snow up the hill to the Johannsen house. Mr Johannsen was sat on a wooden bench, with a large blanket wrapped around him. He appeared to be looking out to sea.

"Good morning, Mr Johannsen. I wondered if Frank was home." He didn't reply. "Er, Jan, it's Rich Froodroy. Is Frank here?" Rich said loudly to the man, but his head didn't even move to acknowledge their presence. The front door burst open; Frank blustered through.

"Hi, Frank," Savannah smiled.

"What are you doing here?" he replied, flustered.

"You keep missing practice. Mr Johnson's going mad," Rich intervened.

"I haven't got time. I'm not well," Frank shouted.

"Well, which one is it? Are you ill or have you not got time?" Rich said defiantly.

"I'm ill," Frank said.

"Is Ava okay? She hasn't been at school either," Savannah asked.

"She's ill, too," Frank said, his face glowing red.

"And your dad's ill, too, is he?" Rich said crossly, looking over to Mr Johannsen, who seemed oblivious to the uproar in front of him.

"We are ill. We are all ill. We just need to be left alone," Frank shouted.

"Fine by me," Rich said impatiently, turning on his heels and stomping back down the garden path. Savannah stood for a moment and watched Frank disappear through the front door, Mr Johannsen still sitting motionless on the front bench. He looked completely different to when Savannah had first met him, in the Woods' family kitchen. He looked tired and dishevelled.

"Too posh to even say hello. Ignorant man, and Frank thinks he's too good to bother practising. Well, I'll speak to Jorg and get him replaced," Rich said angrily as they strode along the sea bridge towards home. Savannah noticed her aloe vera plants were still growing, which gave her some comfort. They had formed a wall-like structure.

"Look, they're becoming a natural sea defence." Savannah pointed to the plants.

"Yes, you really are clever with plants, Savannah. Now you just need to practise your gliding," Rich smiled, his anger at Frank seemingly forgotten.

"Hmm, I need to do some jobs in the orangery first. And I need some hot chocolate. And the wood burner in the orangery needs more wood." She made sure her eyes didn't meet his.

"The Laird!" Rich shouted, interrupting her thoughts. The shiny pearl-white helicopter was parked in the Froodroys' front garden. "They're home, the Sapphires are home!"

As they ran through the door, Rich hugged his father tight. "Hello, son," Mr Froodroy said softly. He looked tired. He had a black eye and clumps of his hair were missing.

Doreen rested her hand on Savannah's shoulder. "It's good to see you, dear. How are you?" she asked.

"We've missed you," Savannah replied.

"I'm pleased to see you're still training, Savannah," Delia said affectionately.

"Delia, you look awful," Rich interrupted. She did look a mess. Her sparkling sapphire glasses were black and she had cuts and bruises covering her face and arms.

"Thanks." She glared mockingly at Rich.

"It's good to have you back, Mrs T," Rich smiled.

"Well, the good news is we got the job done. The Devil's inhabitants are back where they belong. The bureau used all of its resources. Every international society was there in full and, together, we put a dampener on the Devil of the Hudson," said Mr Froodroy.

"Yeah, lucky we were all there. If all the society members hadn't been there, waiting to chase, I don't know what would have happened," said Precious, walking out of the kitchen with a glass of rhubarb fizz. "Hello there, Savannah, how's the gliding going?" she asked, still managing to look glamorous despite wearing muddy clothes.

"Hi, Precious, the gliding is... rather slow progress," she replied feebly.

"Well, matter not, my dear," said Mr Froodroy.

Theodore knocked on the front door and Mr Froodroy waved him in. "Mr Froodroy, delighted to have you home," Theodore said, shaking his hand. "Your timing is rather apt. The Froowind turbine design is finalised," Theodore announced. A loud resounding cheer erupted from the Froodroy house.

"Well, I think I may just have a couple of spare installers," he said, clapping his hands together. "Laird? Precious? Billy? It will take a few weeks, I suspect. Would you be so kind as to assist?" Mr Froodroy asked. Savannah hadn't even noticed Billy tucked in the corner of the room, nursing a broken leg and looking decidedly dishevelled.

"Mr Chairman, you read my mind. A bit of Faroese fresh air is just what the doctor ordered after all that stinking Bronx gas," Billy smiled.

"Christmas in the Faroes," Precious smiled, holding up her fizz to toast the other members.

"And a bit longer than that, I would think. My design is a little complex, I'm afraid," Theodore added, hesitantly.

"Even better," the Laird smiled.

CHAPTER 10

THE WATCHTOWER GHOST

"Rowing in candlelight is a tradition that dates back to when the Vikings first inhabited these islands," Delia said, standing at Waterfall Mile Lake's shore, facing the Strendur rowing team, who were sat in the *Hobgoblin* rowing boat with unlit candle lanterns. "It's quite simple. We have all your costumes back at the school, but they aren't as warm as you might like, so we won't put them on until the last minute. It is our Christmas Eve tradition to row in candlelight around the lake, as darkness falls. We will do one lap of the lake, which will take about half an hour. It's not a race, just a chance to show the community who the Strendur rowing team are and what we can do.

Speaking of which, where are Ava and Frank?" Delia asked.

"Mrs Tuni, Jorg was going to talk to them about their lack of attendance," Mr Johnson quipped. "Savannah was going to do it," Jorg quickly said in his own defence.

"Jorg. You are the captain. It is your responsibility to look after the team, not our newest substitute member." Delia sprung to Savannah's defence. "Savannah, would you go and get them, please?" Savannah stood up. As did Rich. "Not you, Rich, you stay here. We've got enough people missing as it is. And I think Miss Wood has already proven she is more than capable."

Savannah walked past the lake and the school and up the hill to the Johannsen house. Dusk was falling and the charcoal grey light made the house feel eerie. Savannah knocked on the door, moving her legs on the spot to keep warm. She stood for a moment, but no one answered.

"Dana, is that you?" Savannah jumped backwards in shock; the voice didn't come from behind the door, but rather from behind her. Frank's father was sitting on the bench in the front garden despite the oppressive cold. She hadn't noticed him when she walked up the path. "Ava!" he shouted, getting up.

"No, Mr Johannsen, it's Savannah. Savannah Wood. I've come to see Frank and Ava." Just then, the front door opened and Frank stood in the doorway.

"Don't laugh at him," Frank shouted at Savannah, standing in front of his father.

"I wasn't laughing," Savannah replied gently.

"He's not well," Frank said quietly, moving to where his father sat. "Come inside, Pa, it's too cold. People are starting to look at you," Frank said to his father, who brushed him away coldly.

"No. Not until they're home," Mr Johannsen shouted angrily. Frank's eyes filled with tears but Savannah pretended not to notice.

"You'd better come in." Frank gestured to the front door and Savannah walked inside. The house was not how Rich had described it. It was rumoured to be the most glamorous house on the island, but what Savannah saw was a mess. There was no fire in the hearth, it was freezing cold and there was dust covering every surface and washing-up piled high in the sink. Above the unlit fireplace, Savannah instantly recognised a painting of a Selkie, like Liv.

"Have you ever seen one?" Frank asked, pointing at the picture. Savannah didn't know how honest she could be with Frank, so she didn't say anything. Frank hung his head and sighed. "I always thought they were just a myth. Until one day after school, Mum picked up the brown rug next to the fire and walked down the hill. She told us she couldn't live a lie anymore." Frank crumpled to the cold wooden floor. "Then Ava, last month. She went down to the shore to see her, and she hasn't come back. Now they're both in there!"

He pointed to the fjord. "Living as Selkies. Dad's gone mad. He hasn't worked for months. He just sits there, on the bench, trying to get a glimpse of them. He's lost everything. The business is gone. The money's gone." Frank looked down at the floor desperately.

"So that's why you were on the fishing boat and not at school. That's why Ava hasn't been to class, and neither of you have been to rowing practice," Savannah said, bending down to Frank's level.

"Merry bloody Christmas. I had everything, Savannah. A big house. Family. Money. Now it's gone, all gone," he said despairingly. "Why do you care anyway? You don't even know me. And you never knew my mother, or saw how we lived before she left," he said.

"I wondered why you were always so grumpy," admitted Savannah. "And no one our age should have to support their whole family," she added. Frank looked helplessly into Savannah's eyes.

"Now you know," Frank said.

"We might be able to help you," she said.

"Yeah, sure," Frank replied sarcastically.

"Just come with me, please," she pleaded. "What have you got to lose?" After a minute of silence, Frank begrudgingly stood up.

"All right then, let's get this over with," he said.

They walked back to the lake and Savannah pulled Delia aside, telling her of Frank's predicament. Delia didn't even appear shocked.

"We had an inkling there was a Selkie hidden somewhere on the island; Doreen had mentioned it a while ago," she said quietly as they watched Mr Froodroy walk with Frank back towards the Johannsen household, one arm around Frank's shoulder. Meanwhile, Rich came running from the school, with Viking costumes bundled in his arms.

- ▼ -

Despite rowing one team member short, Strendur rowing team were a festive, albeit slightly frightening, sight. The smell of mulled wine and mince pies filled the freezing cold air and scented it like a Christmas candle. Tom, Martha and Theodore stood proudly watching Savannah as she rowed in time with her crew around the lake. It was the most beautiful Christmas Eve Savannah had ever imagined. The candlelight across Waterfall Mile Lake brought back memories of meeting Sid's mother as she carried her candlelit fisherman's lantern. She had never imagined the Selkie Liv spoke of could be Frank's mother.

After receiving a hearty applause, Jorg and his father posed for pictures with the *Hobgoblin* and Savannah and Rich were tasked with taking the costumes back to the school.

"You could have left some lights on." Savannah rolled her eyes to Rich, rubbing her hands together to keep them warm. Rich glanced up to the watchtower.

"I did, though. I know I did," he yelled in defence. Savannah pushed open the huge oak door and fiddled to find the light switch. A flicker of light darted up the corner wrought iron staircase, taking Savannah by surprise.

"Power cut," Rich said, repeatedly flicking the lights on and off with no light appearing in the dark grand hallway.

"I think there's someone here, Rich. I just saw a flicker of light on the spiral stairs," Savannah said nervously.

"Mr Johnson," Rich bellowed.

"It's not him. He's with Jorg having pictures taken," Savannah informed him. The flicker of light again appeared on the staircase. Savannah looked at Rich nervously. "Let's just leave the costumes here and go," Savannah said, backing out of the oak front door.

"Not a chance! We are Sapphires, Savannah. We are brave. If we are going to face our fears out in the fjord, we need to practise with the easy stuff," he whispered.

"Easy?" Savannah gasped. There was a gentle click and the lights in the building all turned on.

"I told you it was nothing," Rich laughed as they continued walking further into the building and carefully stepped up the clinking metal stairs to the watchtower where the costumes were stored.

"You're right, though, Rich. I'm a wimp, aren't I?" Savannah asked, feeling childish.

"Savannah, how can you say that? In the past year, you've changed schools, moved country, joined the Society." He turned around to face her. "Don't get big-headed, but I think you're pretty brave." Rich said.

Without warning, the lights went out again. Savannah exhaled deeply. "You're right. I'm not the person who left England." Savannah smiled to herself.

"You don't even look the same. Your hair covers your ears now, and I'm sure you're getting paler," Rich laughed.

Savannah stroked her silky red hair and tucked it behind her ear, smiling to herself. "I will go first, there's only one flight of stairs left," she said with newfound confidence, still in darkness. Rich held on to her coat from behind and together they reached the top floor, but as they got to the final steps of the watchtower, Savannah caught a flicker of movement out of the corner of her eye. They were not alone. Savannah abruptly stopped walking, and Rich ploughed into the back of her, causing them to topple to the floor in a heap.

Savannah scrambled to her feet, accidently scattering the Viking costumes onto the floor.

"Why did you stop?" Rich yelled, oblivious to the unknown presence in the room. Savannah turned Rich's shoulders to face the corner, where a flicker of light luminated the torso of a woman sitting down, peering out of the window. Rich gasped, "Savannah, it's a ghost."

Savannah wanted to run, but as she flicked her fingers through her hair, she felt a tingle of defiance that she had never felt before. "I'm not running anymore," she whispered in Rich's ear. She took a step towards the lady.

"You are correct on both counts, young man." The woman spoke softly but continued looking out of the window. "I am no longer part of the living." She then turned to face them. "And she is brave," she smiled at Savannah, her blue eyes piercing the darkness. Rich scarpered down the stairs, the old wrought iron stairs erupting with his heavy footsteps as he leapt from stair to stair.

"There are benefits to my existence up here. I see everything. I know what you don't," the lady said.

"About what?" Savannah shook as she replied.

"Out there," the lady replied. As she turned to point out of the window, her silhouette vanished.

"What's out there? What do you know?" Savannah cried, but received no reply.

CHAPTER 11

CHRISTMAS FOG

"I've heard of her; Delia has encountered her once or twice when she's been working late, but I've never seen her myself," Doreen said, the next afternoon, as she poured orange and cinnamon tea from the pot, giving Tricver a stroke as he lay under her round oak table. Savannah felt a little shocked still, not just at meeting the ghost, but also at herself for not running away. "Here, have a mince pie," Doreen said, pulling a tray of golden mince pies out of the oven. Savannah took one and watched the pastry crumble down her ochre-coloured jumper as she took a bite.

"How is the Johannsen boy now?" Doreen enquired thoughtfully, sitting down unceremoniously in the leather armchair by the fire, watching her own mince pie crumbs tumble onto the armrest.

"Frank and Mr Johannsen are staying with the Froodroys for a while until Mr Johannsen feels brighter. Mrs Froodroy thinks some home-cooked food and rhubarb fizz will help," Savannah replied with a mouth full.

"She's quite right; healing comes in many forms. Speaking of which, how have you been getting on while I've been away? Have you been practising?" Doreen asked.

"I've read all of the books and have done some plant orientation with Mai…" Savannah replied.

"Well, there's no time like the present to test out your skills. Here's one of Truffy's stones that needs shining. Would you like to try?" Doreen said, handing over the dull blue tie pin.

"Great." Savannah grabbed her trug. She laid out her textbook under the skylight on the round table and headed outside into the snow. She chose aloe vera from the sea bridge, some angelica leaves, dainty yellow flowers from a *calluna vulgaris* and various stems and berries. Back inside, Savannah prepared the plants in her mixing bowl as directed in her textbooks.

"Ready. Have you got your shining shield, Doreen?" Savannah asked in anticipation as she opened the skylight.

"Ready," Doreen replied eagerly. Savannah dropped the sapphire into the cleansing mixture. "Very quickly you will start to see some bubbles appear on the surface and some gas leakage," said

Doreen, watching the mixture. Doreen's aloe vera plant had shuffled itself next to Savannah's chair, another positioning itself onto the table.

They waited and waited but the mixture showed no signs of bubbling or gas expulsion. Savannah sat herself down in the chair, disheartened. The aloe vera pot shimmied itself to her side and slowly reached out a stem to her hand, as if in consolation.

"Not to worry, it takes time to learn," Doreen said. The smaller aloe vera flew across the table to the trug and flicked the yellow-flowered *calluna vulgaris* across the room. "Aha, I think your plants are trying to tell you something. I thought you said you did some plant orientation with Mai," said Doreen.

"We did. She helped me identify the *calluna vulgaris*," Savannah said, standing up.

"Oh, that is *calluna vulgaris*, but you have the wrong colour," Doreen said. "Only the purple-flowered variety should ever be used for shining." Savannah gave a long sigh and picked the yellow flowers out of her trug. There was a knock at the door, and Rich, Billy and Precious came in. "Let's try again tomorrow. We have a meeting tonight to discuss the events in the Bronx anyway. You go and have some time off this afternoon," Doreen smiled and turned to the new arrivals. "Precious, Rich, Billy, how are you?"

"I'm better now I've found a warm mince pie; Frank keeps eating all of ours, straight out of the oven!" Rich said begrudgingly.

"At least he has his appetite back. I think he's slowly coming to terms with, well, everything," Precious said.

"Yes, the news of Dana and Ava was a shock for all of us, but we can't rightly imagine what it's been like for Frank. What about Mr Johannsen?" asked Doreen.

"Still a misery, understandably, but that chairman of yours has got him to agree to help Theodore assemble the wind turbine in the fjord. Now that his oil drilling business is finished, his oil pipe-laying knowledge should come in pretty useful," Billy said.

"Anyway, we have to dash if we're going to meet Truffy," Precious said, gesturing to Savannah. "I thought we could do some gas-gliding practice, Savannah," she added.

"Oh, I don't know, Precious. I'm not having a very good shining day." Savannah looked at Doreen.

"The trick is not to practise until you get it right, it's to practise until you don't get it wrong," Precious said, putting an arm on Savannah's shoulder.

"Oi, oi," shouted Truffy. Instantly, Savannah felt better for seeing Truffy in the snow-covered removal depot. "While Precious and Savannah practise on the easy ground, me and Billy 'ere have been hard at work making you, Rich, a Christmas gliding obstacle course. Watch out for the rugby scrums and real holly," Truffy added with his hands on his hips, laughing mischievously.

"That's so unfair. Can't I just go for a gentle glide with Savannah and Precious?" Rich winced but looked secretly pleased.

"If you're going to be the best glider on this island, like you keep telling us you will, you need to beat me, too. Take a look. You glide over the van, round the holly bush, over the top of me. All the while, I'll be trying to tackle you down like the green-eyed muted of the Hellson. Then, go through the shed, where a little surprise is waiting, and through the depot doors to the finish line," Billy said.

"Well, Savannah, we couldn't have our Rich getting too big-headed now, could we?" Truffy whispered to Savannah, making her giggle.

"Rich has a natural talent there. Don't feel disheartened it's taking you a bit longer to perfect your gas-gliding technique," Precious said as they walked to the snow-covered grass.

"Perfect it? I can't even get off the ground without crashing. I'm a disaster," Savannah said.

"Savannah, you're just learning. Mistakes are proof you're trying. As long as you are willing to try, I am willing to help. You telling yourself you are going to crash before you start isn't going to do you any good. The art of gas gliding, and it is an art, is to believe in yourself. Think of all the obstacles you have overcome. Use that strength," Precious said.

Savannah looked at the ground. "But what about all the obstacles I haven't overcome?" Savannah said, not able to look Precious in the face.

Precious put her hand on Savannah's shoulder protectively. "You are a natural shiner, Savannah, already you and your aloes are making headlines at the bureau. Some things are buried, not because we cannot overcome them but because they are seeds," Precious said thoughtfully, making Savannah smile.

"Take your sapphire in one of your hands and form a fist. Position your fist towards the ground and think of the strength you have gained from a difficult situation," Precious instructed.

Savannah thought back to herself standing on the stairs and seeing the ghost in the watchtower at school and remembered how good it felt to be brave. "That's it. Now fill yourself up with that pride and self-worth until you can feel it bubbling up and spilling out," Precious said, watching over Savannah. "Now, instead of letting that good feeling spill over, force it out through the hand you are holding your sapphire in," Precious said. Savannah's feet rose gently and gracefully off the floor.

"You've got it!" Precious called. "Now imagine yourself gliding across the field towards the Christmas obstacle course. I will be right next to you," she added calmly. Savannah looked forward towards the obstacle course and did as Precious instructed. She felt a gentle breeze waft through her hair, the snow below her feet remaining untrodden and pure.

"Go, Savs!" shouted Truffy, watching from the sidelines.

"We are going for a glide around the quieter bits of the island," Precious said to him. Rich stuck his thumb up in the air, and Savannah felt more pride overspill. "Well done, Savannah. You see, it really is a matter of believing in yourself. The things that are buried will be resolved at the right time. Given enough inner strength and nurture, you really can find good from pain others have caused," Precious said.

"Yes, I think you're right. I now have true friends in the Sapphire Society. They've helped me see that I can be brave," Savannah smiled.

"Home isn't where you come from, it's where you make it." Precious winked at Savannah.

- ▼ -

The evening sky flooded Strendur Church with a grey haze as Savannah and Rich sat on the shiny church pews.

"The surprise in the shed was only blinkin' Elvis! Truffy asked Pa if he could borrow him to help with my training and he barged me from behind, stabbing his horns straight up my—" Rich was interrupted as Savannah howled with laughter.

"Good evening, Sapphires, Diamonds, Rubies," Mr Froodroy announced from the front of the church. All full members were cloaked; the Sapphires in navy blue, Billy in a burgundy cloak with pale blue trim and Precious in red, standing formally in the church pews. "How nice it is to have international members with us, even more special that they are here for the festive period. Doreen and Terrence are going to give us a brief update on our apprentices' progress, I will give a technical update and then, if there's no other business, we will enjoy some refreshments." Mr Froodroy stood down and Doreen made her way to the front.

"Good evening, all. As you know only too well, the issues in the underwater volcano, the Devil, in the Hudson River, have caused somewhat of a delay for Mai's exam results, but we are all confident Mai will shortly be receiving good news from the bureau examination board." Mai shuffled her feet but was tapped on the back reassuringly by Truffy.

Doreen continued: "Savannah is showing great understanding of shining and has already managed to produce a whole host of aloe vera plants, a feat very few shiners could accomplish. Today, she has been working with Precious on gas gliding, and I can confirm she has conquered the basics very gracefully," Doreen smiled.

"Well done, Savannah. I tell you, her rowing is good, too," Delia chipped in.

Truffy made his way to the front. "Evening all. As Rich's chasing mentor, I can honestly say this boy can glide, Mr Chairman. He really can. Today, with the help of Billy, we put him through his paces. With the exclusion of a minor injury to his jacksie, our boy glided better than most fully cloaked can manage," Truffy announced proudly.

"Wonderful, and how's he getting on with the theory?" Mr Froodroy queried.

"Yes, I'm sure he will be good at that, too." Truffy gave a sideways glance.

"We will look forward to that update early in the new year," Mr Froodroy remarked.

"Yes, Mr Chairman," Truffy replied before turning to whisper something in Rich's ear.

Mr Froodroy made his way to the front again. "I can confirm we have had only one minor Hellson eruption, although we know only too well, that does not mean there aren't shenanigans we are not yet aware of. I can confirm tremendous technical progress, in terms of our gas-dispersing turbine. Our society friend, Mr Theodore Wood, has actioned a team for assembly in the fjord, which will be commencing imminently. I know we already discussed that you would all be willing to assist Mr Wood, but what we will really need are some volunteers to provide security against inevitable Hellson attacks while construction is being carried out," Mr Froodroy said.

"Mr Chairman, I appreciate I am a Ruby and not a Sapphire Society member, but I would be happy to stay on your glorious island a little longer to assist," Precious said.

"We would be delighted, Precious; you are indeed a sparkling addition to our community."

"And me, boss. I'll help, if you don't mind my temporary wonky leg," Billy said.

"Wonky legs are very welcome here, Billy. Assuming our usual fantastic cavalry, Truffy and Delia, are happy to assist?"

"Always, Mr Chairman," replied Delia.

"Count me in," said Truffy.

"Brilliant, then we have a full house. I will let Theodore know he has the best turbine security the bureau has, and I know I'm not exaggerating. For those of you who have fought against the greed of these vile underwater volcanoes here and more recently in the Bronx, I would like to take this opportunity to thank you. The world is a better place because of you all being in it. Others aren't privileged enough to know how much you do for our society and our world, our way of life even, but I do. Thank you all. I was proud of you in the Bronx and I'm proud of what together we are able to achieve here on our little island. I would trust any one of you with my life and I feel deeply honoured to be leading you against the Hellson and beyond."

"Hear, hear. Well said, Chairman," shouted Delia. The meeting drew to a close, and for the first time, Savannah was able to glide proudly off the floor and bow to the chairman, as was customary at the end of each meeting.

"Hello, Theodore." Rich shook Savannah's father's hand as they left the church.

"Pa, what are you doing here?" Savannah gave him a hug.

"Your mother's orders. She wants me to invite all the Sapphires and extended society members to Christmas dinner," he said.

Mr Froodroy, on hearing this, coughed to clear his throat and announced loudly, "Can I have all members' attention please. All those wishing to join the Wood family for Christmas dinner, please let Theodore know, now." Quietly taking Theodore aside, he said, "I know we would be delighted to join you, but I had better check with Mrs Froodroy first."

"No need, your wife has accepted already. She has been planning it with Martha," Theodore replied, smiling.

"But of course, I tend to be the last to know these things," Mr Froodroy laughed.

"Truffy usually has Christmas dinner with me, but I know we would be delighted to accept your invitation," Delia said.

"If you are sure it won't be too much trouble, I would be delighted to come," Precious said.

"Me too," said Billy.

"That's settled then. I'll let Martha know everyone will come. See you at home, Savannah. I have to just pop to Froowind headquarters with Mr Froodroy quickly to grab some paperwork," Theodore said.

Savannah and Rich slowly wandered home, gas gliding when locals weren't looking. "Why are we going this way?" Savannah asked, as he pulled her away from their usual route home towards the opposite direction.

"Just for a change of scenery," Rich smiled. Savannah raised her eyebrows and smiled suspiciously at him.

"Okay. There's something I want to show you this way," he admitted. "Anyway, Christmas at yours then?"

"Certainly seems that way. At least we have a week off rowing practice before Jorg really cracks the whip for our extra training sessions," Savannah replied.

"Yes, and now you've been promoted from substitute to the crew, there's no excuse for you or Frank to skive off," Rich said. The water on the fjord was perfectly quiet; even the gentle lapping of the waves seemed muted.

"Look, there's Mai and Truffy up ahead. It's very foggy near the shore where they are," Savannah said.

"Wait." Rich put his hand protectively in front of Savannah to stop her walking forward. "Look, I don't think we should catch them up; it looks like they're arguing," Rich whispered. They were too far away to hear what was being said. Truffy was waving his hands in the air and Mai had her back to him with her head in her hands. The fog was getting denser, obscuring their vision.

"Truffy's crying now, too," Savannah whispered from behind the large aloe they had used to hide behind.

"Truffy's not a crier, Savannah. I'm sure he wouldn't be crying," Rich replied, disbelievingly.

"He is, look." Savannah pointed to him. Truffy was wiping his eyes, but now his hands weren't gesticulating in the air, they were around his throat.

"He's not crying, he's choking. It's the fog, it's Hellson," Rich shouted as he jumped from behind the aloe vera plant. Rich glided at lightning speed over to Truffy and was by his side instantly. Rich threw his sapphire-studded hat into the dense gas, causing a loud, eerie scream to emanate from the fjord which Savannah knew only too well. Rich began battling against the gas with a sapphire in his spare hand.

"No!" Mai was screaming and kicking and punching at the gas. Purple flowers flew from the ground and stuck to Savannah's face, covering her nose and mouth. She realised she could breathe clearly thanks to the flowers filtering the gas, but Rich and Truffy were struggling. Savannah glided to where Truffy was. His hands were around his throat but he was able to clear some of the stench by moving his head and collecting some of the gas into his sapphire stud earring. Savannah glided around him and removed her necklace, swinging it around the ground in circles to clear the air, allowing Truffy to breathe. The gas was suctioned into her necklace like a vacuum cleaner. As quickly as it had arrived, the fog lifted, the noise stopped and the foul gas began to disperse. Mai, Truffy, Savannah and Rich lay cold and gasping on the freezing snow, the waves lashing noisily at their feet.

CHAPTER 12

SEEDS

"Merry Christmas, darling." Martha stroked Savannah's hair as she awoke from her heavenly slumber.

"It's not often you wake me, nowadays, Ma. It's usually Big Al," Savannah smiled, yawning.

"I think they've been busy," Martha smiled, knowingly. The aloes in her bedroom were decorated with Christmas baubles and slowly hoisted Savannah out of bed.

"Aloes, what are you doing?" Savannah shouted in shock and amusement. The aloes carried Savannah down the metal spiral staircase and into the orangery. Holly, ivy and mistletoe adorned every nook and cranny; it was beautifully decorated. The large dining table's chairs each had their own mistletoe climbing around each chairback, spelling out society members' names. Even Tricver lying in front of the wood burner sat proudly with a red poinsettia flower attached to his collar.

"You aloes never cease to amaze me," Savannah mused, inspecting the beautiful purple-flowering *calluna vulgaris*, aloes and holly which spelt out *Savannah* on her favourite leather armchair, tucked into the side of the table. Tricver trotted over to Savannah and accepted a tickle behind the ears before barking wildly to be let out of the orangery doors. "Okay, okay, hold on," Savannah said as she fumbled in her pocket for the heart-shaped key.

The lock clicked open and Tricver flew out into the garden, which backed onto the Froodroys' house. Tricver began digging. "Tricky, don't do that. Ma will be furious," she hissed, pulling at his collar for him to stop. Tricver still dug, despite her best efforts, until a large hole had appeared. Savannah ran into the orangery to collect a spade to fill in the hole, but as she returned, Tricver barked at the freshly dug hole triumphantly. Inside the hole was a sapphire pot. As she removed it, Tricver dug again, unearthing yet another pot. Eventually, the hole was so wide it had hidden at least seventy new sapphire pots. Tricver licked her face and spun around to rebury the loose soil.

"I think that's a Christmas present from Grandma and Tricver," Martha said, passing Savannah a hot cup of tea. "There's a few more pressies inside if you want to open them. It looks like Tricver has filling the hole back in covered," she smiled as she helped Savannah put the pots on shelves in the orangery.

"Merry Christmas, darling!" Her father handed her a small box wrapped in brown paper with a gold ribbon. She sat on the sheepskin rug in front of the sitting room fire and pulled at the ribbon, making the brown paper unfold. "A little something special from me and Ma."

Under the paper was a blue velvet box. She popped the lid up with a satisfying click to reveal a pair of gold and sapphire rectangular earrings. "We thought now your hair is growing longer, you might like something to draw attention to your beautiful locks," Theodore said. Savannah felt her cheeks burn hot and Martha looked at her daughter with her frequent expectant gaze. Savannah took a deep breath.

"Precious thinks you can use difficult situations to your advantage, even if you haven't yet overcome them. Even the things that feel so dark, it's as if you've been buried." Savannah looked into her parents' worried eyes. Martha took one of the earrings out of the trinket box and handed it to Savannah for her to put on. Tom giggled, amused at all the lights and presents.

"We will never underestimate you, my dear, especially when it comes to plants and seeds," Theodore said, smiling.

"And it's good to see you've stopped underestimating yourself. Which brings me to my next present for you," Martha said, handing over another, slightly larger gift.

"Sheepskin gloves and earmuffs," Savannah said, grinning.

"Mr Johnson reports you're one of the hardest working substitute rowing team members they've ever had, so I thought you would need something to keep you warm during all those practice sessions coming up," Martha smiled.

"Thanks, Ma. I love them," Savannah said, slurping her tea.

- ▼ -

Society members slowly began to arrive and the aroma of roast turkey filled the little cottage.

"Jan and Frank have made the move home. Jan's agreed to work for Froowind to help you assemble the turbine, Theodore," Mr Froodroy said, shaking his hand.

"Great news. How's Frank?" Theodore queried.

"Frank now doesn't have to worry about working after school or at weekends, so he seems to be doing better," Mr Froodroy reported.

"Good for the rowing team too; we can't lose two members," Delia chipped in. Savannah and Rich wandered through the cottage into the orangery. Savannah was keen to show him the aloes' decorations.

"I love the chair name places," Rich said, impressed.

"That's the aloes, they did it all overnight," Savannah replied as they sat in front of the orangery wood burner with Tricver and Tornado.

"Those plants definitely have your back, Savannah. Those purple flowers flew straight to your face when you glided into the gas. I couldn't breathe at all, but you and Mai seemed fine," Rich said.

"Yes, I didn't realise until after the gas was gone that they were even there. They formed a sort of gas mask, covering my mouth and nose, allowing me to breathe through. It's all described in the book, *Facing your Fauna*," Savannah said.

"So how did Mai manage to breathe, then? She didn't have a purple flower mask, but she didn't struggle to breathe at all," Rich questioned.

"You're right. I'll have to ask her to teach me that," Savannah replied.

The Woods, The Froodroys, Delia, Truffy, Mai, Doreen, Precious and Billy all sat down at the table. Ching ching ching, Theodore tapped his knife gently on his glass, cleared his throat and stood up. "On behalf of myself, Martha, Savannah and Tom, we would like to warmly welcome you to enjoy Martha's sublime roast turkey. You have all become such splendid friends and we warmly thank you for your kindness and friendship since we moved here to Strendur. Merry Christmas! Now let's eat," Theodore said. All at the table enjoyed their roast dinner, even Tricver and Tornado who loitering underneath the table enjoyed some scraps passed down by Rich.

"Sherry round the tree?" Theodore asked, once everyone had finished.

"Good idea. I believe there may be some presents still under it," said Truffy, winking.

"Indeed, there are. Everyone grab a glass of sherry off the tray. Savannah, Rich, you had better stick to rhubarb fizz," Martha said.

"Fine by me; have you ever tasted sherry?" Rich guffawed.

"Rhubarb fizz for me, too, please, Martha. I can't get enough of it." Precious clinked glasses with Savannah.

"Rich, here's a gift for you." Delia passed it to him. Rich tore off the paper.

"A watch! Thank you so much, Delia," Rich smiled.

"A sapphire watch, to help keep you on time and out of trouble," Delia smiled.

"We can but try," Mr Froodroy joked.

"Mai, 'ere's a little something from me to you," Truffy said, quietly handing Mai a small box wrapped in gold paper and then gulping the contents of his sherry glass in one mouthful. Mai flicked the box open, making the room audibly gasp. Inside the box was a solitaire teardrop-shaped sapphire ring.

"I don't know what to say, Truffy," Mai said quietly.

"How about, 'Thank you'?" Rich tittered, but no one else laughed at his joke.

"Say you'll wear it, at least." Truffy leaned forward to hold Mai's hand but she turned and sat back down on the chair, clicking the box closed.

"Savannah, this is from me," Mai said, quickly diverting attention away from herself, lifting a heavy object from under the tree onto the floor where Savannah sat. Savannah carefully untied the gold string and pulled off the red paper. Inside was a large grey and blue stone mixing bowl, with a matching wooden spoon, just like the one she had admired at Mai's house when she visited.

"Mai, it's wonderful. Thank you. Thank you so much." Savannah went to Mai and gave her a hug.

"You may be pleased to have us as friends, but we are even more pleased to have someone as special as you protecting our island," Mai said, grasping both of Savannah's hands in her own.

"Hear, hear," said Doreen.

"If nobody objects, I'm going to try and shine Grandma's necklace using my beautiful new mixing bowl," Savannah smiled as the sherry bottle continued its journey around the room. Rich carried the heavy bowl and spoon through the study and into the orangery, where the table and chairs had been removed and it resembled normality. As Rich placed the bowl onto the wooden workbench, Savannah took off her necklace and placed it inside.

"When I was little, Ma taught me to knit. I haven't done it for a while now, but I noticed you were cold at rowing practice and, well, Merry Christmas. Here you are," Rich muttered, pulling a parcel out of his pocket and placing it between them on the sheepskin rug. Savannah got off the rug and paced purposefully over to her plant shelf, where she brought down a green parcel with red ribbon.

"Funnily enough, I have a little something for you, too," Savannah smiled. Together, they unwrapped their respective gifts, Rich ripping his wrapping paper quicker than Savannah.

"Savannah, I love it. I just hope I don't kill it," Rich chortled as he held a small blue sapphire pot with purple *calluna vulgaris* inside.

"You said it was the pretty purple flowers that were covering my face against the gas, so I thought you might like one for yourself," Savannah smiled. She pulled the last scraps of paper and string from the jumbled package and found a navy blue woollen scarf. She instantly wrapped it around her neck and snuggled into the warmth of the wool. "It's exquisite, Rich. You made this?" Savannah asked.

"Don't tell anyone," Rich said, staring at the floor. "It's not a very manly skill, apparently. As I found out last winter. Bloody Toftir lot," he said.

"So that's why you want to beat Sven and the Toftir rowers so much," Savannah giggled.

"It wasn't funny," Rich said defensively.

"No, no, Rich. I wasn't laughing at you, far from it," Savannah said.

"Well, it looks like you are. It was a stupid idea. Why would you understand? Perfect Miss Wood, always on time, always with a special skill," Rich said, standing up and trying to grab the scarf from around Savannah's neck. The mood in the room had changed so abruptly that Savannah didn't know what to do.

"That's not true, Richard," Precious said, appearing in the doorway.

"It is true. Savannah's special. She has special plant powers that even Mai can't beat, and Savannah's only just started learning. Everyone likes her, even bloody Tricver," Rich said, holding back tears.

"Where is this coming from?" Savannah asked, perplexed, but Rich just ignored her. Tricver got out of his bed and put his head on Savannah's lap.

"Ask her why her hair used to be so short," Precious continued, walking into the orangery and closing the glass and metal door behind her. Rich turned directly to Savannah and she blushed poinsettia red with years' worth of Margale High tears beginning to pour from her eyes.

"Where I used to call home, in South Africa, I had a tough time growing up," Precious said, wrapping the scarf back around Savannah's neck and using the blue wool scarf fringe to blot Savannah's tears.

"I was born Jacob, you see, not Precious. I was the boy who played with dolls and wore my sister's clothes when no one was looking. Then I got older, I grew my hair and people at school noticed I was different to the other boys. I was so proud of my jaw-length hair; you should have seen it," Precious smiled with tears in her eyes. "But the girls didn't like it. They called me names and held me down and shaved off my beautiful hair with a razor," Precious said. Rich looked at her in disbelief. "It takes someone who knows that pain to be able to recognise it in others," she said, looking at Savannah. "Savannah and I are different; we have lived different lives and have been affected by bullies in a myriad of different ways. Being transgender, I have been targeted and ridiculed by almost everyone I have ever known. But I am stronger because of it, and I can recognise when others have suffered."

Savannah wiped her tears and nodded. "Kirsty Sharp and the Margale High swimming team cut my hair off. They didn't want a ginger in their team," Savannah sobbed.

"I never knew. I never even guessed, Savannah." Rich stood up. "How could these people be so cruel? This is who we are risking our lives to defend," Rich said angrily.

"If you believe in good, Rich, you must put all your energy into it. Use your energy for good, and the bad and the greed will have no power left. Without fuel, they have no fire. This island is glorious, with beautiful people from many backgrounds and circumstances," Precious said.

"Except Toftir," Rich smiled.

"Everyone has their own battles to deal with; just look at Frank," Precious said.

"Yes. You're right," Rich shrugged, and sat down on the floor next to Savannah.

Precious gently rose her glass of rhubarb fizz into the air and cleared her throat before leaning forward and whispering, "To seeds, and all we may become."

"To seeds," Rich and Savannah vigorously whispered their response through tight lipped smiles.

CHAPTER 13

SELKIES

Savannah's Christmas scarf, earmuffs and gloves made her feel toasty warm as she skipped out of the Wood family home into the freezing February air for her early morning rowing practice around Waterfall Mile Lake.

"Being up this early is stupid," Rich growled as he began power walking around Waterfall Mile Lake.

"What's stupid is that Ava still isn't here. Tell her from me, Frank, she's out," shouted Mr Johnson over the clatter of oars and splashing water.

"Sorry, Frank, I delayed it for as long as I could," Jorg said as he patted Frank on the back, and quickly turned himself around to face Rich and Savannah. "She's visiting family abroad, apparently. We all know what that means; her father sent her to a private school but can't afford to send Frank, too. Poor guy,"

Jorg whispered, but said it so indiscreetly that Frank heard and had a private chuckle to himself, raising his hands in the air and laughing to Rich and Savannah from across the boat.

"Savannah, congratulations. You've been promoted to the first crew. Now, you know the drill: catch and finish, catch and finish. Oskar, put some blinkin' welly in. Victor, if you want to live up to your name and be victorious, you need to put a bit more care into your catch," Mr Johnson shouted from the front of the boat with little respite. The big race against Toftir was getting closer and Mr Johnson's training regime was growing increasingly rigorous.

The day at school passed by, with many groaning yawns from the rowing crew and the usual lunch of fish pie and rhubarb crumble. From the school window, Savannah had a perfect view of the fjord, her father, Jan Johannsen and the assigned society members acting as Hellson security. Progress was slow but gradually the foundations were being laid.

"As you know, the Valentine's ball is approaching and this year will be held in our very own grand hall, due to the Froowind headquarters being unavailable," Delia said. "May I remind you that our friends from Norway will also be joining us at the ball, so we expect your very best behaviour." The bell rang loudly and the class began to pack up their oars and belongings.

"Rumour has it you're on the first rowing crew now, Savannah," Sven said as he shuffled alongside her out of the big oak door.

"Yes, that's right," Savannah replied politely.

"Are you going to the Valentine's ball?" Sven asked as he flicked his blond hair away from his face.

"I'm not sure," Savannah replied, giving a sideways glance to Rich.

"Watch where you stick that oar please, Sven," Delia said as she let the class out of the door.

"Yes, miss," Sven huffed.

"See you tomorrow then, I'm off to Truffy's." Rich looked directly at Savannah before fleeing onto the sea bridge. Savannah strolled along the fields towards Doreen's cottage and dragged her feet through the snow. In the fjord, she could see Sven and the rest of the Toftir pupils from class rowing home. Sven still managed to flick his hair even while rowing. Her eyes were drawn away from the Toftir boat and the sapphire wind turbine crew to a brown blob, bobbing in the water. She stopped and screwed her eyes up for better vision. The brown blob was moving against the current. Savannah walked closer to the shore to get a clearer view. As she got closer, she realised there wasn't one brown blob but three, and they were seals, darting up and down around her father and the wind turbine, circling. Savannah sat down and pulled the flapjack her mother had made her out of her bag, eating it as she sat on her school bag to protect her clothes from the snow. The seals continued, apparently unnoticed by anyone else. Suddenly she became aware of a presence behind her, crunching slow footsteps.

"Just like your grandmother, you don't miss anything." Mai touched her on the shoulder, smiling. "Or so I've heard anyway," she added.

"Do you think it could be Ava and Dana out there?" Savannah wondered aloud; her gaze fixed on the rich chocolate brown fur creatures.

"Anything's possible. Are you heading to Doreen's?" Mai asked.

"Yes, I just got distracted," Savannah replied.

"Good afternoon, shiners." Doreen appeared behind them.

"Have you seen the seals in the fjord? Is it Ava and Dana?" Savannah blustered.

"Very likely, the larger of the three is definitely Liv. They are circling around the turbine. Liv said they wouldn't help us anymore, but luckily she seems to have changed her mind," Doreen added.

"Nearly results day now," Mai interjected.

"I have total faith in you, Mai, as do the rest of the Sapphires," Doreen said reassuringly as they strode through the entrance of the cottage.

"I know," Mai said, looking at the floor. Doreen looked at her students. Savannah had plants surrounding her chair and Petunia the puffin was tapping at the window to try and get Savannah's attention. In contrast, Mai sat in her chair looking forlorn.

"I think we should take our tea, grab some blankets and check out the turbine progress," Doreen smiled.

"Great idea. The only thing I miss from England is watching Pa work. I have so many lovely friends, I don't get time now," Savannah added. They sat by the edge of the fjord resting on sheepskin rugs with warm enamel mugs filled with steaming hot tea.

"How I love this fjord. It's so soothing to watch the water tickling the rocks," Mai romanticised.

Theodore waved from the large boat he was working on to assemble the turbine base. Savannah waved back, holding her warm tea in the air and snuggling into her navy wool scarf.

"Speaking of rocks, I see you aren't wearing the ginormous ring Truffy got you for Christmas," Doreen observed.

Mai sprung up off her warm rug. "Look. The water. It's spiralling around the turbine base. It's Liv. She's up to something." The water was beginning to swell around the sides of the boat, rising high like gigantic towers.

"Pa!" Savannah wailed in distress at the top of her voice. Bodies were being flung from the water out of the tornado into the vast mass of blue, miles from shore. "I have to help them. Doreen. Where's your boat?" Savannah yelled.

"Sid's *Sea Machine* is tied up to the rock, but if we want to get them all in, there will only be room for one of us to row," Doreen said anxiously. The tiny rowing boat was pushed into the water by Mai and Doreen, with Savannah and two old oars attached. Savannah rowed as fast as she could while Doreen and Mai yelled directions as she avoided the vast water tornado and battled against the waves.

"Precious!" Savannah shouted to get her attention.

"Thank goodness," Precious said as she swung her legs over the side of the boat. "Jan is over there." Precious pointed to Jan Johannsen, who was treading water close by. Savannah edged the boat as close as she could to him as he shouted expletives, desperately clambering into the boat.

"Pa. Where's Pa?" Savannah asked, frantically.

"Over there, near the massive wall of water!" Jan shouted.

Theodore was swimming proficiently towards them, waving. "I'm so glad you joined the rowing team," he remarked, as Precious and Jan hauled him on board.

"Savannah, watch out," Mai screeched from the shore.

"What's she on about? We are clear of the water spiral," Jan sneered.

"Billy. Billy's not here!" Theodore stood up, making the tiny boat wobble.

"He's there, and he has company," Precious revealed, pointing to Billy treading water a few metres away, struggling to keep his head above water and encircled by three grey and brown seals. Savannah clumsily steered the boat around, towards them.

"Billy, get in," Savannah shouted. Two of the seals swam in front of him blocking his path. A large thud hit the bottom of the boat, making it shake. Savannah screamed.

"Dana, no!" Jan yelled at the seals.

"I can't push them out of the way; my leg isn't strong enough," Billy spluttered. One of the seals swam away from Billy and vanished.

"It's okay, Billy. It's Dana and Ava; they're going to help us," Jan assured him. Billy tried again to swim towards the boat but the largest seal hissed yellow teeth and forced its weight on top of him, submerging him up to his neck. The other seals appeared at either side of the full-to-bursting rowing boat. "I don't understand," Jan said to the seal. In synchrony, the seals began to rock the boat from side to side, capsizing them all into the water. The freezing water hit Savannah like a blade stabbing into her chest.

Theodore flipped the little vessel back over and dived down underwater to rescue Billy from the depths. "He's a dead weight, Savannah. I need your help," he shouted as he disappeared under the surface.

"I will help," Precious volunteered, diving down, followed quickly by Savannah. Precious and

Theodore put Billy's arms over each of them and began vehemently kicking water to reach the surface.

Underwater, Savannah saw a familiar face. "I warned you, Sapphires. If you don't return our people to us, the king will turn against you." The hypnotic black eyes morphed into human form, revealing Liv's face.

"We did! Ava and Dana are here," Savannah mouthed bubbles underwater.

"Last warning. No more of your vile human trickery. We need all of them," Liv screeched in Savannah's face before returning to seal form. She rounded up the other two seals before diving down into the dark water of the fjord, out of sight.

- ▼ -

"That Hellson of yours is ferocious," Theodore said to Savannah as they sat in front of the orangery fire, with warm tea supplied by Martha.

"But where was the fog and the noise?" Billy questioned.

"Listen, you two," Martha spoke sternly to Savannah and her father, "let the man rest. He's had a hideous amount of water in his lungs. He's lucky to be alive, so if you want your security team back, Theodore, I suggest you do as I say and stop unsettling him even more." Martha slammed the door as she left the room murmuring, "Damn Hellson," under her breath.

Billy closed his eyes and fell asleep next to the wood burner, leaning against the leather armchair and propped up with soft feather-filled cushions. Mr Froodroy gently tapped on the orangery room door to be let in. Theodore stood up and shook his hand. "Please, Theodore, sit down, sit down. How are you feeling? How's Billy?" Mr Froodroy enquired thoughtfully.

"Just having a snooze," Theodore replied. "Martha is insisting he stays with us until he's fully recovered. He's now got two damaged legs, I'm afraid. A seal bite now on his good leg, but Doreen's given him some sort of tincture to help it heal."

"Yes, very peculiar indeed," Mr Froodroy said quietly, so as not to wake Billy. "It was Doreen and Mai I was trying to locate actually."

"They went straight to Mai's house. She was very distressed by it all," Savannah added.

"Madam Wood," Nigel leaned around from behind Mr Froodroy and bowed his head.

"Yes, Nigel has come to see Mai," he added quietly.

"On behalf of KAPOW, you understand." Nigel said KAPOW in the style of a superhero, making Mr Froodroy cringe.

"Yes, well, we shall look there, then."

Mr Froodroy steered Nigel away, but Nigel's eyes were fixed on the orangery. "So here we are. Meinhild Simonsen's legendary orangery." He walked around Mr Froodroy, inviting himself in for a better look.

"It looks like you're doing pretty well here," Nigel said to Savannah.

"Thank you," Savannah smiled.

"The pots, look at your pots!" Nigel threw his hands up over his mouth. "Tell me that isn't *calluna vulgaris*, in this climate, in full bloom," Nigel said excitedly.

"Yes, it seems to quite like it here. In fact, I thought it might look quite good as an addition to our roof, if my parents agree, of course," Savannah said, raising her eyebrows to her father.

"You're the green-fingered one, Savannah. You do as you see fit." Theodore rested his hand on her shoulder.

"Green-fingered?" Nigel snorted. "Your daughter is more than green-fingered, Mr Wood." He wagged his finger at him reproachfully. "A *calluna vulgaris* roof would be exquisite, not to mention a potential lifesaver to its occupants if Hellson boundaries are ever breached," Nigel said passionately. He turned around to face Mr Froodroy. "I can see **KAPOW** won't need to audit this young lady. I only wish the same could be said for Mai. Now, can you take me to her, please, Chairman?" Nigel said authoritatively, spinning on his heels and departing. "Good day, Madam Wood," Nigel said, tipping his head as he left.

CHAPTER 14

VALENTINE'S BALL

"Beautiful," Theodore announced as Savannah strode barefoot down the orangery staircase in a navy-blue velvet gown. The sumptuous fabric accentuated her pale skin and matched her elongated sapphire earrings and her grandmother's sparkling necklace.

"Precious, you can certainly choose a ball gown," Martha said.

"Doesn't she look majestic?" Precious smiled. "There's just one thing left to do. You need to learn how to walk in heels. Here we are, I've got a pair here in your size to start you off. No friend of mine can go to a ball in trainers," Precious scoffed, handing her a pair of blue satin kitten heels. Savannah slid the heels onto her feet and walked gracefully around the orangery. Tricver wagged his tail and sat up for the performance.

"As I suspected, Precious, she's a natural," Martha said proudly.

"That was easier than learning to gas glide, that's for sure," Savannah said.

"Well, come on, come on. Precious is going to take a family picture for us," Martha said. Tom sat on top of Tricver while Martha and Theodore positioned themselves on either side of Savannah.

"What about Tornado?" Martha called. Precious picked up Tornado and handed the disgruntled cat to Theodore.

"Can all the Woods say cheese?" Precious called out.

"Cheese!" they cheered, in time with a click of the camera.

Billy hobbled into the room on his crutches. "So who are you going with, Savannah?" he enquired.

"Astrid and the other rowing girls are meeting me at school, but Delia's walking there with me," Savannah smiled. Billy looked at Precious, questioningly.

"I know, Billy, I know." Precious rolled her eyes.

"What about next door?" Theodore asked.

"Oh, Rich is walking with Frank," Savannah replied.

Delia tapped on the door and entered. "Evening all. I guess you're going to have a nice evening in front of the fire while I try to control this glamorous lot." Delia pointed to Savannah, winking.

"No offence, but I don't know why Savannah didn't go with that rower from Toftir. Now there's a sportsman. My contacts in the sporting community in England reckon he's going to be one of the best rowers in your generation. He keeps coming to the door, asking for Savannah, but she keeps pretending she's out. He leaves her a box of chocolates and rows home. Not that it takes him long to row back to Toftir, he's so fast," Billy shared with the room.

"Yes, well, Billy; good sportsman or not, you can't always trust what you see; even salt looks like sugar!" Delia smiled to Savannah.

"I couldn't have put it better myself, Delia," Precious added.

"Come on then, Savannah, grab your dress coat. To the ball we go!" Delia opened the door and proudly waved goodbye.

"Hold on, hold on!" Billy hopped to the door. "Can I eat the chocolates the rower boy brought for you, then?" he called out.

Savannah swung her sheepskin cape over her shoulders. "Too late, Precious got to them first!" Savannah laughed as she closed the door.

"So, you've been with us a while now. How are you finding it?" Delia asked as they strode along the sea bridge.

"I like it better than the last place, that's for sure. English is my favourite lesson, as you can probably tell from my grades," Savannah replied.

"Actually, I meant the Sapphire Society," Delia smiled.

"Ah," Savannah looked up. "I think I'm doing okay."

"When you first joined, you were given a choice between shining and chasing," Delia stated.

"Yes. I feel like I made the right choice. My aloes are doing really well and the purple-flowering *calluna vulgaris* I added to our roof has worked out a lot better than I imagined," Savannah replied thoughtfully.

"Pretty spectacular actually, that roof of yours." Delia tapped her on the back.

"Thanks," Savannah grinned modestly.

"Rich told me about you and him seeing Truffy and Mai after the society meeting a while ago," Delia said.

"Oh, I didn't think we were going to mention that. Yes, it was the same flowers that helped me breathe through the gas that day that I've planted on the roof," Savannah said.

"Yes, yes, but you gas glided and rounded up Hellson gas with that," Delia said, pointing to her grandmother's necklace.

"Yes," Savannah replied, stepping carefully to avoid splashes on her new shoes.

Delia threw her hands in the air. "I knew it," she said triumphantly.

"I was just trying to help." Savannah stopped walking, looking at her new shoes.

"Savannah, Sapphires can't do both," Delia said impatiently.

"I knew Rich and Truffy could handle it – it wasn't much gas. I just thought I'd help and speed the process up," Savannah said defensively.

"No, you don't understand, Savannah. I'm not saying you're not allowed to do both. I mean, no one else has ever been *able* to do both," Delia said, with a huge grin.

"Oh, I see," Savannah beamed.

"No one, that is, except one person. Can you guess who?" Delia asked, wide-eyed.

"Grandma?" Savannah laughed.

"Grandma, indeed," Delia confirmed as they approached the watchtower school entrance.

- ▼ -

The school was a hive of activity. The rowing girls, Astrid and Freya, both looked so different out of school uniform and sports gear, in shimmering gowns. Delia slotted into school mode and quickly organised matters inside. Frank and Rich strolled up to Savannah, both wearing full black dinner suits.

"Doesn't he look great?" Astrid smiled in their direction.

"Yes, he does." Savannah had never seen Rich looking so well turned out.

"He actually seems happier now his mum and Ava have moved to Australia to live with their aunt. Strange really, I always thought Frank and Ava got on okay, but I guess not," Astrid chatted.

"Oh, I see, yes." Savannah swallowed hard.

"I see Rich, on the other hand, forgot to clean his shoes," Freya said, rolling her eyes.

Savannah looked down at Rich's shoes and noticed a heavy covering of dust.

"Evening, ladies," Frank said.

"You scrub up all right." Rich nudged Savannah, making her wobble on her heels.

"Thanks." She leant on him to steady herself.

"So do you," she smiled.

"Thanks," he leant in and whispered in Savannah's ear, "except I had to go to Froowind headquarters in my suit to collect the turbine base plans for Pa on the way, and I got my shoes covered in dust. You don't think anyone will notice, do you?" he asked, wincing.

"No, no, no. Not at all," Savannah lied. Mr Johnson stood at the school oak door in a full black dinner suit, at the top of a sweeping red carpet. The evening was cold but bright and the helicopter escorting the visiting Norwegian students made the ball feel more like an awards ceremony. A group of Norwegian students in full ball gowns and suits exited the chopper with much more sophistication than Savannah thought she would ever be capable of.

"Are you coming in, Froodroy, or are you just going to ogle the pretty girls from the doorway?" Mr Johnson barked, taking the tickets out of his hand.

"Isn't it something?" Rich nudged Savannah as he watched them dismount. "I mean, the helicopter, not the girls, Mr Johnson," he added, blushing as he breathed in to make his tailored shirt fit.

"Good evening," one of the girls with flowing golden hair said as she wafted past in a purple silk floor-length gown.

"Good evening," Savannah smiled, tucking her hair behind her ears.

"Your earrings, they're so beautiful," the girl complimented Savannah.

"Oh, thank you. I'm Savannah and this is Rich," Savannah beamed.

"I'm Olga," she said. "Are you from here? Is this your school?"

"Yes, I joined last year," Savannah replied as Rich shuffled by her side.

"You're so lucky to have a school like this; our school in Norway is so small and boring." Olga and her friends looked captivated by the stone gargoyles and vast rooms, which Savannah still felt proud to be a part of.

"Olga, hey!" Sven, who had been lingering near them, now pushed in front of Savannah and extended his hand. "Careful who you associate with,

Olga, these two will bore you to death with their knitting stories." Sven sneered at Rich, who promptly walked away to speak to the rowing team. "So, where are you from?" Sven continued, looking sideways at Savannah.

"Utsira, a little—" Olga replied but was quickly interrupted by Sven replying dismissively, "Never heard of it."

"Hold on," Savannah interjected. "I have. My friend Mai is from Utsira. It's a tiny island off the west coast of Norway, isn't it? You have strange seaweed that makes your breath smell—" Savannah said excitedly.

"Ugh, sounds delightful," Sven interrupted again, sarcastically.

"Yes, Savannah, that's right. We call it sea stench," Olga said, frowning. "But there's no one called Mai from our island."

"You must know Mai. Long brown hair, my height. She's about twenty-five," Savannah continued, trying to jog Olga's memory.

"Definitely not our Utsira. There must be another island with the same name. Wait until I tell the others." She started walking off into the grand hall to find her friends.

Sven stared at Savannah defensively. "If you had just come with me to the ball, you wouldn't have to try and make new friends with sea stench people," he sneered.

"I've got friends. Good ones, thank you very much," Savannah hissed quietly in his direction, her hands shaking. Rich ran over at seeing the commotion.

"Oh look, what are you going to do, Froodroy, hit me with your knitting needles? You should have chosen better friends, Savannah, then they might tell you where they actually come from instead of making up a stinking island with stinking seaweed." Sven turned around only to bump into Frank's large muscular build, blocking his path.

"Problem with my mates, Sven?" Frank reared up to Sven, causing him to step backwards in shock.

"You used to be all right, Frank. But not now. You're a Strendur loser like the rest of them," Sven spat in response. From behind, Rich gas glided into the back of Sven, forcing him at great speed out of the grand hall and past Mr Johnson into the cold night. Sven turned back and looked aghast.

"On you go, Sven, you got what you deserve. Now get rowing," said Mr Johnson. Crepe paper hearts flew around the room due to the commotion, causing a cheer from the other students as they danced, oblivious to the altercation.

"Like my dad says, mate," Frank said, having witnessed Rich gliding through the air, "I don't know, and I don't want to find out. Got it?" Rich nodded in response.

Delia appeared out of nowhere. "Richard, did you just…?" Delia looked down her glasses at him.

"No, miss, no." He fumbled his reply, looking over her shoulder.

"Good. I thought not, because if you had, I would have to report you," she glared.

"Yes, miss." He looked down at the floor and put his sapphire quickly back into his suit jacket pocket.

"Go and find Frank and stop him bragging about it," she ordered.

"Yes, Mrs Tuni," Rich replied as he shuffled back through the front entrance.

"And you, Savannah," she continued, "since you seem to have such good bravery and chasing skills, you can go up to the watchtower and find some spare crepe paper hearts. Richard just glided half of them out of the door," Delia directed. Savannah paused, remembering the ghost. "Now, please." Delia pointed to the spiral staircase in the other corner of the entrance hall.

"Can't I use that one?" Savannah pointed to the central oak staircase.

"No, Savannah, that will only take you to the second floor, you know that. The costumes and decorations are stored in the watchtower, six floors up. Get moving!" Delia pointed to the metal spiral staircase.

CHAPTER 15

KAPOW

Savannah began the ascent up the cold black metal stairs, hitching up the front of her mermaid tail ball gown as she gingerly strode step by step. Savannah stopped halfway and peered out to the fjord. Liv and the Selkies had damaged the base of the turbine foundations, and future progress was going to be slowed down considerably without a full security team. Her kitten heels clicked up the final steps, giving her a clear view of the room. She paused and took a deep breath while visually searching the room for the ghost's presence. The room was clear, so she began fumbling in cardboard boxes for the spare crepe paper hearts.

"They are in the other box," came a voice from the stairs. Savannah gasped, spinning around on her kitten heels to see the ghost standing on the stairs.

"I've been right behind you since you stopped to admire your work out in the fjord," the lady called out with an echo. The ghost was a fluid-like mass of smoke, hazily wafting on the spot, making her face difficult to see, but she was very much real. "I think you will find lots of things are right under your nose; you're just not looking properly, you're not *seeing*," she taunted. Savannah didn't feel quite so scared now the shock of her presence was wearing off.

"What is it? What am I missing?" Savannah plucked up the courage to ask.

"You looked out of the window, but you did not see," the ghost said benevolently. Savannah hitched up her ball gown and climbed over the boxes to get closer to the window looking out over the fjord.

"The turbine, I can see the turbine, but it's getting dark. I can't see anything else," Savannah said feebly.

"You're looking," the ghost corrected. Savannah looked again; the house lights from Toftir opposite twinkled across the water, but not enough to give a clear view. "Your new friend Olga was right," the lady added. Savannah was slowly lifted off the floor, her kitten heel backs dangling off her feet as she was gently pushed closer to the window, her face close up to the glass. Then, finally, she saw. She looked away from the fjord and onto land where Mai was running along the sea bridge, carrying something. She reached the shore where the aloes were planted and began removing her clothes.

"She has suffered long enough." The ghost was now behind Savannah, watching her. Mai hung her clothes onto an aloe stem and put on what appeared to be her brown fireside rug, transitioning herself into a seal.

"There's the missing Selkie their king is so angry about losing," the ghost revealed. Savannah's breath shallowed and her heart thumped. She grabbed the box of crepe paper hearts in distress, gasped a deep breath, and turned. She ran straight through the ghost in her effort to escape, and was overcome by a freezing cold sensation when she did so. She ran down the stairs, losing a shoe as she ran. "You need to see, Savannah; you need to learn to see!" the watchtower ghost called out as Savannah ran.

Savannah ran into the crowded grand hall and found Rich chatting to Olga. "Rich, we need to go. Now." She spoke as quietly as she could, but there was panic in her voice.

"Why? I'm just chatting to Olga," Rich replied, confused.

"Now," Savannah gulped through gritted teeth, tears beginning to well in her eyes. They walked discreetly out of the building, but Savannah was grabbed on the shoulder by Delia at the door.

"Delia—" Savannah began but was interrupted.

"I know, I know there's a rogue Selkie. Did the lady in the watchtower tell you who it is?" Delia asked Savannah quietly with her face close to hers.

"It's Mai," Savannah confided.

"It can't be!" Delia objected.

"The lady in the watchtower didn't tell me; I saw it with my own eyes. Mai's gone," Savannah said, swallowing hard.

"Richard, run home immediately and alert your father," Delia instructed Rich who ran, skidding over the snow in his leather-soled shoes.

"Mr Johnson, you're in charge. I have to go," Delia shouted behind her as she pulled Savannah to walk with her. "You had better come with me. I don't want Truffy to hear this from anyone else," Delia mused sadly.

- ▼ -

They arrived at the removal depot and Delia banged on the door for several minutes with no response. "That's odd, I know he must be home," Delia said. They began to look around the yard.

"He's not here, Delia. What should we do?" Savannah asked.

"Let's try Doreen's," Delia replied, and they ran over the fields to Doreen's cottage. The lights were on and smoke was coming out of the chimney. Petunia was nestled for the night in the roof flowers. Bursting through the door, they found Truffy sat at the table, with his head in his hands.

"Sorry, Doreen, but we need to speak to Truffy," Delia said. "Urgently."

"I already know, Delia. I know what she is. I didn't care about that, but now she's gone," Truffy gulped.

"You knew?" Delia asked, breathing noisily through flared nostrils.

"I saw her, before Christmas, walking into the sea and changing herself into a seal. Then, after one of our society meetings, I confronted her. She said she had no choice; her father is the king, and she had to do something on the island to protect him and their kind," Truffy blustered, his bottom lip quivering.

"What did she have to do?" Delia's voice got louder.

"I don't know," Truffy said, hiding his head in his hands. "I tried to persuade her to stay, to make a new life here, but then when I saw she had given her mixing bowl to Savannah, I knew her mind was made up."

Delia put her hand on his shoulder.

"What can we do?" Savannah looked to Doreen.

"There's nothing to do, my dear. An emergency meeting will probably be called by the chairman, so just make sure you're at the church tomorrow night."

- ▼ -

Mr Froodroy banged his sapphire flower on the church pulpit, although the sombre atmosphere in the room made it an unnecessary action. "My Gems. Thank you for your precious time at such short notice. It is with deep regret that I have the task of telling you that we have had a traitor in our midst." Truffy looked down, unable to stand. "It has finally come to our attention that our shining apprentice, Mai, was actually a Selkie in disguise, the Selkie king's daughter, no less. She was sent here on a mission, the goals of which are still unknown to us. The bureau has confirmed that Utsira, the Norwegian island Mai claimed to be from, has no society linked to them or to us. Her presence here was all a lie, in order to gain our trust and a place in these pews."

"If the king didn't know where she was, it obviously wasn't him who sent her," Doreen noted.

"That charade in the fjord, the Selkies pretending to be angry with us, was all a hoax," Mr Froodroy attempted to explain. "That's my guess. They knew Mai was failing her shining exams, and they knew Truffy was aware of her secret, so they put on that show to distract us from looking too closely at one of our own. They were just buying time." Mr Froodroy's voice began to crack.

"They seemed pretty angry to me, Mr Chairman," Billy said, pointing to his bandaged leg.

"Princess Mai. Now what do us land lovers have that they would want?" Delia spat.

"Liv is the only Selkie I know well enough to give a character reference for, but my opinion is they are still resentful of us," Doreen said calmly. "Due to the men on this island tricking their most beautiful Selkie ladies into living on shore, which they have done for generations now. They want nothing to do with us. A brief hello once a year is more than enough interaction for them. Their emotions are different to ours. They are wild and it is imperative that they live a wild life."

"So, I'll never see my Mai again?" Truffy looked at Doreen for answers.

"She can only touch dry land once a year, like the rest of them." Doreen rested her hand on his shoulder.

"Emotions aside, there are formalities to be met," Mr Froodroy interjected. "Doreen, as the only cloaked shiner, you must attend the bureau to return Mai's books. KAPOW are already grumbling. The bureau president, Nanuq Samossen, is coming here for a meeting at first light tomorrow. We need to explain ourselves. Since Doreen will be at the bureau and unavailable, could you be free to assist?" Mr Froodroy asked Delia.

"Of course, Chairman," she replied.

"What about me?" asked Truffy. There was silence.

Billy raised his walking stick in the air. "You come with me, mate. I know a thing or two about healing, and I know just the person who can help."

"Yes, indeed. Well done, Billy. Martha Wood will, I'm sure, be happy to assist as always," Mr Froodroy smiled, gliding himself off the pulpit. "No refreshments tonight. Get home safely, my gems," he said weakly. The society members glided upwards and home as swiftly as Savannah had ever known.

- ▼ -

Gliding the *Fortress* was easy this time. Precious' tuition with gas gliding and her rowing skills had come to her just in time.

"Park in front of the gates, please, Doreen," the security guard said at the Hudson steps. Through the rose archway and into the glass palace, it still felt as magical as before, lifting Savannah's depleted spirit. Rich had let Savannah borrow his hat to avoid the bird droppings and she glided, wearing her new kitten heels and jeans topped with one of Martha's handmade jumpers.

"You've learnt a lot from Precious, haven't you?" Doreen smiled at her new interest in fashion.

"And from you! I copied your beautiful roof. Well, sort of. Mine has *calluna vulgaris*, not angelica. I hope you don't mind," Savannah added.

"Mind? I'm pleased. What a clever idea to use that plant. You're learning fast," Doreen said. They made their way down to the basement. Nigel was in his usual position with his feet on the desk, delegating tasks to a short man in an ill-fitting suit. "Good morning, Nigel," Doreen called out, placing Mai's shining books on his desk. He swung his legs off the desk, this time managing not to fall off his chair.

"Isn't it just. Move aside, Brian," he said to the man, making flicking gestures with his hands. "Give these legends some room," he smiled. "Was I right? Was Mai a total and utter failure?" Nigel asked, leaning forward expectantly, like a dog requesting a pat on the head.

Doreen's eyes narrowed. "Suffice to say we are all very upset, Nigel," Doreen retorted. Nigel inspected Mai's books before taking them individually and blowing on each of them.

"*Society Handbook*, return. *A Shining Field Guide*, return. *Facing your Fauna*, return. *Purifying Plants*, return. *The Little Latin*, return." The books flapped and swooped at differing speeds. Savannah watched *Facing your Fauna* flap to a shelf; the other books wriggled to either side before the flapping book circled on the shelf, the way Tricver did before lying down, and positioned itself neatly in between two other books.

"It's amazing, isn't it?" Savannah said to Nigel.

"No more amazing than what you do with plants. You've got the glory of nature; I've got the glory of words. Rather less acknowledged, but I like to think we do our part against the evils of the world, in our own way." He smiled without showing his teeth. "Have you got time to see your grandmother's books? She has a whole book dedicated to green roofs," Nigel asked.

"You go ahead, Savannah. I will grab some tea from the cafeteria and bring it down to you both."

"Bring a sugar pot, Doreen," he said, slowly dislodging himself from his swivel chair.

"Don't these books float like the others?" Savannah asked, noticing Nigel's actions.

"Not these ones, Savannah. We have to go down a level for these. Come with me." He rubbed his hands together.

"Down from the basement?" Savannah screwed her eyes up. They walked through rows and rows of bookshelves, until they had passed through so many different rows, they were the only two people in the vicinity. The rest of the library was immaculate. Every book had a place, but the end of the shelves where the two of them now stood looked unkempt, like a charity book shop. A floor-to-ceiling vast wall of higgledy-piggledy books, some of which were twitching, was in front of the unlikely pair. Two of the books flew out of the pile, growling like Doberman dogs, and flew into Savannah's face. Nigel held out his palm, into which the books flew, and he spoke a language unfamiliar to Savannah, "*Tantum dignus ut intra*," before the Doberman books flew back onto the shelf. A red leather book flew out of the wall and landed in Nigel's outstretched hands. The pages were frantically blowing along the spine of the book, until abruptly they stopped.

"Well, of course," he said. The book's pages had stopped turning on a reference page and the words *Latin for Beginners* were raised off the page, as if floating. He put the red leather book back in the vast piles of books and moved his head from left to right, looking for something. "Aha!" he said, pulling another book out of the book wall. "Now, stand still, Savannah," Nigel instructed, pointing at her feet on a threadbare Venetian rug. A thundering sound was before them. The floor began to shake and the wall of books began plummeting down; where to, Savannah could not tell. The noise made Savannah feel claustrophobic. Dust flew into her face. The floorboards were now visible in front of Savannah, on which the books had been piled only moments before, and their removal revealed an enormous cave. Books inside were shelved in a spherical fashion, up and over the inside ceiling of the cave. She walked in with Nigel, covering her head in case one fell down on top of her.

"Welcome to my world. KAPOW headquarters," Nigel said. At the end of the cave there was a waterfall, through which Savannah saw daylight. "I'm bending the rules bringing you in here. But hey, I'm the boss." Nigel threw his hands up in the air.

"That waterfall is incredible. I don't remember a waterfall in the Hudson."

"No, you wouldn't. We aren't in the Hudson. Society members can gas glide. We can't do that but we can turn a page and be wherever we choose. We really do escape in books, you see. Well, not you. You're not KAPOW. Today, we have escaped to

Canada. I think maybe Egypt tomorrow; this cold weather is chafing my lips, but I digress. Meinhild Simonsen's books."

They walked through the breezy cave and stopped on the right where they reached some glass shelves, mounted on an apothecary cabinet. "Yes, erm... I should explain this. Your grandmother's books and cabinet weren't receiving the care and attention they required when the Froodroy family were supposed to be looking after the house, so," Nigel paused with a grimace, "okay. Hands up. I sort of stole this cabinet and its contents when the Froodroys weren't looking. Which wasn't hard, because they weren't there much. They never even noticed, so we at KAPOW feel it was the right thing to do," Nigel said pompously.

"This was hers?" Savannah smiled, running her hand over the top of the walnut burr wood apothecary cabinet, with its tiny, intricate drawers and sleek glass shelving.

"I couldn't leave it in that cold house to rot. I was having nightmares about it and the unpublished work disintegrating. All that greatness just... mouldy. It was too much to bear," Nigel said, folding his arms into his chest.

"Well, thank goodness you did. Our house is nowhere near as glamorous as this anyway. It looks at home here. May I?" Savannah asked, gesturing to the glass shelving containing the books.

"Please do. As long as your hands are clean," Nigel said, peering at Savannah's outstretched hands. "Yes, go ahead. All her published work is here. First editions, too. *Seaweed as Defence*, *Facing your Fauna*, *Mixing by Eight*, all of her famous work and even one that was yet to be published. The manuscript is in her own handwriting before she…" Nigel stopped himself.

Savannah wished so much that she could have met her. The questions she could have answered, the tales she could have told, none of which Savannah would ever know. Savannah admired her grandmother's handwriting, which flowed like calligraphy.

"She even sketched some watercolour illustrations at the back of a newly discovered plant species," Nigel said, pointing to the fern print, green leather-bound journal. Savannah wished she had Nigel's enthusiasm, but all she felt was sadness. "Look. There's a chair here. Anytime you want to come and see this cabinet and browse, you just come and find me and I will bring you here. Just don't try and get through the book wall yourself; you saw those guard books! You're a friend of KAPOW now," he said warmly.

"Thank you, Nigel."

"Let's find that tea." He gestured for Savannah to walk with him towards the waterfall.

"Through there?" Savannah asked in confusion, but Nigel had already pushed her impatiently through the waterfall and they found themselves back at Nigel's desk, where he was already repositioned in his swivel chair.

"Finally," Doreen said, loitering at the desk. "I've drunk my tea and had a Danish pastry. Yours is in the pot, Nigel, but Savannah, we have to go, I'm afraid," Doreen said, ushering Savannah out of the library.

"Come back anytime, Madam Wood, you're a friend of KAPOW now!" he said theatrically. Savannah turned around and replied, "Thanks, Nigel" as she glided off.

"Hold on, Doreen! You forgot the sugar pot," Nigel yelled.

"The cafeteria staff said to get it yourself." Doreen smiled to herself as they glided around the corner, out of sight.

CHAPTER 16

THE LAIRD

Savannah laid out the knives and forks for nine people along the long farmhouse pine dining table, a number ever-increasing thanks to Martha's nurturing of broken people, in both body and mind.

"Not those ones, darling; get the silver cutlery out of the cabinet," Martha heckled as she pulled a tray out of the oven.

"Why? It's only Rich and his parents." Savannah turned her head unenthusiastically; the extra rowing sessions were beginning to take their toll on her energy levels.

"Only Rich and his parents, one of whom happens to be Pa's boss, Savannah," Martha said sternly. "Anyway, it's not just the Froodroys; Truffy is coming to dinner as is one of Mr Froodroy's friends from Scotland," Martha said.

"Brilliant, did you say the Laird is coming?" Billy hobbled past the dresser and manoeuvred himself into a dining chair, leaning his crutches next to the dresser.

"A laird? No, his name is Stuart. Stuart Douglas," Martha replied.

"Yes, Ma, that's the Laird," Savannah snickered, knowing the thought of cooking for someone with such a title would worry her, being the reason her father didn't tell her.

"Theodore!" Martha yelled in a fluster.

"Hold on, Martha. I can see the chopper! Stuart is here." Her father hopped down the stairs, missing every other step.

"If I had known…" Martha stood in front of Savannah's father with her arms crossed.

"Yes, I know, dear, you wouldn't have cooked casserole. You would have done something fancy, which none of us want anyway, so that's why I didn't tell you." He smiled cheekily at Martha, giving her a kiss on the cheek. The vibrations from the helicopter blades made the house shake violently; the silver cutlery bounced around the table. The Laird ducked as he strode through the front door of the cottage.

"Good evening, all. Mrs Wood, it is a treat to meet you. I understand you run somewhat of a society safehouse for the sick and impaired." The Laird grinned, while thrusting a bunch of flowers and a large cut-glass bottle of whisky into her hands. "Smells divine. Where's the boss, then?" He waved to Billy, Savannah and Theodore, his eyes glistening with mischief.

"Good evening, all. We heard you landing, Laird," Mr Froodroy said, walking through the front door. He shook the Laird's hand jovially.

"Sit down, sit down and I will dish up," Martha ordered.

"Just waiting on Truffy, Martha," Billy said.

"Yes, I heard about all that kerfuffle with Mai. I did not see that one coming," the Laird said with his hands on his hips.

"Princess of the Selkies no less, Laird," Mr Froodroy added. Unknown to those in the conversation, Truffy had walked through the front door. Everyone fell silent when they realised he was there.

"I didn't know she was a Selkie, but I always thought of her as a princess," Truffy said, his eyes red and swollen. Martha walked over to Truffy, hugging him tightly.

"I know, Truffy. It's a terrible shock. That's why we are here. We're here to help you," Martha said protectively as she ushered him to a seat next to Billy.

"I can't sleep, I can't eat," Truffy said.

"My legs are on the mend," Billy said, in an attempt to redirect the conversation. "And I'm sure Martha's getting sick of having a great oaf like me kicking around. Can I come and stay with you until the turbine's finished, mate? It would do us both a favour," he asked, patting Truffy on the shoulder.

"Thanks, mate," Truffy smiled, for the first time since Mai's departure. "That'd be good."

"Well, we will miss you, Billy. Now sit down, everyone," Martha said, putting dinner onto the table.

"So, Laird. News travels fast if you've heard about our Selkie issues," Mr Froodroy said.

"Aye. Ripped your turbine base straight out of the sea, I hear, injuring Billy boy at the same time," the Laird said, with a mouth half full of casserole and half full of whisky.

"Yes, indeed, leaving us with only a skeletal team of chasers and security," Mr Froodroy added with a sideways glance.

"I knew it! I knew there was a reason you invited me for dinner," the Laird said, smirking and taking another gulp of the amber-coloured liquid, which was disappearing quickly from his glass.

"The turbine's ready," Theodore said quickly. "We just need to patch up the foundations and hoist it into place. Then, the island has good protection from random gas bubbles. The new turbine will have sapphires attached to each sail. Buckets on the end of each sail push the gas through the sapphires, filtering it and keeping control of it on a day-to-day basis. It won't cure the problem, but it will certainly improve the lives of people unsuspectingly flying or boating over it."

"Indeed, Theodore. What we need you to do, Laird, is fly that lovely chopper of yours over it while we are working, to keep the Hellson at bay. You will be like a whole hoard of defending society members with the gems you've added to that thing," Mr Froodroy said, pointing outside to the pearl- and gem-encrusted helicopter.

"You supply the meals, Martha, and I will be the Sapphires' saviour," the Laird roared jovially.

"Brilliant. We start next week," said Mr Froodroy, clinking glasses with the Laird.

- ▼ -

Spring had arrived in the Faroe Islands and the longer daylight hours made the ever-increasing rowing practices much easier in the early mornings. The Woods' roof that Savannah had planted with dainty flowers was beautifully in bloom, while daffodils, bluebells and tulips were scattered across the fields as Savannah walked Tricver to Doreen's for shining theory practice. The angelica field displayed hints of white buds as Savannah glided carefully to avoid the new blooms with Tricver at her side.

"He's become quite attached to you," Doreen observed, patting Tricver on the head. Tricver scanned the work surfaces for crumbs, his nose scanning the sides of the wooden worktops, but he retreated to the fireside rug after receiving a swat on the nose from a melissa plant.

"The president visited me yesterday," said Doreen.

"Nanuq Samossen? Oh, about the turbine progress?" Savannah looked out of the round window looking out to the fjord, the Laird hovering over the Hellson in the pearl helicopter as her father, Jan Johannsen and the Sapphires worked to replace the foundations previously attacked by the Selkies. "Pa said in a few days they should be ready to raise the turbine into place."

"No, although he was very impressed with your father's work. He wanted to arrange your first shining exam," Doreen smiled.

"Already? But it's only been…" Savannah sat down, her teacup shaking on the saucer in her hand.

"It's been nearly a year since you first joined us," Doreen replied, looking over her glasses.

"Yes, I suppose it has. When is the exam?" Savannah asked.

"August the first. The date you first came to a society meeting. Precious is going to help, too, since she's here to help me shine all the extra sapphires that need cleansing from putting the turbine up anyway. She agreed to help by escorting you to the bureau regularly and helping you navigate the library. Although to be honest, I know Nigel will help with that, too," Doreen said.

"Well, at least rowing practice will be over soon. That will give me a chance to revise more," Savannah said positively.

"Yes, not long until the big race now. The chairman says poor Rich was very irate at losing last year, and the year before," Doreen sniggered. Savannah grimaced, dreading Rich's reaction if Strendur lost again.

They passed the afternoon in Doreen's cottage practising a shining base recipe and learning the history of shining. As Savannah left with a befuddled brain at all the new information it had streamed, she saw Rich riding towards her at full pelt on his rusting bicycle.

"Savannah, the president went to see Truffy yesterday. I've got my first exam booked in. What am I going to do?" Rich panted as his back wheel braked, nearly forcing his body over the handlebars.

"Me too. August the first," Savannah replied, raising her eyebrows.

"At least we'll have time to celebrate winning the rowing race. There's no way Toftir will win again; we've got them this time," Rich beamed. "That fuggleschmuck Sven can eat my oar," he added, gesticulating wildly with his hands towards Toftir across the fjord. Savannah laughed so much she nearly dropped her trug.

"See you tomorrow, don't be late!" Savannah said to Rich, who had nearly made her late for school the week before.

"Yeah, yeah, I won't be." Rich rolled his eyes.

- ▼ -

Savannah and Rich skidded through the oak classroom door at 08.22, two minutes late. Their classmates were sitting quietly at their desks, except Sven, who sat upright, arms across his chest, laughing at them.

"Savannah, Rich, congratulations. You have earned an after-school detention with Mr Johnson this afternoon for being late," Delia said, without looking away from the board.

The day passed without too much annoyance from Sven, whom Savannah, Rich and Frank avoided for the most part. Everyone was excited for the boat race at the weekend, and the younger children had made a selection of bunting to hang around the lake. The school bell rang, signifying the end of the school day and the start of Savannah and Rich's detention.

"You may as well do something useful while you're here. You can clean and wax the *Hobgoblin*, ready for the race this weekend," Mr Johnson barked, pointing at the slimy, dirty vessel, parked on chunks of wood outside the watchtower.

"Enjoy. I'm off to help the conservation volunteers with the wind turbine," Delia said, winking to Savannah.

"Yes, I will get these two shipshape and rebuking of their bad habits in no time." Mr Johnson waved Delia off. The hot soapy water was at least warm as the pair soaked their sponges to reveal the boat's clean and slime-free exterior.

"Don't forget the brass polish for the nameplate," Mr Johnson indicated with his pipe as he sat and watched them scrub as he smoked and drank his mug of tea.

"We're going to win this year," Rich said to Mr Johnson.

"Yes, I think we will," Mr Johnson replied. Footsteps could be heard in the watchtower.

Savannah looked up, thinking she could see someone in the window.

"Did you hear those footsteps, too?" Rich asked, noticing her diverted eyes. "What did you just see up there? Was it the ghost lady?"

"I'm not sure, probably nothing. I'm so tired. I'll be relieved when this race is over," Savannah said.

"Last practice tomorrow before the race on Saturday. Don't let me down, you two," Mr Johnson said at the end of their detention, peering down at them.

CHAPTER 17

THE RACE

The bunting was blowing carefree in the wind. The sheepskin gloves Savannah had acquired for Christmas kept her freezing hands mobile. All of the Strendur village community was braving the cold wind in the hope that this might just be the year that Strendur win. Even the Sapphire Society had come to Waterfall Mile Lake's edge.

"Even the doomed widow's here. That shows you how their luck is going to pan out," Sven sneered from the other boat.

"Ignore the competition. You are here to uphold Strendur's good name." Mr Johnson knelt forward, facing the Strendur crew.

"Except our reputation is for losing," Oskar pointed out.

"We are going to change that," Jorg said. "The

Hobgoblin is in top form and has even had a polish-up, thanks to Savannah and Rich's detention." The two rowing boats balanced side by side, bobbing surreptitiously in the freezing cold lake. The Strendur team wore pale blue tunics; Toftir wore yellow.

Strendur rowing crew were sat in the boat, oars ready in hands. The mayor of Toftir stood ceremoniously on a platform with a loudspeaker. "Ladies and gentlemen, I welcome you here to Waterfall Mile Lake for the 87th annual Strendur versus Toftir rowing race. The course is as follows: To begin, here at the starting line coxswained by Mr Johnson for Strendur and Mr Madsen for Toftir. The crews will continue straight for exactly one mile to the finish line. Mr Anderson is this year's independent adjudicator and will be in the motorised boat directly behind both of the competing vessels. Mr Anderson…" The Toftir mayor handed over to the adjudicator.

"Good afternoon. Toftir, Strendur, I want a clean race," Mr Anderson began.

"Tell that to Sven," Frank whispered to Savannah.

Mr Anderson continued, "If a boat strays from its own path, I will call out to the offending team to move over and I expect immediate corrective steering to be deployed. Coxswains at the ready!" Mr Anderson shouted from a megaphone in the motorised boat. Savannah and the Strendur crew were poised.

"This is it, Strendur. This is our year. I want everything you've got, now let's win!" Mr Johnson shouted.

"Ready, Toftir?" shouted Mr Anderson.

"Ready!"

"Ready, Strendur?"

"Ready!"

A loud bang echoed from the starting pistol and both boats careered over the starting line.

"And they are off, Strendur off to a lightning start, the brawn of the Strendur team being Frank Johannsen," the announcer called. "Toftir currently a whole pace behind as we pass the first 250-metre mark."

Savannah felt the cold air blast down her throat into her lungs and lunged herself forwards and backwards.

"Toftir!" shouted the adjudicator from the boat. Toftir was gaining on them and was now alongside and veering into the *Hobgoblin*'s rowing line.

"Toftir are trying to close in, veering into Strendur's rowing line," shouted the commentator from the bicycle, riding alongside the boats.

"Maintain position!" shouted Mr Johnson. Victor was panting and Savannah could see sweat trickling down the back of Rich's neck. "Toftir!" shouted Mr Anderson, the adjudicator, with great urgency. Savannah glanced across and saw Sven, within arm's reach, and then a sudden smash.

"And we have an oar clash, just within the Strendur lines," jeered the commentator. Savannah kept going, determined not to let the crash throw her concentration but soon realised the head of her oar was gone. All she had left was a stick with no paddle. "And Toftir have equalised at 100 metres to go, but Strendur are slowing. It seems middle rower Miss Wood has lost her oar." Savannah felt the stick in her hands but was powerless.

"No!" yelled Mr Johnson. All Savannah could do was sit and watch as Sven and the Toftir crew glided past, despite the rest of the Strendur crew maintaining pace. She let the stick go into the water past the 1,500-metre mark and heard the Toftir villagers cheer as Sven and the Toftir crew glided under the finish line bunting to win the race. Savannah felt her cheeks burn as she sat, unable to help, as the rest of the *Hobgoblin* panted to their defeat. She could feel the crowd's eyes lasering into her. The *Hobgoblin* sat motionless under the finish line in the cold water as the crew leant forward in their rowing seats, their heads in their hands at the humiliating defeat.

"What the hell did you do?" Rich shouted at her, spinning round in his seat.

"Bad luck, Savannah. Come on. Get out of the boat," said Mr Johnson. Martha rushed over to the *Hobgoblin*, raced knee-high into the water and grabbed Savannah by the hand. Savannah couldn't process what had happened but found herself wading through the water to the edge, then in Martha's arms being carried over to the Sapphires as she watched Mr Johnson run over to the adjudicator, unable to hear what was being said.

"It was the other boat. They veered into your rowing path. That's not a fair match," Billy said, hobbling towards her. Precious wrapped a blanket over Savannah's shoulders. Mr Johnson had lit his pipe and was stood with Delia, arguing with Mr Anderson on the shoreline. Rich was still in the boat, leant back with his blond hair stuck to his head with sweat.

After a few minutes, Delia walked over to them. "Mr Anderson said no one was able to guarantee Toftir was in Strendur's rowing line, so they are putting Savannah's oar break down to accidental damage with no one team at fault. Toftir's victory stands," Delia said, sighing.

"Ladies and gentlemen," the mayor began, "following an adjudicator enquiry, it gives me great pleasure to announce that for the fifteenth year running, Toftir have won the race and maintain their winning title." Sven was being thrown into the air in celebration by the Toftir rowing crew.

"Are you okay?" Jorg asked Savannah as she sat in the mud at the water's edge. It took all of Savannah's strength not to cry, but she nodded in response.

"The gold rowing cup, victory again for the Toftir rowers. Well done, Sven and teammates," the mayor continued, handing the large gold chalice to Sven, who promptly thrust it into the air, much to the crowd's delight.

"Go on home, Savannah. Astrid and I will get the *Hobgoblin* back to school," Jorg said, tapping her on the shoulder. Precious put her arm round Savannah and without saying a word, they walked home, leaving Rich sat on the shoreline.

CHAPTER 17

FORGIVENESS

The light spring evening made the walk from home to the Sapphire meeting at church interesting for Savannah. Puffins and oyster catchers were busily flying over the hedgerows and gliding over the fields looking for food for their newborn chicks. Savannah arrived to be faced with the church gargoyles, which she had now affectionally named Mahmud and Genghis after conquerors she had learnt about in history at school. The angel statues inside were still awaiting names. She pushed open the solid oak door to find the other society members chatting and laughing.

"All right?" Rich asked when he saw her.

"Yes, thank you," Savannah replied formally, before walking towards the back of the church to sit with Precious and Doreen, who were waving in her direction. She and Rich hadn't seen each other since the race.

"Savannah," Rich said, standing up.

"Yes?" she replied coldly, still having not forgiven him for blaming her for Strendur's rowing defeat. Rich gave her a sideways glance.

"Do you want to… I mean, please… will you sit with me?" Rich quickly shuffled along the shiny pew, making room for her. Savannah sheepishly sat down, opened her bag and removed her shining revision book. She flicked through the pages but didn't manage to take any of the information in.

"I was an idiot," Rich whispered while staring straight ahead.

"Yes, you were," Savannah replied, looking directly at him. "But so was I. I should have watched that stupid oar. I should have remembered I'm just a beginner. I got too big for my boots, too confident in my minor ability. I must have hit the Toftir boat so hard to smash it. I'm an idiot, too," Savannah said, curling her lips together.

"Who cares about that now? Elvis is missing Tricver, so… we better just get back to normal so he doesn't start head-butting people with his dreadlocks," he grinned.

"Deal." Savannah returned his smile.

"Anyway, I heard stupid Sven put the gold chalice on his head and got it stuck over his ears for an hour," Rich laughed.

"Good evening, gems." Mr Froodroy glided into the church, tipping his head as the society members glided off the floor in a Sapphire greeting. "As I'm sure you are aware, we have a turbine base!" he announced, thrusting his fists in the air in a celebratory fashion. Whistles and cheers emanated from the room. "Thank you, thank you. It is estimated that the turbine can be positioned this week, so we are looking at going live with the turbine this weekend. I will pass you over to Delia, who is managing that side of the project."

"Thank you, Mr Chairman. Now the Laird has kindly agreed to spend the next week here, hovering, and will need all hands on deck to raise the turbine into position. Please bear in mind we have non-Sapphires on this project, so gas gliding, gas bubbling and blue talk are off limits." Delia looked directly at Truffy, who promptly looked to nobody behind him.

"Thank you, Delia. Doreen, Truffy, would you please be able to give some progress reports for our apprentices?" Mr Froodroy requested.

Doreen slowly glided to the front of the church and cleared her throat. "Hello, all. Following a visit from the president, I can confirm Savannah has her first shining exam in a few months' time. Savannah has been working very hard at the theory behind shining, both the history of shining and present-day techniques…"

"Yeah, nice roof you've put on the house, Saveloy!" Truffy shouted.

"I'm not sure Savannah likes being referred to as a Saveloy sausage, Truffy." Doreen looked at Savannah, laughing while rolling her eyes, before continuing. "However, it's good to have you back to normal, Truffy." Doreen smiled affectionately at him.

"Hear, hear. Well said, Doreen," shouted Billy, patting Truffy on the back.

"I will continue. Savannah is now a competent gas glider and has made quite an impression on KAPOW, the minister of which, Nigel, has offered to assist with any further reading which she requires. She has finished reading all the mandatory books and is now furthering her knowledge with wider subject reading. Practically, she can now produce a steady shining solution with a 60% success rate. Bearing in mind the current filthiness of the gems we are being given, that is not to be sniffed at. All in all, Savannah is way above target for her first shining exam on August the first," Doreen concluded, making her way back to her seat.

Rich turned to Savannah in disbelief, scoffing, "Teacher's pet. When have you had time to do all of that?" Savannah smiled coyly but didn't respond, knowing her tired eyes probably gave away the answer anyway.

The Sapphires applauded. "Well done, Savannah," Delia said, while clapping.

"Truffy. You were going to update us on Richard's theory progress?" Mr Froodroy enquired.

Truffy shuffled on his seat before finally standing up, although he did not make his way to the front of the church. "Yes, I was. Richard is making superb progress in his gliding. He can complete complex jumps, side turns and can glide many metres from the ground while avoiding obstacles, even flying ones," Truffy said, sitting down.

"You told us that last time, Terrence. The theory stats progress report?" Mr Froodroy looked in turn to Truffy and Rich, who both looked at the floor. "Truffy, without the theory, Richard will not pass his exam in August. We know he can glide, but can he theorise his skills and prepare for battle with a rational and observational pathway?" Mr Froodroy questioned.

"Not sure, really," said Truffy, cringing.

"Next meeting, you two, I want evidence of battle technique theory."

"Yes, Mr Chairman," Truffy said as Rich raised his eyebrows.

"Any other business? No? Well our visiting shiner, Precious, has been learning a new potion herself, from Mrs Froodroy, and has made us all some rhubarb fizz, so if you would like to head to the back of the church, refreshments will be served. Goodnight, Sapphires." Mr Froodroy tipped his head and glided off the floor, to which the rest of the society members, including Savannah, did the same.

- ▼ -

The spring school holidays gave Savannah a chance to put her theory into practice. The turbine was nearly complete, although only full members were able to participate, leaving Savannah and Rich time to study for their upcoming exams. Rich lay on the tartan wool blanket, basking in the mild sunshine, and Savannah foraged in and around the angelica field for ingredients for her shining recipe.

"Come on, I've finished, and all you seem to be doing is sunbathing out here," Savannah said sternly.

"Listen. You have to make the most of any sunlight you can get here in the Faroes. Rhubarb fizz?" Rich responded light-heartedly, passing Savannah a bottle. Savannah sat down and took a swig from the sticky bottle, gazing out to the fjord. The Sapphires, her father and Jan Johannsen were well on their way to completion.

"I think they will finish tonight," Rich said.

"That should make life a lot safer," Savannah said.

"Yes, but it's only a filter, really. If it explodes, you are still reliant on us chasers to contain the explosion; it just assists with dispersal," Rich corrected her.

"Right, well, in that case, shift your backside and become a chaser instead of sitting and daydreaming," Savannah said, grabbing both of Rich's hands and hoisting him off the picnic blanket.

"Okay, okay. I need to quickly go into school to collect my school bag. I managed to leave it there last week," Rich huffed.

They walked carefree along the sea bridge to the school. It seemed strange, seeing it so deserted and quiet.

"Mr Johnson," Rich shouted, hoping he would let them in. They tried the oak front watchtower door but it was closed.

"There he is," Savannah said, pointing to a cloud of tobacco smoke wafting from the school boatyard. They went around the back to find Mr Johnson washing the *Hobgoblin*.

"I was hoping to see you two." Mr Johnson put his hands on his hips and stopped scrubbing.

"I'm sorry I ruined the rowing race, Mr Johnson," Savannah said, looking down at his wet shoes.

"Yes, about that. At the time, I didn't see what happened," he said, continuing to puff.

"I hit the Toftir boat too hard with my oar; it was a stupid mistake." Savannah shook her head.

"No, no, no. Go up to the watchtower; she wants to see you," Mr Johnson said.

"She?" Rich quivered.

"Yes," Mr Johnson replied, pointing to the watchtower spiral staircase.

"Rather you than me," Rich said to Savannah, wide-eyed.

"Both of you," Mr Johnson smiled mischievously. Savannah strode up the stairs, reluctantly followed by Rich who scuttled behind.

"Shh, I can hear something," Rich hissed, putting his hand onto Savannah's shoulder. Savannah turned her ear towards the top of the stairway.

"It's singing," Savannah whispered in reply.

"*'Row, row, row your boat gently through the fjord',*" came a gentle singing from the top floor. They continued clinking up the steps; Rich's hand remained on Savannah's shoulder. They reached the top floor and saw the ghost. She wasn't hazy like the last time Savannah had seen her at the school Valentine's ball. She had a clear outline and wore a pale blue pinafore dress with a white waist apron. Her hair, which sat quaffed around her shoulders, was golden blonde. She smiled at Savannah, her piercing blue eyes locking onto hers.

"Nice to see you, Miss Wood," she beamed.

"Nice to see you, too," Savannah said hesitantly. "I'm sorry, I don't know your name."

"You lost the race. I knew you would," she smiled.

"It wasn't her fault," Rich chipped in, peering around Savannah's shoulder.

"I know," she replied, moving over to the window and beginning to sing. "*'Row, row, row your boat, gently through the fjord, if you race the Toftir crew, you will lose your oar.'*" She turned around, her eyes locking onto Rich's.

"How do you know that?" he spluttered, looking uneasy.

"Kenneth looked but didn't see," the ghost said, tilting her head and squinting.

"Kenneth?" Savannah asked.

"Mr Johnson's first name is Kenneth. Do you mean Kenneth Johnson, downstairs?" Rich asked her.

"He needs glasses; his eyesight is failing him now he's getting old," she said, continuing to look out of the window.

"He said you wanted to see us," Savannah said.

"I wanted you to see me. You see me properly now, don't you?" the ghost asked. Savannah nodded. "You're learning. I didn't learn to see until it was too late," she said, pulling a handkerchief out of her pocket and dabbing her eyes.

"I think I saw you the day we were cleaning the boat," Savannah said eagerly.

"You looked. What did you see?" she said curiously.

"I thought I heard someone moving about in the tower, so I looked up and thought I saw you at the window," Savannah said.

"Did you hear me moving about today?" asked the ghost.

"Yes," said Rich.

"No, you heard me singing," she replied sharply. "Did you hear me moving around the first time we met?" She spoke sharply, moving towards them.

"We saw a flash of light," Savannah said.

"When I make no steps, how is it you could hear me walking?" she said, pausing for their response.

"It wasn't you," Savannah said.

"Correct. And your oar didn't break by accident. There are people out there that do see. They saw you were fast. They saw your oar," she said.

"Everyone saw Savannah's oar," Rich mocked. The ghost made a cutting action with her hand, as if sawing a piece of wood.

"I get it! They sawed her oar. I knew it. The cheating fuggleschmucks," Rich shouted.

"It was Sven you saw in the watchtower, on the day of your detention. Just after you left, he took his wood saw and cut halfway through Savannah's oar," the ghost said before vanishing into a thin haze. Rich raced down the spiral staircase, two steps at a time, closely followed by Savannah and ending up in the boatyard with Mr Johnson.

"Where is it? Where's the oar?" Rich demanded. Mr Johnson pointed to the floor and Rich immediately picked up Savannah's broken oar. On closer inspection, tiny serrated cutmarks were visible on either side of the splintered oar.

"How did I miss that?" Savannah said forlornly.

"We take it for granted that everyone is as honest as us. But that just isn't the case," Mr Johnson said.

"We need to alert the judges and get the win overturned," Rich shouted.

"The adjudicator won't accept the oar as evidence. They will say we did this to the oar after the race, so we could try and overturn the win. No. We will just beat them next year. They won the battle, but we will win the war," said Mr Johnson thoughtfully, patting Rich on the shoulder and removing the splintered oar from his hands.

CHAPTER 18

THE DEVIL

"Danish pastries, a large pot of tea and a full bowl of sugar," Savannah announced, placing the laden copper tray on Nigel's desk.

"Madam Wood, I only wish every society member was as well-versed in etiquette as your good self," Nigel sighed, indicating for Savannah to pull up a chair.

"Not you, Brian, interns can get their own." Nigel flicked away the short man in a suit as he leant into the tray to take a pastry. "To what do I owe this pleasure?" Nigel said, cramming a huge spiral of cinnamon-coated pastry into his mouth.

"Just some more revision practice papers, please. That and some peace and quiet. Now the turbine is up and fully working, our house is full of Froowind employees and I just want some peace. I've only got a month," Savannah said nervously.

"You didn't come alone, my dear?" Nigel said sympathetically.

"I'm not allowed to yet. Truffy and Rich are over there doing some chasing cramming," Savannah replied, pointing to the other end of the library, where, to the untrained eye, it still appeared more practical revision was being conducted by the Sapphire Gruesome Twosome, as they were now commonly known.

"I'm afraid chasers are usually more brawn than brains," Nigel said cattily. "Brian, hold the fort and try not to destroy anything in my absence." Nigel heaved out of his chair in a rocking motion, to persuade his buttocks to part from their comfortable flattened cushion. He gestured for Savannah to follow him through to **KAPOW** headquarters before shouting, "And I've counted those pastries!" over his shoulder to Brian.

They stood again at the wall of untidy books, the guard books this time shooting off the wall and into Savannah's arms, the pages of which appeared to pant. Nigel held out his palm, and the guard books flew into it.

"*Tantum dignus, ut intra,*" Nigel announced dramatically.

"What does that mean, Nigel?" Savannah enquired.

"It's Latin. Only the worthy may enter. If you weren't worthy, the wall wouldn't let you in," Nigel said. The red leather book flew out of the wall and landed in Nigel's outstretched hands.

"And the red book?" Savannah asked.

"It's a wall reference book of all the titles on the shelves here. It gives you suggested reading. On discovering the book you are required to read, it will then dissolve all others and pave the way to headquarters. Last time, you may remember it guided you to *Latin for Beginners*." The pages were frantically blowing along the spine of the book and stopped at a reference page with the words *Sabotage Interception* floating in the air off the page.

"Ooh. That sounds adventurous. Does it mean anything to you?" Nigel asked.

"It's a long story," she coughed, not wishing to disclose her failure to spot her sawn-off oar. Nigel put the red leather book back in the vast piles of books and moved his head from left to right, looking for the corresponding title.

"Aha!" he said, sliding the black book out of the book wall. "You know the drill, my dear. Be still."

Savannah was poised and froze her feet to the threadbare Venetian rug. The cacophony produced by the books plummeting downwards caused the floor to shudder and made her wince. When the thundering noise finally reached a quiet conclusion, Savannah gingerly opened her eyes to discover her new location couldn't be further away from noise and chaos.

"You're in luck. Welcome to Tenryu Shiseizen-ji, the head temple of Buddhism and calm in Kyoto, Japan," Nigel said, lowering his shoulders and inhaling deeply. The books were dotted around on sleek glass shelves positioned on raked pure white gravel. The silence was overwhelming.

"Here we go. Practice exam papers," he said, handing them over. "Take your time, just exit through the temple doors when you're ready."

Savannah sat on an ebony wooden bench and spent the whole morning working through her practice exam papers. Nigel returned and brought a pot of tea, which he put on the bench next to her.

"You know, you're going to be fine in your exam," Nigel said thoughtfully. "I've seen what you've read and how hard you have been working. You've got it covered." He poured Savannah a cup of tea from the pot. As Savannah leaned forward to pick up the cup and saucer, she saw a ripple of movement across the tea's surface. Then the cup and saucer shook so violently they fell off the bench. The ground was shaking, causing the gravel to tremor and smear the precisely raked pattern. Explosions could be heard in the distance.

"What's happening, Nigel? What's going on?" Savannah yelled as she saw KAPOW members running to the exit through the temple doors.

"Now the reference book showing me *Defence Against Imminent Danger* as I came in makes sense!

- 231 -

Savannah, the bureau is in danger!" he shouted over the noise and ducked as bits of rock and pure white gravel flew through the air. They ran to the temple, where Savannah transported back to the library.

"Rich, Truffy!" she shouted.

"Looking for Truffy?" A short man with brown hair, mostly covered by a tweed cap and a goatee beard, looked at her. "I'm his big brother, Scott. Come on, this is no time for apprentices to be down here. It's the blinkin' escapees again. Come with me, we will soon find Truffy and get you home. I'm guessing you're Saveloy," Scott said.

"I'm Savannah," she gasped, the usual niceties forgotten given the chaos of the moment.

"Scruffy!" Truffy shouted, running over and embracing his brother. "There's only two devil absconders, me and you, plus a couple of observers. We have to put the escapees back in there now," Truffy shouted, grabbing Rich.

"I'm not sure the president would be very pleased if he knew we took your apprentices along." Scruffy tilted his head.

"Come on, Scruffy, they need to see what the job's really like. There's only so much you can learn from a book." Truffy slapped his brother on the shoulder. "And we can't very well just leave them here."

"Okay. But this is a Sapphire decision. Don't drag us Diamonds over the coals if we get told off," Scruffy replied. They glided out to the Hudson River in the *Sapphire Fortress*, where it appeared a jacuzzi sat under water, blowing gentle bubbles and gas around the lake, causing a thick fog.

"It seems so gentle; why is it causing so many problems in the bureau?" Savannah asked Scruffy.

"The bureau is fine above ground, but the subterranean levels like the library are on the same foundations as the underwater volcano, so it always looks worse than it is from down there," Scruffy explained.

"Yep – drill a few hundred metres outwards from the library level and you would be in the underwater volcano, we call 'The Devil' of the Hudson," Truffy said. "Now, an abscond is quite different in characteristics to an explosion. If the Devil had exploded, the drains, sewer and underground rail system would have flooded, like happened a little while back. The water would be shooting approximately ten times the volcano's size up into the air, which is how we can estimate the size and population of an underwater gas volcano… There's one!" Truffy pointed to a well-camouflaged person, bobbing up and down in the water at the side of the river. They rowed over and Truffy put his hand full of gems into their face.

"Wait, wait, wait, Truffy. Can you see, this person has the usual luminous green eyes. They are always very pale-skinned, due to the lack of light, and they can't speak. Their voice boxes get dissolved by the gas," Scruffy said, leaning forwards. "Okay, now you can grab him and we will literally push him back through the central bubbles."

"Won't the boat get dragged in?" Savannah asked.

"A normal boat would, but not our *Sapphire Fortress*. We have enough protection on here to glide over several times until the sapphires and other gems need shining," Truffy said. Truffy didn't bring the escapee into the boat but held him alongside and glided the *Fortress* to the jacuzzi-like bubbles, where he firmly pushed him down. The man spiralled several times through the water and gas before being sucked down with a satisfying squelch.

"That was easy enough," Rich smiled.

"Yes, in the water they are fine; it's when they are out of the water that they cause problems. They start to remember their old lives, but by the time their eyes are fully green, there's no helping them. I just heard a rustle in the bushes over there. One of them may be out of the water," Scruffy said. As the *Fortress* glided towards the noise, the silhouette of a girl was visible. She wore a pair of jeans with old-fashioned blue sneakers and a Yankee baseball jacket. Savannah stared at her as Scruffy got off the *Fortress* and onto the water's edge. Suddenly a leg flew from the bushes and kicked Truffy in the head, knocking him over. Scruffy grabbed the girl from behind and put her in the *Fortress*, although she made no sound. She sat opposite Savannah and fixed her gaze upon her. Savannah leant forward to examine her features; white, hollow complexion with a distorted bone structure securing her startled green eyes, which bore at Savannah like lasers. Without warning, the girl launched herself towards Savannah, breaking free of Scruffy's grasp and beginning to snatch Savannah's sapphire necklace, still attached to her neck. The next few seconds played out as if in slow motion; the girl gasped into the necklace, causing her eyes to roll back into her head and temporarily muting all other sound. The inhale of breath felt torturous to listen to. The searing pain caused by the suction of harsh, cold air against her raw and bruised, bleeding trachea was somehow audible. The girl's fragile legs crumpled and she hit the floor of the *Fortress* with a thwack.

She lay deadly still, but her eyes remained fixed on the necklace.

"Scruffy, one of her eyes has turned brown," Savannah whispered.

"Impossible." He shook his head.

"I'm certain. Look!" Savannah pointed towards the girl, who had a green left eye and brown right eye. She began gesticulating with her hands, as if she was trying to communicate. The look of fear in her eyes was palpable.

"In all my days, I've never seen this. Is it even possible? It can't be right, bruv." Truffy peered at the girl's eyes.

"I don't like this. I don't like it at all. We need to get her back in the underwater volcano now." Scruffy's voice shook as he spoke.

"We can't give up on her, Scruffy. If she has a flicker of life, we need to at least try to see if she can be restored back to life. Let's get her to Sister Angeline at the bureau hospital right away." Truffy put his hand on the girl's shoulder. "It's all right, love, you're safe now. We'll get you sorted," Truffy said to the girl reassuringly, watching her closely as she began to breathe out plumes of black gas. They quickly fled the chaotic scene and made their way to the bureau hospital.

- ▼ -

Sister Angeline was a rotund lady with dark skin and a tall white hat. "Da poor girl. She looks like she needs a good meal. How long has she been down there, Scruffy dear?" Sister Angeline said, putting her hand on the girl's back and pulling back the crisp white cotton sheets from a hospital metal-framed bed.

"Not a clue. But I've not seen a Yankees baseball logo like that before," said Truffy.

"Hell's bells. That logo hasn't been used since the 1960s. Either she has a vintage top on or this girl is over fifty years old," Sister Angeline said, stroking the girl's braided hair. The girl looked like she was trying to say something, but no words came out.

"Shh, don't try and talk, just rest," Sister Angeline said to her, pulling the covers over her and placing gemstones around the bed. "How on earth did you get her eye to change back?" Sister Angeline asked.

"She grabbed Savannah's necklace and sort of sucked air through it," Rich said. When Savannah looked down at her necklace, she realised it was no longer blue but black, like a lump of coal.

"Ha ha. Now that's gonna take some serious shining to get its colour back," Angeline laughed.

"She's one of the best shiners on our island. It won't take her long," Rich said, sticking out his chest as he spoke.

"What do you think caused the escape, Scruffy?" Angeline asked.

"No idea. There seems trouble around at the moment."

"Rumour has it, that turbine of yours, Truffy, is pushing gas to other underwater volcanoes," Angeline said with her hands on her hips.

"Nah, no chance," Truffy said, and turned to his brother. "We better get back, mate. Say hello to the Diamonds for me. Come on, you two." Truffy embraced Scruffy.

"Yeah, well, now you've got your turbine, you can let Billy boy come home," Scruffy shouted at Truffy, a chuckle in his voice, as they walked through the hospital doors and back to the *Fortress*.

CHAPTER 19

A NEW SAPPHIRE

"Good evening, gems," Mr Froodroy said from the church pulpit. They had returned from New York the night before, and Savannah's mind still whirred with all of the events that had taken place there. "First on tonight's agenda is the fantastic news of our fully working turbine," he said, with cheers from the congregation. "Also, this week, I had a visit from the bureau president, Nanuq Samossen. Since we have unexpectantly lost a shiner, it was agreed we could recruit from the bureau for a new shiner for the Sapphires. Interviews have been conducted by myself and Doreen and I can confirm we have recruited a most suitable candidate."

"Who is it? When can we meet them?" Truffy asked.

"Our new recruit is not Faroese but loves this country and culture like it is her own. She is one of the best practical shiners known to the bureau, with years of battle-shining experience. She will remain in her old cloak until the next cloaking ceremony in December," Mr Froodroy grinned.

"Yes, yes, yes, we know the drill. Who is it?" Delia yelled impatiently.

"Sapphires. Please be glided, for our new member of the Sapphire Society. Precious!" Mr Froodroy announced.

"Hooray." Savannah ran over to Precious, hugging her tightly.

"Like I said, home is where you make it," Precious winked.

"I didn't want to lose my Mai, but I honestly can't think of a finer replacement," Truffy smiled, shaking Precious' hand.

"I always thought you would be better suited to a blue cloak," Delia said to Precious.

"Indeed, and now my wife has taught her the rhubarb fizz recipe, she said she's not allowed to leave the island," Mr Froodroy jested. Everyone settled down back into their seats. "Tonight, we say farewell to Billy, who is now fully recovered from both injuries and will be returning to rugby and the Diamonds next week. I know we are all very grateful for his support, but Scruffy is keen to have his top chaser back in Blighty. After tonight's meeting, we have arranged for a little shindig to celebrate, with the fizz made especially for the occasion by our newest shiner, Precious," Mr Froodroy said.

"Next on the agenda, Truffy. Your report on Richard's theory practice," Mr Froodroy said, looking over his glasses at him.

Truffy swaggered to the front of the church. "Good evening, Mr Chairman. In the last couple of weeks, Rich and I have spent considerable time in the bureau's library." Truffy turned the page on a large wooden flip chart to reveal a pie chart display. "Here, you can see in red, 50% of young Richard's time has been spent in practical training. Putting this practice into theory—" Truffy was interrupted.

"Sorry, Truffy, I think you mean putting the theory into practice," Mr Froodroy corrected.

"No. As chasers, our strength is the practical side. He can do the moves but what he found challenging was interpreting why the theory was relevant at all. Putting the practice into theory, in other words."

"Well, yes, I see. That does make sense now you explain it, Truffy," Mr Froodroy replied, straightening his cloak.

"So, 25% of our time has been spent reading and the other 25% has been spent using this information in live time, such as assessing the characteristics of a gas-mutated absconder. Richard has completed a considerable amount of the mandatory reading and is on target to have skimmed the rest of the text by his exam date," Truffy finished with his chart and sat down. There was silence in the room. "Was that okay, Mr Chairman?" Truffy asked, swallowing hard.

Delia stood up from her seat and began clapping. "Superb, Terrence. I knew we could count on you."

"Without further ado, we will move on to the final items on the agenda, celebrating Precious' arrival and partying Billy back to the Diamonds. Thank you, Billy, we hope to see you again very soon," Mr Froodroy cheered. The celebrations went on into the early hours of the morning, supplemented by Precious' rhubarb fizz and a bottle of amber-coloured alcohol the Laird had given to the chairman for the occasion.

- ▼ -

Mai's old home, Mountain Cottage, had a new lease of life now that Precious had moved in. "Ready for inspection?" Precious asked Savannah. Savannah proudly held up her necklace, which shone its regal blue once more after a whole day in the beautiful mixing bowl Mai had given her and a huge amount of aloe vera and patience.

"I'm impressed. Even an absconder can't get the better of you, it seems," Precious said, reviewing the stone. Precious' beautiful soapstone mixing bowl and mango wood furniture made the little cottage seem quite exotic.

"No one is ever going to think that's a Selkie rug," Rich laughed, pointing at the zebra hide rug in front of the fire.

"Ziki the zebra was my childhood pet. I was devastated when she died, so I saved her skin so she can always be with me on my adventures," Precious said, stroking the rug affectionately. Rubber tree plants, beautifully scented wild malva and exotic palms adorned the interior. "I wondered if you could give me a hand with the roof. I have some confetti bush seeds to plant up there to give it some style," Precious asked.

"Brilliant," Savannah replied, grabbing the seeds and a ladder. Mountain Cottage was halfway up Strendur Mountain, boasting superb views over the fjord. On reaching the roof, Savannah found something peculiar. "Precious, there's a chair up here." Savannah pointed to a wooden armchair, balanced in between the two chimneys.

"I know. I'm going to cover it in moss and keep it between the two chimneys so I have a comfy warm seat with the most beautiful view in the world. And I can keep an eye on the superb turbine, too," Precious said with her hands on her hips.

"Look! Seals!" Rich exclaimed, pointing to the sea.

"Yes, they are here regularly. I like to think it's Mai keeping an eye on us," Precious said.

"You can see everything from here. The school, the church, my house, the turbine and every inch of the fjord," Savannah marvelled as she scattered the seeds.

"Come back tomorrow after school and you can test out the armchair. I guarantee it will be the cosiest seat on the island. I will help you revise as you sit; only a couple of weeks to go now," Precious said.

"Only a couple of weeks until the summer holidays," Rich cheered, waving his hands in the air.

"That just means our exams are getting closer." Savannah wrinkled her nose.

"Don't remind me," Rich winced.

CHAPTER 20

THE HELLSON

History was the final lesson of the last day of the summer term. The hypnotic motion of the wind turbine maintained Savannah's gaze out to the fjord, not making her essay on Genghis Khan any easier. The sea bell's ferocity shook the classroom and despite Delia's best efforts to finish the lesson, the students were inevitably already packing their belongings into their bags. Everyone seemed to have plans for the summer. Frank and his father were redecorating their house to include a pool table, Freya was visiting family in England and Sven bragged to everyone that he was going on a sailing holiday to Portofino.

"At least we don't have to see his ugly mug for a couple of weeks," Rich spat. Savannah and Rich waved goodbye to Frank and walked along the sea bridge. Savannah was eager to visit Precious and see how the moss armchair and confetti bush roof had transpired.

"Hello, you two." Delia caught up to them. "I bet you're ready for a break. It's been quite a year. I heard about you catching an old relic from the Devil. Is your necklace okay?"

"Yes, thanks. It's as good as new now, thanks to these aloes," Savannah replied, brushing her hand along the top of the aloe plants.

"That turbine really is something," Rich said, stopping to admire the large humming structure. The sapphires were not visible unless you looked inside the turbine, but it had an unusual shimmer like a blue beacon.

"Fugschmuckles," Delia yelled, then began laughing, her shoes and ankles drenched in water from an unexpected wave.

"Apologies for my bad language, gems."

"Delia, that can't be right," Rich said, pointing ahead of them. The sea path was flooded. Savannah's shoes filled up with water instantly.

"This path has never flooded. Not once," Delia said, looking around her and turning on the spot. "Can we get up over the bushes?" she asked.

"No chance, they are filled with brambles and over 6 feet high," Savannah shouted.

"Delia, that cloud looks really familiar." Rich tapped on her shoulder. Over the middle of the fjord, a black cloud had appeared which was slowly moving towards the sea bridge. The sky had become abruptly dark. The fear of impending doom sat deep within Savannah's chest. She didn't know whether to run or fight, but even if she wanted to run, there was nowhere to go. The brambles made escape over the sea path impossible. She watched as the cloud swept over the sea bridge ahead of them. She stepped backwards only for her legs to meet slicing thorns. The lapping sound of the water was replaced with a high-pitched shriek.

"Hold on, gems. Hellson's coming for us," roared Delia, grabbing both of their hands with an iron grip. It hit. Savannah tucked her head into Delia but felt the water smash into her face and up her nostrils, the ice-cold water pummelling her body and weakening her legs until she was pushed down onto the path. The water tumbled over and over her exposed face, preventing her from breathing. The saltwater in her throat made her gag, and she frantically waved her arms to try and reach Rich or Delia, to no avail. It seemed the Hellson was determined to further its cause and it was desperately seeking new victims. Savannah could hear faint noises of struggle from Rich and Delia but was unable to move. The pounding of the waves was relentless and after a short amount of time, the lack of oxygen in her body meant its flight or fight response was beginning to fade. She forced herself to keep going, to keep kicking and screaming and trying to unpin her body from the path, but the insurmountable weight of the sea on top of her and the lack of oxygen made her feel confused. Her hearing was going; the only noise audible was the lub dub noise of her own heartbeat, and it was gradually slowing down. She could feel something stroking her leg, then with a firm embrace around each limb, she felt her body being hoisted from the sea's grasp.

Finally, out of the water, she still couldn't breathe. The Hellson gas cloud was on top of her and the stench engulfed her lungs. She stumbled ahead, still gasping for air, and almost tripped over Rich who was being pushed to the ground, still underwater. Her stinging and burning eyes could just make out Rich's agonised face through the water and gas. She tried to heave his arms free but with no success. Through the water, Savannah could now see the aloes and realised it must have been the plants that freed her.

"Help me, little aloes!" she shouted. In a flash, the plants surrounded Rich and as if in military formation, their stems wrapped around each limb, ceremoniously forcing Rich's body out of the water. Rich gasped a long lungful of filthy gas but had at least not drowned.

"Thank you!" Savannah shouted. Another metre along the path they made their way to Delia, who blasted out of the water like a spurting fountain. She caught her feet back into the water with her right arm in the air, a sapphire bracelet glistening. The water calmed as instantaneously as it had erupted. The three of them sat aghast on the path, the cloud slowly passing over them, back into the centre of the fjord and sloshing over the turbine. Creaks and screeching of metal against metal and an intense quickening of speed from the turbine filtered some of the smog away, but an almighty shroud of gas drifted inland. The sea bridge cleared of water.

"Come on, gems. Get gliding, no time for walking. We need to get back to school and call a code blue. This is it. Hellson has called us to war."

CHAPTER 21

CODE BLUE

Delia, Savannah and Rich glided almost vertically up the spiral stairs. "The time has come," the ghost called from the corner.

"We discovered that for ourselves," Delia snapped as she began ringing the huge brass bell in the centre of the tower.

Savannah looked out of one of the windows. "The gas has moved over to the Froowind building," Savannah shouted in alarm. The gas engulfed the building, making it impossible to see the structure under the gas.

"It's war. It's not just after one-off victims or society members – it wants to fight. It's seeking total control of the island," Delia shouted over the noise of the bell, which she continued to ring.

"That's not all..." The ghost pointed to the

Hellson, which was erupting and spewing bursts of water hundreds of metres into the air.

"Delia. There are people. People are swimming out of the Hellson," Savannah yelled in panic.

"Pa." Rich ran over to his father, who was gliding up the stairs.

"Ma, the Woods and the Johannsens are at the Woods' house. Thank heavens for your protective roof, Savannah; that should keep the non-society members safe for a while," Mr Froodroy said, embracing Rich and Delia.

"There's an absconder, right next to the school entrance. I put as many local non-society members in my house as I could. My confetti roof will buy them a bit of time," Precious assured them as she entered the watchtower.

"Well done. Did they ask questions?" Mr Froodroy asked.

"I followed protocol; I told the locals it was an underwater volcanic explosion due to oil drilling. Mr Johannsen backed me up," Precious said. "Any sign of Truffy?"

"Look!" Savannah shouted, pointing out of the window to the solid oak school entrance door. Truffy could be seen grappling with someone. Rich glided down the stairs and out of the window. Savannah saw Rich circle the fighting men, tipping his hat. The muted absconder disintegrated into dust, which was sucked up into Rich's sapphire, sewn into his hat. The pair of them glided up the stairs.

"Evening, all. Nice weather for a ruck," Truffy smiled, wiping blood from his ear.

"Door locked and emergency procedures in place, Truffy?"

"Yes, Mr Froodroy. Emergency tunnels clear. The *Fortress* is fighting fit and protective roofs are glowing like beacons. Even the old bird Petunia is hovering the fjord," Truffy smiled.

"Right then, my gems. Everyone is now present and correct," Mr Froodroy began, formally.

"What about Doreen? She's not here yet," Savannah said. Mr Froodroy's eyes locked onto hers.

"Sit down, everyone. Conserve your energy. Savannah, Doreen isn't coming," Mr Froodroy said gently.

"But those people out there; she can't defend herself alone," Savannah gulped.

"We have a code blue protocol. We had hoped to high heavens we would never have to use it, but the Sapphires are ready, and ready ourselves we must. Doreen is safe, Savannah. It is bureau protocol that apprentices do not learn of such things until they are cloaked, but I'm afraid fate has not granted you the luxury of ignorance for long. We are at war. Savannah, Rich, if you want to sit this out in a safe house, we will all understand." Mr Froodroy looked at Savannah and Rich in turn.

"No chance," Rich insisted through pursed lips. Savannah shook her head.

"Then I will explain. A code blue is only called when three categories are simultaneously met. One, when the Hellson erupts; two, when the Hellson inhabitants not just abscond, but attack; and three, when we have had communication from their leader, Ragnar, that causes us concern," Mr Froodroy explained.

"That's mad. How does a dead Viking communicate?" Rich asked.

"Through me," the ghost said. Savannah looked at her; she almost looked as solid and lifelike as a living person, but the chill she gave off, in temperature and temperament, was unnerving. "He wants what you have," she said to the room.

"What is it?" Savannah asked.

"We don't know. We've been trying to figure out what he wants from us for some time now," Truffy said.

"Whatever it is would undoubtedly have a sinister effect on the island. Ragnar came to conquer these islands hundreds of years ago and he will not rest until he fulfils his bequest. We cannot let that happen," Delia added.

"With this code blue comes our action plan. Our first is to ready our secret tunnels, which Truffy has done," Mr Froodroy explained. "We have a network of sapphire rock tunnels from the school cellar to

Doreen's and Meinhild's orangery, spanning across the island and beyond. These tunnels provide safe passage to chief shiners, so they can cleanse a high volume of stones under their protective roofs. Because you shiners need so much fresh plantation, it just wasn't viable to keep a store here. The *Sapphire Fortress* plays a vital role in collecting supplies from the bureau. Our plan of attack is to wait for the waters to calm then directly attack at close range to the Hellson. This requires security, and a lot of society members. I need a volunteer to glide to the bureau and alert the president to seek other societies to assist, collect weapons and speak to **KAPOW** about what on earth it could be this crazy Viking is seeking."

"I'll go," Truffy volunteered.

"Thank you, Truffy. Can you speak to Nigel?" Mr Froodroy asked.

Truffy rolled his eyes. "I can try, but who knows if he'll listen to me?"

"Okay. Take Savannah with you. She knows Nigel well enough to ask a favour. We need them to urgently investigate what it could be that Ragnar wants. When we know, we can protect it and make sure he doesn't get it. Delia, Rich, I want you in charge of the tunnels. Use them to visit Doreen and brief her. Precious, we will stay here and monitor what's occurring. Until we get bureau back-up, we cannot attack, so for the moment we are just firefighting," Mr Froodroy said.

"Right, come on, Savs," Truffy said, getting up from his seat.

"Be careful." Rich rested his hand on Savannah's shoulder. Savannah and Truffy glided down the stairs, through the grand hallway and into Delia's office.

"Ladies first," Truffy said, pointing to the stationery cupboard. Savannah tilted her head and squinted with bemusement.

"Ah, I forget you're not fully cloaked," Truffy responded. Truffy put his ear to the door and spoke assertively: "*Sola recedat fortis*."

"Repeat," came a voice from inside the cupboard.

Truffy raised his voice. "Walter. Let me through."

"No. There's two of you, but only your sapphire key. Plus, your accent destroys that beautiful language. I shouldn't let you pass for that reason alone," the voice said.

"Savannah, I'm sorry about this. Could you place your '*medal of light*'," Truffy shouted for effect and continued, "onto the door so jobsworth Walter can verify it, please?" he finished, disgruntled.

"Sorry, Terrence, but you know I can't break the rules, especially when there's trouble afoot," said the voice from behind the cupboard door. Savannah held up her necklace to the keyhole and quickly the stationery cupboard door sprung open, revealing a man with a wolf's head, the sight of which made Savannah gasp.

"Savannah, this is Walter, chief protector and groundsman of our underground network," Truffy introduced. Walter was at least 8 feet tall, with kind brown eyes, and was covered in grey fur from his shoulders up.

"Pleased to meet you, Walter. I love your mask," Savannah said, holding out her hand to shake Walter's in an attempt to be polite.

"What? They haven't told you about me?" Walter said, looking at Truffy.

"She's new," Truffy replied swiftly. "Look, I promise I will tell her all about you on the way to the bureau but we need to hurry; we have a code blue," Truffy continued.

"Oh, I know, the stinking, half-dead creatures make such a hullabaloo. The *Fortress* is already in Cod Cove for you. I gave her a polish-up, so she's ready to rumble. Keep up; I'll take you right away." Walter indicated for them to follow him. The tunnel system was vast and hugely complex, with fishbones scattering the floor like crunchy white turf.

"How many different tunnels are there?" Savannah shouted to Truffy, while running to keep up with Walter.

"Thousands. That's why we need Walter. Anyone else would get totally lost down here. Plus, he likes to keep a low profile, for obvious reasons," Truffy said.

"Yes, about that. What is he?" Savannah said, lowering her voice.

"He's a wulver. A wolf-headed man. Originally, he's from the Shetland Islands, but evidently, he came for a holiday fifty years ago and decided to stay because the fishing is better," Truffy said. Finally, the tunnel opened out to a beautiful cove, where resting majestically above the water floated the *Fortress*. "Here we are. Careful as you go. Make sure you are slow and steady while gliding out of the cove, Terrence, or the bottom of the *Fortress* will catch the high rocks," Walter said, helping Savannah onto the *Fortress*.

"Yes, yes, will do. We'll be back in an hour," Truffy shouted as they glided slowly out of Cod Cove, leaving Walter waving from the water's edge.

CHAPTER 22

MEMORIA MANEAT

The *Fortress* glided gracefully out of the cave towards the evening sky of the open water. Suddenly there was a thump on the bottom of the boat.

"Don't worry, there are jagged rocks everywhere so we sometimes catch the bottom. Nothing to worry about; we will soon be clear from the rocky cove," Truffy smiled. Another thump, this time on the side of the boat, making Truffy glide even slower. Suddenly a familiar face appeared at the side. "Mai!" Truffy shouted. Mai was sodden, her brown hair slicked and framing her attractive features, albeit this time half-covered in brown fur.

"I can't stay like this for long. Truffy, I'm so sorry," she wailed.

"It doesn't matter, love. Get in," Truffy said, his eyes filled with tears.

"You don't understand. It's Ragnar. He's trying to take over the island. There's something he wants. He has been searching the waters for decades, but every possible avenue has been unsuccessful, so he forced me on land. Truffy, you have to forgive me but I had no choice. He kidnapped my mother and refused to give her back unless I went on the island and tried to find what he wants. He was going to destroy the Selkies if I refused; I had no choice," she spluttered.

"What is it, what does he want?" Savannah said with urgency as Truffy continued to hold on to Mai's shoulders with both hands.

"It's a type of seaweed that grows in fresh water. It's totally non-toxic wet, but when burned, it produces a gas that spreads like a disease, killing every living creature in its path. It was thought to be wiped out in the Ice Age, but Ragnar is convinced the island has some growing in secret somewhere. His plan is to find it and burn it, releasing the toxins into the air, killing every living human in the Faroe Islands and far beyond. This gas is a thousand times more powerful than your people's most powerful nuclear weapon," Mai said with wet eyes, though Savannah couldn't decipher whether they were caused by sea water or tears.

"Where is it? What's it called?" Savannah asked.

"*Memoria Maneat.* I couldn't find it; I don't know where it is," Mai said calmly.

"Hold on, Mai. You're telling me you went looking for this? To give him? So, he could kill every person on this planet?" Truffy said, letting go of Mai's shoulders.

"He threatened to kill every Selkie in the fjord if I didn't try and find it. It was us or you. He only let us live if we agreed not to help you when they attack," Mai said through gritted teeth.

"It doesn't matter now. Come home," Truffy shouted.

"What else could I have done? I had to save my own home," Mai said, flicking her head around and swimming off as a seal.

"Come on, Saveloy. Enough. Let's get to the bureau and see what weapons we can get to kick this half-dead Viking into finally getting some manners," Truffy panted. They sped through the oceans and the Hudson River and swiftly arrived at the bureau's security.

"Code blue, mate. We are in a rush," Truffy shouted to the security man in a dinner suit.

"Glide straight through to the arch, mate. Here's a permit," he replied. They ran through the archway of roses into the vast glass structure. Its splendour still took Savannah's breath away, despite her panic.

"Right, first stop is the bed to collect weapons," Truffy shouted.

"The where?" Savannah recoiled.

"Here. The flower bed. Everyone knows, if you've got something precious and you need to hide it, you put it under your bed. So, the bureau did the same. All our best sapphires are stored in cellars under our flower bed. Ours have the blue flowers on top," Truffy indicated.

"Irises. They are beautiful. There must be at least a few thousand iris flowers here." Savannah marvelled at the vast field of blue irises bathing in the brilliant sunshine.

"Hello Sergeant," Truffy said to a tall man in a black uniform. "Sapphire, code blue. Pull out the good stuff for me, mate. We need cannons, gem grenades, sapphire spears, AK blues, combat cloaks, absconder alert goggles and just fill the rest up with loose sapphires, mate."

"Right away, Mr Truff. We shall load it onto the *Fortress* for you. The task will be completed fully within fifteen minutes," the sergeant said, saluting to Truffy, who merely said "Cheers" in response before turning on his heels to face Savannah.

"I need to alert the president and get some other societies to come and back us up," Truffy said. "While I'm there, I need you to speak to that plonker in charge of KAPOW. See what he knows about that seaweed thing. Meet me back at the *Fortress* when you're ready," he shouted behind him as he glided off towards the president's skyscraper. Savannah glided frantically at full speed, dodging other gliding society members and swooping birds, until she arrived at the library desk.

"Nigel!" Savannah yelled, slamming her hands down on the desk, causing Nigel to physically jump into the air.

"Madam Wood, what on earth…" Nigel got up out of his chair, protectively placing his hand on her shoulder.

"I need KAPOW's help, Nigel. We are under attack, we've got a code blue," Savannah blurted out with much less decorum than she had intended. Nigel put his hand in a stop gesture to Savannah, then flicked his hands into the air at the bookshelves, which enclosed his desk from the sides, and swirled the pile of books on his desk into a mini tornado before shooting them into the air, where they formed a ceiling.

"Now our conversation is private. Sit down, my dear, tell me your woes," Nigel said, standing authoritatively and pressing his hands together in front of him.

"We are under attack from the Hellson. Its inhabitants are leaching out and attacking us. Then Mai—" Savannah was interrupted.

"I knew that traitor was up to no good; her shining hygiene was abysmal," Nigel quipped.

"She told us on the way here that Ragnar is trying to locate something called '*Memoria Maneat*'. He thinks it's growing on the island somewhere and wants to find it so he can destroy the Faroes," Savannah said.

"And destroy it would, but not just the Faroe Islands, my dear; it would blast the whole of humankind into oblivion. But that has been extinct since the Ice Age. In fact, some theorists and philosophers in **KAPOW** concluded it caused the Ice Age," Nigel pondered, flicking at the surrounding bookshelves and ceiling of books to reinstate them into the library. He walked over to his desk, unlocked his top drawer and threw out donut boxes and biscuit wrappers before pulling out a mustard yellow leather book, which he tucked under his arm. "Follow me," he said, gliding the now familiar route through the library to the untidy bookshelf. Instead of the usual process of pulling out the required books, Nigel simply patted the guard books and said, "Code blue," at which the books crumpled, leaving Nigel and Savannah standing on the rug, in the middle of a beautiful Georgian library with a large polished mahogany table sitting centrally. Nigel took the mustard yellow leather book from under his arm and laid it on the table. He sat down at the head of the table into a Queen Anne red velvet chair and leaned over the pages, booming, "KAPOW. This is your minister. We have been called to assist with a code blue, I repeat, a code blue, my friends. Our world as we have come to love and cherish it needs your power of knowledge. All past and present, please attend," Nigel said with such pomp and ceremony, it made Savannah brim with pride.

There was a tap on the door and in shuffled an elderly maid in black and white, pushing a chrome tea trolley. "Hello, Nigel. I heard the call, so I brought extra sugar and Garibaldi," she smiled and bowed before back-stepping out of the room.

"Thank you, Nigel, thank you so much. Where are we this time?" Savannah took a seat next to him.

"KAPOW headquarters, Downing Street. It's where you always come, but usually we are escaping to other places, so you don't see where we actually are. But not today. Today is too important for us to hide from our duty," Nigel smiled, raising his eyebrows.

"We are at number 10 Downing Street?" Savannah questioned, aghast.

"No! The British Prime Minister gets the smaller house at number 10. KAPOW headquarters is the largest in Westminster, number 13. Ahh, here they come," Nigel said, pointing to a bookshelf which slid across, revealing a secret door, which at least ten people walked through, all chattering and nodding. Books began flying off the shelves and glided mid-air, hitting chairs and opening to reveal ghosts wafting out of them, who all faced Nigel and nodded. A year ago, Savannah would have run in fright, but she found herself being less surprised at the amazing things she encountered through being a Sapphire apprentice.

"KAPOW," Nigel announced, clearing his throat as all eyes, living and departed, gazed on at him expectantly. "So often we are overlooked, ridiculed even, due to others' ignorance of our true capabilities. But here sits Madam Savannah Wood, granddaughter of one of KAPOW's missing, Meinhild Simonsen. A Sapphire apprentice now herself, she and the Sapphires have been plagued with recent deception and now face a full code blue attack." Gasps were audible from members around the table. "They seek our assistance in their time of need; it is only us that can truly save not just their nation, but our world. Ragnar is seeking *Memoria Maneat*."

"That seaweed has been extinct for thousands of years, Nigel," a lady with grey hair and a British accent said.

"It appears not. Meinhild spoke of this before her departure. She was researching this very plant before she went missing. I need all you can bring me. I need all of your knowledge. Where is it located and where is the antidote we know our very own Meinhild was seeking? You have five minutes," he boomed, as members walked back through the bookshelf's hidden door and back into the books from where they came.

"Do you think we stand a chance?" Savannah asked Nigel as he poured out two cups of tea into fine bone china cups and saucers. Nigel sighed, moving his gaze into the corner of the room.

"Sig, get on with it," Nigel spat, to the ghost of a young boy around Savannah's age.

"Mr Nigel," he looked at Nigel's cup of tea as he spoke, "I know how you can find out where it is, but I promised not to tell. I crossed my heart and hoped to die if I ever spoke of it," Sig said, managing to look frail and pale, even by ghost standards.

"Sig, you're already dead, and so will the rest of us be if you don't tell us," Nigel said.

"The day I drowned, I was out with her, you see, Meinhild. She rowed me out to the fjord to see the Selkies, and the book fell out of her bag while she was chatting to one of them. I was only reading it because I didn't want to look like I was eavesdropping…" Sig said quietly, his hazy appearance flickering as he spoke.

"It doesn't matter, child. You were trusted to carry this burden until it was the right time to disclose it. Now is that time," Nigel soothed uncharacteristically.

"Her new book. The one she hadn't yet published," he said.

"*Aggressive Aquaponics*?" Nigel queried.

Sig nodded. "In her private notes on loose pages tucked into the front cover, the answer to your question, it's in an envelope. She was on her way to bring it to the KAPOW safe, except I know she never got here," Sig said, still looking at Nigel's cup of tea.

"Well done, Sig. Now at least we stand a fighting chance. Madam Wood and I will get the book. You regroup and debrief with the others," Nigel smiled at the boy.

Sig nodded and said, "Your grandmother saved me," directly to Savannah.

"But you died," Savannah exhaled.

Sig smiled. "Dying isn't a problem, but half-living in Hellson is. I owe her everything," he said solemnly.

"Consider your debt repaid, Sig," Nigel said.

"Thank you," Savannah smiled as Sig vanished into the bookcase. Nigel had already walked over to the beautiful walnut apothecary cabinet with its exquisite glass shelving.

"Maybe I was meant to steal this cabinet and bring it here, after all," he said, flicking through the books and pulling out the fern-printed leather-bound journal and handing it to Savannah. She took it into her hands and untied the leather bow, opening the pages. Just as Sig described, a yellowing letter with *KAPOW, CODE BLUE* handwritten on the front.

"I think you should read this," Savannah said, her eyes feeling full.

Dear KAPOW Minister,

The long-forgotten lethal seaweed of oblivion, Memoria Maneat, has been located and now quarantined in the Sapphire Society's designated quarantine area. I have conducted many research studies to acquire the antidote to this seaweed and have found the cure to be Fungai Mortem Toxicus, the indigenous blue mushroom.

Yours faithfully,

Meinhild Simonsen, Sapphire

Nigel sighed. "All this time, the answer has been right here under my nose." He slammed his hands down onto the table, making the teacups shudder. "I've let you down."

Savannah took the letter. "No, Nigel. You found it at exactly the right time. Now I have to get to the *Fortress*; I need to find out where this designated quarantine area is," Savannah smiled. Nigel said nothing but took Savannah back through the secret bookcase door of Downing Street and back into the library.

CHAPTER 23

MINEFIELD

The reflective clear water splashed and sloshed around Walter's legs as he strode knee-deep into the water of Cod Cove. The *Fortress* glided steadily towards him, the heavy burden of weaponry making no dent in its transatlantic crossing speed.

"Ragnar's totally manic; he's even torn up Waterfall Mile Lake." Walter's hands trembled as he helped them out of the *Fortress*, tying it up with a hemp rope to a tall brass pole at the cove edge.

"The Scottish Pearls and the Diamonds are on their way to the watchtower as we speak," Truffy reassured him with a slap on his back. "Walter, first of all we need to get to Doreen, then I need you to unload the weapons and take them to the watchtower."

Walter could only manage a nod in response before gesturing to them to follow him. Truffy and

Savannah ran at full speed to keep up with Walter as they sprinted behind him and quickly arrived at a trapdoor, which sprung open. They climbed down a small underground opening into the foot of Doreen's fire. "I'll collect you in five." Walter bolted off back through the warren of tunnels.

"You're safe." Doreen quickly walked over to the fireplace, helping Savannah and Truffy out of the tunnel, before clicking it shut behind them and covering it over with the sheepskin rug. "This must be such a shock for you, Savannah, and so early on in your training," Doreen panted, with black circles under her eyes. The cottage was dimly lit, but flashes of fire and booms from outside lit up the night sky. The plants shuffled, leaning at the windowpanes. "They've started attacking houses." Doreen swallowed while continuing to stir several pots of shining liquids on the round oak table. "The muted stalked around the garden and tried to scratch their way through the front door, but my roof managed to be too difficult for them to break through; it looks like they've given up, for now."

"*Memoria maneat*. My grandmother found it; it's what Ragnar's been looking for," Savannah spluttered, out of breath.

"Heaven help us." Doreen stopped stirring and stood motionless.

"It's true, Doreen, but she also found the cure. Savannah found it in the library," Truffy smiled.

"Actually, it was Nigel and **KAPOW** who found it, in Grandma's book. She had the *memoria maneat* seaweed safely contained in a place called the Sapphire quarantine, and the antidote called *mortem toxicus*, too." Savannah smiled so broadly, her dry lips cracked. Doreen lunged forward and held on to her tightly.

"Before she went missing, I had a feeling she was close to discovering something big. I knew it." Doreen's eyes glazed over.

"Where do you think this quarantine could be?" Truffy asked.

"It's obvious when you think about it. Where would one of the world's best shiners hide her most treasured possessions?" Doreen smiled.

"In the ground," Savannah guessed.

"You really are so much like her, Savannah. Correct," Doreen laughed.

"You're having a laugh? The deadliest weapon ever known to mankind is just buried somewhere without security or protection," Truffy said.

"Oh, it has protection," Doreen said.

"Do you have a map so we can find it?" Savannah asked.

"Tricver is guarding it. That's why he would never leave your grandmother's house." Doreen looked to Savannah with raised eyebrows.

"So how can we locate it? How can we get the lethal seaweed and its antidote?" Savannah asked.

"Walter and Meinhild trained him well. You need to feed him a piece of freshly caught cod, then he will retrieve it. But you can't do it without security," she said.

"That's no problem," Truffy assured. "We collected an arsenal of weapons from the bureau bed and the president has arranged for the Pearls and Diamonds to come and help us. They should be arriving any minute now. While I'm here, can I give you my dirty gems for shining? I had a battle just getting in the watchtower." He emptied his pockets of blackened sapphires onto the table then answered a knock at the trapdoor. Truffy pulled the rug away from the secret entrance and clicked open the door to reveal Walter. "Perfect timing, mate. We'd better get going, Walter; we need your fishing skills," Truffy said, helping Savannah back down into the sapphire crystal tunnel heading towards the watchtower.

- ▼ -

"Mr Froodroy," Savannah shouted from the bottom of the spiral staircase, freshly caught cod in hand, thanks to Walter.

"How did you get on?" Rich asked. Savannah and Truffy explained their progress and the contents of her grandmother's unpublished book.

"Well, I never. Meinhild saves the day and she's not even here. The Diamonds can support ground forces. The Pearls can provide security from the air," Mr Froodroy said, rubbing his chin.

"The Diamonds and Pearls will be here any minute," Truffy said.

"And not a moment too soon," the watchtower ghost interjected, indicating out of the window. In the darkness outside, car headlights glowed in the distance.

Truffy ran to the window and leaned out. "Yes, Scruffy, mate! What a legend, he's only gone and brought the whole crew." With glowing yellow headlights, a black taxi cab glided to the window.

"Am I dreaming, Savannah? Is that a London cab that's at the window, six floors up?" Rich said.

"All right, sunshine," came a voice from the cab window as it was wound down. Savannah recognised the man as Scruffy. "You're lucky, mate. You caught us down the pub watching the Hammers win against United, so we were all together anyways. The whole crew is here. Me, Tony and big Dave will drop the gems off here then park the wheels downstairs."

Mr Froodroy pushed to the front of the window. "Thank you, Scruffy. Thank you very much," as men with tattoos and maroon and pale blue velvet cloaks clambered out of the cab and through the watchtower window. Behind the burly men was an elderly lady, with a maroon and pale blue hand-knitted scarf, using a walking stick.

"'Ello, love, what's this? Are you dead then?" the elderly but stocky lady with white hair in a beehive said to the watchtower ghost.

"How observant you are," the ghost replied sarcastically.

"All right for you then, love, innit? You can sit back and watch the rest of us earn a livin'," the elderly Diamond member said, giving Savannah a wink.

"Saveloy, meet Edna, known by those who love her as Heavy Ed. You need a bodyguard, she's the best there is," Scruffy smiled.

"Yeah, she knows the score, Scruffy. Look at her, she even looks like Minefield." Edna beamed a smile of missing teeth.

"Ahh, I'm Savannah. Do you mean I look like my grandmother? Only her name was Meinhild," Savannah corrected the lady gently, taking into account her nickname as Rich snickered behind her.

"Yes, love, but if you'd ever gone chasing with her, you'd have called her Minefield, too. She was a belter of a chaser," she said, slapping Savannah on the back. "'Ello, Delia, tell Doreen to put the kettle on," Edna said to Delia, who hugged her affectionately.

"Thanks for coming, Edna. No time, I'm afraid. We need to wait for the Pearls and get a move on to the Woods' house," Delia replied.

Despite the severity of the situation, the Diamonds brought a sense of camaraderie to the watchtower's trials that lay ahead. Scruffy glided up the spiral stairs, followed by Billy and two other Diamond members.

"What's the plan then?" Scruffy asked, clasping his hands and rubbing them together, his gold medallion encrusted with diamonds jingling as he did so.

"Ragnar is seeking a deadly weapon. A seaweed called *memoria maneat*, which we now know is located in the Sapphire quarantine…" Mr Froodroy announced.

"Oblivion awaits?" queried Scruffy.

"Yes, that is the plant's layman name," Mr Froodroy replied sombrely, making the atmosphere in the watchtower seem abruptly very serious. "Ragnar plans to set fire to the seaweed, killing not only the Faroe Islands' inhabitants, but intending the wind to carry the gas across the oceans," he continued.

"Human genocide," Delia added.

"Precisely. Well, not while I'm the chairman, he's not. Not only did Meinhild locate and quarantine the deadly weapon, she also found the antidote…"

"God rest 'er soul, wherever she is," Edna interrupted.

"A blue mushroom, native to our island, *fungai mortem toxicus*…" Mr Froodroy continued but was again interrupted.

"Underwater death mushroom," Scruffy blurted out, wide-eyed.

"Oi, Scruffy, when did you learn Latin?" Truffy said indignantly.

"Saveloy's gran," Scruffy said, indicating to Savannah.

"Diamonds, may I conclude, please?" Mr Froodroy announced, staring at Scruffy without blinking.

"Yes, Chairman, sorry," Scruffy answered quietly, raising his eyebrows.

"I will continue. This blue mushroom is the antidote. What we need to do is locate the quarantine and bring both the weapon and antidote to the watchtower. Once this has been done, we can alert the KAPOW minister so he can collect them and ensure they are securely escorted into the KAPOW safe with a chasing team. This is the first time we have ever had such access into the Hellson. While the entrance to the Hellson is open, we must take our opportunity to remove Ragnar for good. Our final task will be to chase the muted from our island and remove Ragnar from the Hellson, disintegrating him with the biggest sapphire grenade we have. However, we are already overrun with muted absconders. Richard and Precious have estimated a stronghold of Hellson escapees to be approximately 300, with numbers rising."

"We are outnumbered at least ten to one," Precious said informatively.

"Yes, which is why we need the Pearls," Mr Froodroy continued. "The Laird's helicopter has proved it can hold a 2-metre protective field directly below its path. Diamonds and Sapphires will go on the ground, Pearls in the air, giving Savannah and Precious, plus Sapphire and Diamond chaperones, time to locate the quarantine and bring its contents back to the watchtower," Mr Froodroy announced proudly.

Savannah couldn't decipher whether he was proud of his well-thought-out battle plan, or simply pleased to get through his sentence without being interrupted by a well-meaning Diamond.

"Easy-peasy," Edna said jubilantly, throwing her hands in the air.

"Here the Scottish Pearls come now," Mr Froodroy announced, raising his hand to his ear. The helicopter vibrated and gleamed a pearlescent white across the midnight sky. On the ground were rumbles, felt even in the watchtower.

"You're looking, Savannah," the watchtower ghost said crossly. Savannah's eyes flickered across the panoramic view, past the beautiful helicopter. "See," shouted the ghost with acute shivering urgency as Savannah's eyes ravaged across the sky and land to find what she needed to see. It was too late; a vast explosion over the fjord smothered the Laird and the helicopter. Screeches and screams exhaled from the Diamond and Sapphire Society members as they helplessly watched the helicopter plummet down, straight into the Hellson entrance below, belching flames and black gas as it withered out of earthly existence. Absconders with green eyes clambered through the windows of the watchtower, the stench of their Hellson noxious breath knocking society members backwards. Society members were gliding and chasing the green-eyed vagrants, but more appeared.

"Precious!" Mr Froodroy screeched while fending off an assailant. "Take Savannah and Rich to Walter, you've got to go it alone!"

Savannah grabbed Rich by the hand. "We can't let them follow," Precious whispered, leaning in to them and slowly ushering them down the staircase.

"It's okay, Precious. This is my school and I will make sure there are no unauthorised entries," Delia said, flashing an absconder with her glasses and disintegrating him to dust as she stood guard at the spiral staircase.

CHAPTER 24

THE WOLVES

"*Sola recedat fortis,*" Precious whispered, clicking the three Sapphires to the stationery cupboard door in Delia's office. The door swung open.

"Walter, we have a problem," Precious said, trembling.

"I heard fighting." Walter stepped back to let them through.

"They've taken the Laird and all the Pearls. They've crashed straight down through the fjord into the Hellson," Precious exclaimed.

"It can't be," Walter said, the fur on his nose twitching. He stood momentarily, panting.

"We need to get to the orangery, but we're surrounded and have no further society protection." Precious managed to stay calm.

"I can't leave the tunnels, but I can help. Get the Sapphire armour on, get loaded up with weapons."

Walter indicated towards the weapons chest. Walter threw his head back and howled; a long, smooth call. His previously kind eyes looked wild and ferocious. "Stay here," he grunted, running in the opposite direction. Savannah, Rich and Precious loaded themselves with as much armoury as they could carry. Savannah looked up and saw Walter standing before her, in front of a pack of snarling wolves. "I will lead you to the orangery, but once there, I cannot pass the tunnel door. However, they can." Walter pointed behind him, one of the wolves spitting with minute slits as eyes. "They have lost many in their pack due to Ragnar, who takes great delight in mutilating them for sport. They are angry, Savannah. They will protect you, but you may not like their tactics that you encounter," Walter growled.

"We understand," Precious nodded. The pack of snarling wolves skulked behind them; the sound of their dipped bellies dusting against the fishbone floor and the smell of their metallic tainted breath shifted the atmosphere to feel inherently dangerous.

"I brought Doreen here an hour ago; she will be waiting for you. Good luck, my friends," Walter growled as the orangery trapdoor clicked open. Savannah crawled in but was pushed aside by the snarling wolves, battling to get past her. She finally pushed through and saw Doreen, holding her sapphire to the floor towards them.

"We're surrounded, Sapphires." Doreen blinked. The black night sky was illuminated by hundreds of electric green eyes peering through the glass panes of the orangery.

"Tricver," Rich whispered. The wolves surrounded him, Tricver's sheepherding traits suddenly becoming apparent as he too dipped his underside and peered up to the ferocious, snarling pack. "They're going to kill him! Walter said he'd protect us, but we forgot to mention Tricver," Rich said, breathing quickly through his twitching nose. The wolf at the head of the pack walked slowly towards Tricver, moving his head from left to right as he got ever closer to him. Savannah could bear the performance no more, of her trusted dog about to be mauled, and ran over to the centre of the orangery where the breath of the wolves was beginning to steam up the surrounding glass.

"He's a Sapphire," she said, looking directly at the pack leader, clutching Tricver around the collar. The leader of the pack moved his head sideways, sticking his long nose directly over Savannah's hand and nuzzling Tricver's sapphire, dangling from his collar. The wolf's tail began to wag and his shackles came down. The rest of the pack backed down and began tapping Tricver with a playful paw.

"This lot have met Tricver before; there was no need to panic," Doreen smiled, affectionately ruffling the fur on the head of the pack leader.

"Blue thunder, you could have told me," Rich exhaled, putting his palm to his forehead.

"It's that lot you want to worry about." Doreen pointed to the roof and windows, smothered in the offensive green haze expelled from the absconders' eyes. Rich backed into the centre of the room; scratches of absconders' fingernails audible over the wolves' frantic breath. Doreen nodded to Savannah, who knelt down to Tricver and pulled the wet cod fish out of her armour pocket. On seeing it, Tricver's tail immediately stopped wagging. Tricver stalked towards the door, scrapes from the roof and windows frantically moving as the green eyes followed his old, coarsely haired body towards the metal-framed doors.

"Surely not. It can't be outside," Rich said.

"Yes, it can. You always laughed that for a botanist my grandmother had a rotten back lawn full of moss. Now we know why," Savannah said quietly, still watching the muted absconders outside, waiting to pounce.

"You need to open the door, Savannah. You must have faith." Doreen nudged Savannah's hand, which gripped the heart-shaped metal door key. Tricver sat, waiting at the door, as if she was simply letting him out to go for a walk.

"Ready?" Savannah whispered.

"Doreen, you stay in the orangery. I will help Savannah, and Rich will defend Tricver," Precious instructed. Savannah leaned over Tricver and fitted the key into the door lock, turning it anti-clockwise until it clicked and opened outwards towards the deathly enemy awaiting them. The wolves charged, in every direction, but the pack leader stayed next to Tricver, Savannah, Precious and Rich. Tricver paced, ignoring the howls and tearing of flesh that surrounded him as Savannah could barely watch the blood being spilled. Tricver went to the centre of the garden, next to where he had unearthed the sapphire pots, and began digging. The wolves were showing no mercy and already, many of the muted absconders' bodies lay still, until Rich leaned over them, tipping his hat and transforming them to dust, which he hoovered up with his sapphire as he edged past. The green moss began to consume the absconders' blood, turning it scarlet and squelchy as the wolves condemned the muted to a grizzly end. Dirt and moss scattered in the air like confetti.

Tricver stopped, turned and barked, allowing Savannah and Rich into the newly dug hole to remove two gold and sapphire-encrusted terrariums, one the size of a tennis ball, the other much larger, the size of an outstretched broadsheet newspaper, and radiating a startling blue light. Savannah gave the smaller terrarium to Precious and pulled the glowing terrarium into her chest. Immediately, she felt an intense, searing pain in her legs, forcing her to the ground. One of the muted had grabbed her leg and was biting into it. Rich dived over her, his hat flying over her head while a green-eyed noxious face staring straight up at her exploded into minuscule green dust particles.

Rich scooped Savannah off the blood-sodden ground and carried her in his arms while running towards the orangery door. He fumbled with the lock, eventually clunking it open. Rich, Savannah, Tricver and Precious pushed through the blood-smeared and -splattered orangery doors.

"Those things. Are you leaving those poor wolves out there with them?" Martha said as she stood in the orangery kitchen doorway, Theodore placing his arm around her shoulder. Savannah wanted to run to her, to feel protection in her mother's embrace, but her legs were oozing blood and were not moving as quickly as she hoped. Martha ran to her, cupping Savannah's face into her warm, soft hands.

"It's okay, Martha; I can heal her legs," Doreen said tenderly, guiding Savannah down by her hand onto the sheepskin rug, next to the log burner.

"I've heard that before. I'm trusting you with my only daughter; how do I know you're not a traitor, too?" Martha shouted, her hands clutching Savannah protectively.

"I think you know I'm not a Selkie in disguise," Doreen replied calmly, holding out a bowl containing a herbal mixture. Martha wiped her eyes and nodded, taking the bowl and pouring the contents onto Savannah's lacerated lower limbs. "Quickly, you two, I will shine your armour and gems. I have the remedy waiting," Doreen said. Steam rose from Savannah's wounds and the aroma of aloe vera and lavender filled the orangery.

"I'm sorry, Doreen," Martha said, holding out her hand towards her. "This has all been a shock."

"Your family has paid a high price for our islands' freedom," Doreen added, her eyes locking onto Martha's.

"As has yours," Martha replied.

"We need to get back to the chairman. We need to get this *memoria maneat* deadly seaweed into the KAPOW safe, to make sure it never sees daylight again, and ensure the *fungai mortem toxicus*, blue mushroom antidote, doesn't leave its side," Precious said.

Savannah's leg wounds were neatly bandaged. "You're not going back out there, Savannah. I thought the Diamonds were coming to help?" Martha said.

"I have to, Ma," Savannah replied.

Martha paced around her and stroked her trembling hand across Savannah's cheek. "I will be watching from the sea view window. I'm not letting you out of my sight." She locked eyes with her. "You're so brave," she added, holding her close.

"Come on, Savannah, we have to leave," Rich said quietly, putting his hand on her shoulder. Precious flicked over one half of the sheepskin rug, revealing the trapdoor.

"*Sola recedat fortis,*" Precious announced and in turn, each of them clicked their sapphires onto the keyhole. The door sprung open and Walter stuck his head through without crossing the threshold into the room.

"How are they getting on?" Walter asked Precious, nervously.

"It's safe to say the wolves are winning," Precious said.

"Ugh," Walter gagged. "So I see. It's a shame the wolves can't disintegrate the muted like the sapphires do; they are making a terrible mess." Walter winced at the blood-splattered orangery and promptly turned his head away, covering his eyes with his hand.

"To the watchtower, please, Walter. How are they getting on over there?" Savannah asked.

"I will take you straight away. I think they could use some help," Walter replied.

CHAPTER 25

LEARNING TO SEE

"You took yer time, what did you do? Stop for a midnight snack on the way back?" Edna shouted as they stumbled through the stationery cupboard.

"Did you find the quarantine?" Delia asked as they reached the top of the spiral staircase. Savannah nodded.

"Edna, keep watch on the door," Delia ordered.

In the watchtower, Mr Froodroy was pacing. "Thank goodness you're safe." Rich reached into his pocket and pulled out the small terrarium containing the *memoria maneat* seaweed and passed it to his father. The black seaweed looked so insignificant – its slimy, gel-like appearance giving no hint of the perils that would be unleashed in the wrong hands. "*Fungai mortem toxicus*, the antidote," Savannah said, handing the larger terrarium to Mr Froodroy.

Mr Froodroy stared at the terrariums momentarily before raising his eyebrows to the corner of the room where Nigel emerged from a dark corner.

"I will ensure it makes its final journey to the KAPOW safe. I assure you, this vile creation shall never see daylight again," Nigel said.

"Delia will chaperone you, in case of unforeseen dangers," Mr Froodroy said.

"Much appreciated. Walter has kindly arranged to escort me there personally via your sapphire tunnel network. I will return immediately to let you know it's been completed. Good luck, Mr Chairman." Delia put her glasses on and ushered Nigel, who took the terrariums and bowed humbly before leaving via the stationery cupboard.

"Any news on the Laird?" Savannah asked.

"Not yet. The Hellson was bigger and more highly populated than any of us imagined. We've turned hundreds of muted absconders into dust, but still more of them are escaping through the Hellson entrance every second. They are attacking in packs so as to overrun the villagers. Doreen is shining as quickly as she can, but we desperately need Precious back on shining duty before we run out of cleansed gems." Mr Froodroy shook his head.

"I will go to Doreen's now." Precious nodded to the room before departing, her red cloak sailing through the air behind her.

"Without the helicopter, how do we get sapphire grenades directly into the Hellson?" Rich asked.

"We do it the old-fashioned way. We will row our sapphire weapons in," Mr Froodroy answered.

"Lucky we've got the best rowers Strendur has right 'ere, then." Truffy put his hands on his hips triumphantly.

"Time is running out, Terrence. The island cannot take much more. If we don't get to the Laird soon, the green-eye disease will be irreversible," Mr Froodroy said.

Savannah walked over to the window, where the watchtower ghost was sitting in contemplation, her cold gaze transfixed on the Hellson. Ferocious fjord waves climbed so high they were drenching the top of the turbine. The dark night sky had a peculiar green tinge of light that illuminated the carnage trail left by the muted, while the thick, choking gas smothered the land. She looked over the dark fields, the protective roofs gleaming a pulsing blue light, except for her house, where the blue light was beginning to randomly flicker. Her eyes widened in panic.

"You're learning fast," the watchtower ghost said, observing Savannah's face.

"Mr Froodroy!" Savannah screamed. The chairman ran over to the window and Savannah pointed to her home, the protective roof fading fast and smothered by the muted Hellson inhabitants.

"The Hellson can wait. Edna, Truffy, Scruffy, the others will have to defend without you for a while. We're going tunnelling," Mr Froodroy said.

Walter was ready and waiting at the stationery cupboard. "Terrariums escorted safely with Nigel into KAPOW safe, Mr Froodroy, but the noise from Meinhild's is deafening. It's not going to hold," Walter shouted as they ran to the orangery trapdoor.

"No, no, no, Chairman. I'll go first," Scruffy said, ushering Mr Froodroy back from the orangery trapdoor entrance. "Edna, you stick with Savannah and make sure the Wood family are safely underground in the tunnels. We will take them straight to Precious; her roof hasn't even been targeted yet."

"Good idea." Edna stuck her thumb in the air. "Rich, Scruffy, Truffy, help me secure the tunnel entrance and get as many people as possible underground. Walter, stay near; we will need a quick escape." Edna reached into her burgundy velvet cloak's pocket and removed something. It was like a small vase that fitted into the palm of her wrinkled hand. She slotted a sapphire into the top narrow end, held it to her mouth and blew. A large blue bubble appeared, floating in front of her.

"Trojan bubbles. This will knock the little blighters out." Edna raised her eyebrows up and down mischievously, the wrinkles around her eyes growing longer. In her other hand she was armed with a walking stick, which Savannah noticed now had a sapphire on top, instead of the diamond which was in place when they first arrived. "Right, Walt. Let me at 'em," she said, with her head down like a charging bull.

With a click, the door sprung open. Edna flicked the sheepskin out of the way of the trapdoor entrance and bulldozed into the room. As muted absconders were beginning to smash their way through the glass, a high-pitched noise deafened them. Bubbles soon filled the orangery, and absconders disintegrated into dust, falling into neat piles onto the floor. Savannah ran to the kitchen door, covering her ears. A mask of *calluna vulgaris* instantly appeared over her face as the smog hit her. The kitchen was filled with gas, and as she fumbled her way around the dining table, she found her father leaning over her mother and Tom, who had both collapsed on the floor. Tricver sat next to them. Edna's head was now enclosed in a blue bubble, and Savannah picked up Tom and threw his limp body over her shoulder.

Suddenly in front of her stood a man with green eyes. He tilted his head and silently exhaled, forcing more noxious gas into Savannah's face, causing her to stumble backwards. The menacing green eyes gazed over her shoulder and the muted Hellson absconder inhaled, preparing to exhale over Tom's face. Savannah wanted to scream, to run away, but her little brother's limp body would not survive more gas. Savannah leaned towards the absconder, allowing her necklace to dangle in front of his face, and watched incredulously as the green eyes and mutated body disintegrated and were swallowed by the sapphire on her gold chain.

"Tom, wake up, you have to breathe!" she yelled, though nothing could be heard through the unearthly noise. Theodore was gasping; his wide eyes were rolling back into their sockets as the gas took hold. Edna blew a trojan bubble over his face and began guiding him through the orangery. Truffy pulled Martha but was himself struggling to breathe. Scruffy grabbed Martha by the legs, and together, they manoeuvred her through the orangery into the trapdoor. Walter was waiting, as promised.

"They need shining, Walter. Take us to Precious. This is going to need some intensive shining treatment," Mr Froodroy said.

By the time they had struggled to Precious' cottage, Martha and Theodore were regaining consciousness, albeit through spluttered and gasping breaths. Tom was not breathing. Savannah flew through Precious' trapdoor. Precious immediately took Tom and laid his limp and pale body onto the mango wood table.

"Confetti bush, grab me two handfuls with plenty of flowers, Savannah. It will keep him going until Doreen gets here," Precious said calmly. Precious lifted Tom's eyelids and felt for a pulse. Savannah stumbled as she got herself onto the roof, collecting pale pink blooms from the bush she had planted just days before. Savannah thrust them into Precious' hands as Martha and Theodore could only clutch at their youngest child and weep. Precious frantically pummelled the petals in a pestle and mortar and used the paste it produced to smear lines, like warpaint, onto Tom's forehead, cheeks and wrists. Martha was still disorientated from the gas but wept, holding Tom's hands and kissing his head.

"Nothing's happening!" Martha screamed. Edna stood close by, her beehive flattened, and Scruffy could only stand in the opposite corner, facing the wall and covering his eyes. Suddenly a flicker appeared in Tom's left eye, then his right.

"It's working," Precious said, her shoulders visibly dropping as Tom's eyes flickered.

Suddenly he gasped. "Mama," he said calmly, as if waking from a mid-afternoon nap. The room exhaled a sigh of relief and Tom promptly sat up, smiling.

"Thank you. You saved his life. Thank you," Martha cried, hugging Precious.

"Well, we had better cancel Doreen, then," Mr Froodroy said.

"Too late," Doreen said, as she gingerly climbed out of the tunnel entrance.

"Bad news, I'm afraid, Mr Chairman," Walter said.

"What's happened, is everyone okay?"

"Everyone is fine, but there's been an almighty fight, and we lost. It's the school. Ragnar has taken it over. He's in the watchtower," Walter said, the wild look returning to his eyes.

CHAPTER 26

A HIDDEN DIAMOND

"It doesn't even look like home anymore," Savannah said, rubbing her long fingers along the side of the moss armchair on the confetti bush rooftop as she attempted to gather her thoughts. She looked out across the island she now considered home. Her grandmother's beautiful orangery was smashed to smithereens, muted green-eyed absconders still scavenging through the wreckage in the hope of finding people with souls intact, to kidnap and drown in the Hellson gas. The water was ferocious; waves as big as double-decker buses assaulted the lands and any building stood upon them. The only buildings left standing were protected by sapphire shining roofs. The Froodroy house had long been forsaken by the water and the debris was still visible, floating and being blown around in the storm. Martha poked her head out of the skylight, holding two cups of tea, and perched herself on the arm of the moss armchair below the starlit sky. She said nothing but handed Rich and Savannah hot mugs and wrapped an arm around Savannah's shoulder.

"The Sapphires need Rich and I to row out to the Hellson and throw in a sapphire grenade. It's the only way. It's dangerous, but we are the best rowers here." Savannah looked at her mother, expecting her to forbid it.

"I know. I know it's the only chance we have and I know you are our only hope," Martha replied, without looking at her.

Mr Froodroy leaned his head out onto the roof. "If there was any other way, I would do it. Savannah and Rich are our only hope now, Martha." Martha spoke no words but hugged Savannah the way she had on her first day of school, before sitting back down onto the moss chair and wrapping a scarf around her shoulders.

Mr Froodroy paced the wooden floor in the living room as he prepared to speak to the Sapphires and Diamonds. "The Diamonds will protect the house. Savannah, Rich, it's down to you to glide the *Fortress* and then row close enough to allow Truffy and Delia to detonate the sapphire bombs into the Hellson's entrance."

Mr Froodroy passed Delia a huge sapphire bomb, covered in gold and diamond-encrusted stars which omitted a blue-coloured haze. "Walter will take you through the tunnels to Cod Cove to collect the *Fortress*, but after that, you're on your own. Those of us left will keep the shoreline clear to stop absconders returning to the fjord, but we don't know how many are left down there. Once the Hellson is destroyed, the muted can't survive in our air. An hour tops, but get straight back; we don't want to take any chances. Good luck, my gems," Mr Froodroy said defiantly, ushering them towards Walter in the passageway. Savannah looked at Rich, who seemed uncharacteristically calm.

"Ready?" Rich asked, squeezing Savannah's shoulder. Savannah nodded, her fiery red hair swaying triumphantly as she did so.

- ▼ -

"Here we are, Sapphires," Walter said, as they reached Cod Cove.

"Go on, Walt, mate. You get to safety," Truffy said, patting Walter on the back as he stepped back in reverse up the tunnel.

"Do you know what to do, you two?" Delia looked at Rich and Savannah over her sapphire glasses, which balanced on her nose. They both nodded. The *Fortress* glided slowly out of Cod Cove, its protective gems reflecting on the roof of the cave.

The water became increasingly dangerous as they got to the open water. Savannah looked down at the water beneath them as they glided silently over it. The deep ocean appeared like a black hole with no bottom. Delia held on rigidly to the glowing sapphire bomb and breathed out a mist of warm air in the freezing temperature of the cold night, which quickly turned black in the gas. *Calluna vulgaris* slowly spread over Savannah's face, assisting her breathing as the gas intensified.

Rich coughed. "I'm almost getting the taste for this foul air now. You don't know what you're missing, Savannah," he whispered jovially. As the *Fortress* glided over the vast waves with ease, they arrived a metre from the turbine.

"Here we go. We can't glide anymore; it's down to you two to row us the rest of the way," Truffy said. Rich looked at Savannah on the opposite side of the *Fortress*, oars clutched in their hands.

"On the count of three, we will cease gliding. Ready. One, two, three," Rich shouted. The *Fortress* hit the waves with an almighty smash, throwing Truffy and Delia onto their knees to the floor of the boat. Saltwater hit their faces; the waves lashed into the boat. "The storm, it's too strong," Rich yelled.

"We are the storm!" Delia jeered.

Savannah and Rich rowed with such vigour; their limbs pleaded for respite, yet their mammoth effort yielded only minuscule progress towards their target of the Hellson. Underneath them, a green speck of light manifested. Despite the sea's turbulence, the speck of menacing green light grew steadily larger and brighter until out of the inky blue water the evil rose. Their ears were assaulted with a noise so offensive that Truffy's right ear began trickling a gelatinous bloodstained ooze, which travelled slowly down his jawline, pooling into gloop on his shirt collar. The Sapphires' nightmares had morphed into reality, except what surfaced to the water was worse than they had imagined. A rotting Viking longboat was nose-to-nose with the *Fortress*. Twenty green-eyed Viking carcasses with rotten flesh were protected by their round shields, which they banged with the remnants of human skeletons. Savannah trembled and nausea overtook her chest as even the tips of her ears filled with a heart-deadening sensation she had never experienced before.

"Keep rowing," Savannah spluttered across the *Fortress* to Rich. Truffy and Delia pounced, disintegrating the vile Viking creatures as they boarded. Delia held on to the sapphire grenade, but a Viking loomed over her. Truffy swung for him but was grabbed by another green-eyed creature from behind and was pulled over onto the longboat.

"They are taking us down with them. Make sure Ragnar gets this," Delia shouted to Savannah, hurtling the glittering sapphire bomb towards her as she too was tackled down onto the floor and dragged into the longboat as it slowly bubbled and fizzed its way back from where it came, into the deep black ocean. Savannah caught it mid-air and clutched it to her chest.

"Don't let it go. Whatever happens. Savannah, there's another boat coming this way; I can see a light." Rich looked towards the shore as an ominous glow gradually grew closer. "It's Sid's sea machine," Rich yelled above the insurmountable noise, craning his neck closer towards it.

"Ma?" Savannah whimpered. "What are you doing? I don't understand."

Martha defiantly swung her legs over the side of Sid's sea machine and shuffled into the *Sapphire Fortress*. "I couldn't help you when the bullies got to you. This time I can help!" Martha stood squarely as the *Fortress* rocked.

"Martha, you're not a Sapphire. How will you defend yourself?" Rich asked.

"I choose to be peaceful, Richard. That doesn't mean I don't know how to fight," she spewed as if her very words were molten lava. "Three of us rowing will be easier."

Savannah, Rich and Martha rowed, the Hellson continuing to erupt just metres away. Suddenly the darkness was ignited by a green haze which electrified the water surrounding them. "I will do it, Savannah. I will swim it in," Rich spluttered, holding his hands out, indicating to the sapphire bomb that Savannah was clutching. Savannah held it close to her chest.

"No. Let's throw it in," she said, tears flowing down her cheeks.

"It won't work. We must hit Ragnar, or this is all for nothing." Rich shook.

"Give it here, Savannah. I will decide." Martha held out her arms and Savannah passed her the sapphire bomb. Her mother moved to the end of the boat, closest to the Hellson entrance. She began to gag and cough while the gas attacked her lungs. "Look after her for me, Richard!" she ordered.

From the depths of the water came an explosion. And from this devastation he rose. Ragnar leached out of the water, marauding 7 foot tall, with a satanic smirk smeared across his predatory face. His scarred and pitted skin exuded putrid grey gas from its pores. Ragnar represented an evil so triumphant that decency and innocence had never visited his being.

"Ragnar." Martha's eyes burned with rage as she stalked towards him with stealth-like precision.

"You can't even fight," Ragnar taunted. "You pathetic excuse of an islander. Worthless back-up to my future army standing behind you." His loathsome voice cracked into a convulsing laugh. "You should have saved your own measly life and stayed on that roof."

Martha threw Savannah the bomb.

"You haven't even got the shining gene," he bawled, throwing his hands into the air. "This is going to be an easier defeat than I thought."

Martha stood her ground at the front of the boat. "I didn't get the shining gene from my ma," Martha hissed, leaning upwards ferociously into his warped and mutated face as Ragnar laughed at her condescendingly.

"Rubbish. You're nothing but a disgrace to your mother and the Sapphires. You coward. Too scared to be a little sapphire shiner. Poor little Martha," he leered.

"I wanted a family. Meinhild was proud of me, even if I wasn't a shiner, so, she gave me this…" Savannah looked towards her mother's hand. She had never taken any notice of her mother's engagement ring before. A cluster of tiny blue sapphires encircling a huge diamond.

"So what? You're still not a sapphire shiner!" Ragnar mocked.

"Very observant, cretin." Martha leaned into Ragnar so closely, she began to inhale his foul breath.

"I was already living in England when I heard about the Sapphires. So Froodroy senior had a suggestion…"

"Ha, that old codger," Ragnar sneered.

"He suggested I support London's answer to your foul gas." Martha's lips curved into a melancholic smile.

"I don't care about London, you fool."

"You should do. Because I'm a diamond chaser." Martha suddenly lunged forward, blasting her left hand over Ragnar's face and dragging him into the water. "Throw it, Savannah!" she cried as she blasted Ragnar with her engagement ring, down towards the depths of the ocean.

Savannah fumbled with the sapphire bomb. She was unable to conquer the sensation of impending doom; however, fear left her, and pulling her right arm behind her shoulder she hurtled the gleaming blue bomb into the spewing mass of smog surrounding Ragnar as he and Martha tussled. The sapphire bomb hit Ragnar's left shoulder, causing green light to shatter across the sky. Waves erupted from the fjord, capsizing the *Fortress* with Savannah and Rich still on board, forcing it all the way back to the school building. Savannah found herself trapped underwater. The weight of the *Fortress* forced her body down underwater to the fjord floor. She looked around her, underwater, her vision was blurred but she could still make out green masses exploding and vanishing. She could hear the wind turbine screeching, metal grinding on metal and creaking with the force against it. Her breath was slowing; she kicked up off the bottom but was forced down again by the mighty force of the water. Her eyes were beginning to close when she felt a sharp grasp around her right shoulder.

"Aloes," Savannah mouthed bubbles. She bobbed to the surface, where she saw Rich and her mother lying on moss, below the watchtower.

"Not this time," Ava said in Selkie form as she dragged Savannah's limp body onto the shoreline and effortlessly swam back down to the dark waters where a rookery of seals bobbed in the water, their brown eyes glistening. Out of the water, Delia's unconscious body was being dragged by another Selkie, who nuzzled Delia's body onto the shore.

"She's in a bad way, but she's breathing," Dana said. "Thank you for looking after Frank and Jan," she said to Savannah before diving back into the fjord to join the other seals.

Mr Froodroy ran over to them, accompanied by the Diamonds. "Well, I see you can still kick backsides when you need to, Martha. You took that Ragnar down like a sack of—" Edna smiled but was interrupted by Truffy's body being tossed unceremoniously onto the shore by a large seal Savannah hadn't seen before. Truffy's face was grey and lifeless. Precious loomed over him and began to smear confetti bush paste along his brow, joined swiftly by Mai, who swam ahead of a larger male seal, who pushed her back, flicking his tail.

"Help him, Mai!" Scruffy pleaded. Mai hissed at the larger Selkie and he moved aside. Mai produced some red seaweed from under the water. Her chocolate-coloured wet hair stuck around her shoulders as she looked up to the sky, raising her hands, which were filled with the blood-coloured sludge, as if in offering. Blue swirls of light floated into her hands, into the seaweed, turning it purple in colour. She thrust the purple slime onto Truffy's chest. Truffy's pale face began to appear warmer; shards of purple electric shocks appeared to soar through him, making him jolt. Then unexpectedly he gasped, inhaling the blue haze and gazing straight into Mai's deep brown eyes.

"Enough, Mai," the largest Selkie ordered. "Sapphires, we are now even. We shall resume our yearly meetings only. Usual night and place."

"Your cooperation is appreciated. Thank you, your Highness," Mr Froodroy responded to the King of the Selkies, bowing courteously before ushering the Sapphires towards the only home untouched by the muted: Mountain Cottage. The island drifted into darkness as the ominous Hellson gas slowly departed from their lands. As the Sapphire Society members dragged their battered bodies up the gruelling mountain to Precious' home, the nocturnal wildlife around them carried on as normal. Despite winning the battle, the survivors suffered such exhaustion that, on this night, no moon or star in the sky seemed capable of illuminating the battered island.

CHAPTER 27

THE RETURN

Savannah woke to a tickling sensation. Her warm body felt the cosy warmth of a fire on her legs, and she tucked her chin back into a warm wool blanket. "Honestly. It's like this every morning," Theodore said jovially. Savannah slowly opened her eyes to find the aloes stroking her face and Tom crawling around her, gurgling. The Sapphires and Diamonds were mingling in Precious' kitchen, eating breakfast and drinking tea.

"Oh, Tom." She scooped him into her arms; the thought of nearly losing him the night before was too much to bear.

"You did it, Savannah. You and Richard bombed the Hellson into peace." Mr Froodroy stood in Precious' kitchen. Savannah ran to the window and gazed out. The fjord was calm. The turbine stood still.

"There's no gas to push it around now," her father said, putting his hand on her shoulder.

"I'm so proud of you," Martha said, taking Savannah's face into her soft, warm hands and kissing her on the forehead.

"You're a chaser!" Savannah said to her mother.

"Only when the Diamonds really need me. Edna roped me in as a part-timer. I didn't get Grandma's shining skills, but it seems she did pass down a protective gene that comes in pretty handy during gas-fighting battles," she smiled mischievously.

"It looks like the aftermath of a tsunami out there," Rich said solemnly. Most of the houses were gone; debris lay scattered across the previously beautiful fields.

"Never mind the houses, I'm going to have to go shopping for another new chopper," said a familiar Scottish accent, its owner gingerly limping down the stairs.

"Laird!" Savannah smiled.

"We thought you were stuck down there," Rich said.

"A strange thing happened. As the chopper went down, there was light underwater. I couldn't breathe anyway, so I thought I may as well follow it. I was in this weird bubble. There were others in there, but I couldn't breathe. Then your school caretaker found me. The rest is such a blur," he said, quietly scratching his head.

"You're safe now," Mr Froodroy said, nodding to Doreen, who put a mug of tea into his hands.

"What about Ragnar?" Savannah asked.

"He can't survive without the gas," Doreen said.

"So that's it! The Sapphires have won, no more stinking gas," Rich said.

Mr Froodroy glided off the floor, as if giving himself a soapbox, and addressed the room. "The Sapphire Society will always be needed. While there are humans, there is greed. Where there is greed, there is gas. This existence of ours is balanced on a knife edge of good versus greed. The good news is, we are winning," he smiled, raising his mug of tea in the air.

- ▼ -

The clear-up and rebuild of the island was scheduled to take several months. Apart from the smashed glass in the orangery, the Wood house was miraculously untouched by the ferocious Hellson eruption that the newspapers had dubbed the worst tsunami since 1977, and few people knew the truth about the real version of events that summer's night. The church, Doreen's cottage, the school, the Wood house and Precious' cottage were, for the most part, saved by their shining rooftops.

"Now everyone really believes Doreen is the doomed widow," Rich laughed as they sat on their picnic blanket in the glorious summer sun. "And guess what the locals are calling your house? *The Doomed Wood!*" Rich rolled around the floor, his textbook flapping in the breeze. Savannah tutted, giggling.

"We've got more important things to worry about. Our exams are tomorrow," Savannah replied, still trying to cram as much information into her weary head as possible. Despite the debris covering the shores and damaged homes, Strendur was home.

"Come on, your ma is cooking dinner for us all at five thirty sharp, and since I've seen what she did to Ragnar, I'm certainly not getting on her bad side," Rich joked, getting up from the picnic blanket and pulling Savannah up. Their bikes had been destroyed by the Hellson eruption, so Savannah and Rich strolled to the Woods' house, where the Froodroy family were staying until their own home was rebuilt.

"Ready for tomorrow, then? We have to be at the bureau for the 9 am exam start," Savannah asked Rich.

"Yeah, yeah, yeah, I'll be fine," Rich replied, grimacing.

- ▼ -

The Diamonds' black taxi glided back over the fjord, dropping off Savannah and Rich after their bureau exams. "Nigel said he would visit in a few weeks to give us our results," Savannah said.

Mr Froodroy raised his eyebrows. "You two must be special if you are getting your results delivered by the minister of KAPOW."

"He's interested in the refurbishment of Grandma's orangery," Savannah smiled.

"Yes, he always did lurk around there." Mr Froodroy scratched his head, at which Savannah stifled a grin.

The rest of the summer holidays passed, much of which was taken up with rebuilding the houses on the island, but Savannah and Rich made sure there was still time for long, lazy picnics, walks along the fjord and foraging for plants. The glass had been replaced in the orangery; the steel frame had not one dent on it, despite the muteds' best efforts. Savannah sat stroking Tricver as she admired the plants on the oak shelving, which were growing at lightning speed.

"Is that a mushroom I see in the corner?" Rich asked.

"Yes, *fungai mortem toxicus*, the antidote to that destructive seaweed. It sort of self-seeded after the Hellson gas dispersed," Savannah smiled.

"Well, I wish it would sort out Tornado's gas problems; this cat of yours really does stink." Rich looked offensively at Tornado, who simply wafted his tail as he slunk out of the orangery door, rubbing up against Nigel's leg as he knocked on the open door.

"Amazing, it doesn't look any different from when I last visited," Nigel swooned as he strode around the orangery, inspecting every crevice.

Rich exhaled a long sigh and spluttered, "Have you got them?" Nigel handed Savannah and Rich a navy envelope each. Rich tore his open.

"71%, I passed!" He jumped and whooped, grabbing Tornado and kissing him.

"You need 70% to pass." Nigel spoke softly to Savannah, while rolling his eyes in Rich's direction. Savannah's heart felt like a heavy weight and she felt almost faint with worry. She tucked her little finger into the gap of the sealed envelope to tear along the crease and pulled out the folded paper.

"Well?" Rich said, poised and motionless, but still clutching his own letter.

A broad smile spread across Savannah's face. "100%," she said.

"Teacher's pet! Well done, Savannah!" Rich exclaimed, clapping her on the back.

"There is another letter here, which I need to deliver to Delia. Do you know where I could find her?" Nigel enquired.

"She's at school. We can walk you there," Rich said.

They strolled along the sea bridge path. "I almost miss jumping the waves, now the Hellson has gone quiet," Savannah said to Nigel.

The gargoyles guarding the watchtower glared down on them as they arrived at the large oak door. A waft of pipe tobacco smoke wafted around the corner, spilling sideways out of Mr Johnson's mouth.

"The headmistress is in her office," Mr Johnson said to Nigel.

"Many thanks. White, caramel-colour and plenty of sugar, please," Nigel replied, walking through the grand hallway, his leather brogues clicking on the tiled floor.

"Bloody cheek. While you're here, you two…" Mr Johnson pointed up to the watchtower. Without a hint of anxiety, Savannah and Rich ran up the metal spiral stairs.

"'*Row, row, row your boat gently through the tide, if you see the Sapphires coming, you will surely hide*'," the watchtower ghost sang playfully to them.

"You were stuck in here with Ragnar. Were you okay?" Savannah asked the ghost.

"I saw your mother take him down; he wasn't expecting a woman to fight like that," she smiled.

"I wasn't expecting her to fight like that either," Savannah smiled, raising her eyebrows.

"We both passed," Rich said.

"Well, of course." She wafted in between them. "Did they find the Laird's helicopter?" she asked.

"No," Rich replied anxiously.

"I saw Martha push Ragnar down into the fjord. She gave a good fight, but her ring and the sapphire bomb weren't enough to disintegrate him before those Selkie friends of yours helped her onto shore after the Hellson exploded," she said.

Savannah knew there was more to this conversation than she wanted to hear. "Where is he? Where did Ragnar go?" Savannah fumbled her words as her hands shook.

"He filled the helicopter with the muted and Hellson gas, threw the Laird out and used it to escape underwater," she said.

"Miss Wood, Froodroy, the man is leaving. He's waiting at the front door for you," Mr Johnson said, appearing at the top step. "God knows why, but Helga has taken a shine to you two," Mr Johnson said as he stood at the top of the metal stairs.

"Helga, so that's your name." Savannah smiled at the ghost.

"Helga. Helga Johnson?" Rich looked at the ghost, then at Mr Johnson. "Your missing wife?" Rich pointed at Helga.

"Meinhild saved me from becoming one of the muted. She was out rowing in the fjord with little Sig, when that vile Ragnar attacked them. He was dragging little Sig down to take him into the Hellson, but your grandmother, she wouldn't have it. She fought Ragnar off and threw little Sig to me. He was already dead, but at least he wouldn't be muted. Then those muted creatures all jumped on me. I tried my best but they killed me out there in the fjord. The Selkies put mine and Sig's bodies on the moss at the bottom of the tower here. Nigel took little Sig's soul to London, where he would be safe and looked after. I visit him at Downing Street, when they call me to report what I see, but my place is here with Kenneth.

I told him to go and find a wife that was living, but he wouldn't have it." She smiled at Mr Johnson.

"I will never leave you," he said, his eyes filling up with tears, as he reached forward to touch her hand. As he did so, she vanished. Mr Johnson wiped his eyes. "There. Now you know why I can't go back to England. Now come on, they are waiting for you."

Nigel stood by the front door, looking out over the fjord. "Congratulations on your results," he said.

"Ragnar is still out there," Savannah said, still in shock. Nigel nodded solemnly.

"What will happen?" she asked.

"We will keep fighting. We will keep protecting the good and fighting greed. We hold our heads up high and remember what we believe in," Nigel said. Savannah sighed and watched Nigel tip his head and walk off into the distance.

"Come on, we've got a few days left until school starts again and there's a load of debris to make a gliding course out of." Rich tugged at Savannah's arm as they walked slowly home, along the dry, aloe vera-lined sea bridge.

ACKNOWLEDGEMENTS

Despite being a work of fiction, this story has been inspired by an unbelievably real place. The Faroe Islands, where my inspirational Grandmother was born and raised have always been a place of wonder and intrigue to me. My Grandmothers' stories and traditions inspired my own vision of this magical group of islands intertwined with real land marks and my own obscure take on Faroese myths. Of course, being a story means the characters are all fictional, however my friends and relatives may recognise some familiar character traits hidden between the lines. In fact, this story arrived to me quite by accident. Following the death of my Grandmother I felt determined my own daughter should also benefit from the magic of these islands and so the 'Sapphire Society' was born, to pass the mystery on.

I have been blessed with many wonderful people who have supported and guided me during the process of putting my ideas into a book. My unconditionally supportive mother has read every edit with no loss of enthusiasm, and my wonderful father has unwavering faith I will do his mothers islands proud; for their love and support I am truly indebted. One of my many life blessings is my dear friend Kate Johnson. As a children's librarian who has dedicated her career to children's literature, we have no less than 26 years in cahoots for whatever mischief we feel is achievable. Thank you. Laura Bramley, Nishma Patel, Joanna Faustino-Kemp, Mel Hill, Richard Jago and the glamorous rose scented lady who is too modest to allow me to mention her invaluable guidance of transitioning- I am whole heartedly grateful for all of your time and wisdom.

Thank you to Matador publishing team for putting my little story into print. Last but by no means least are my wonderful family. My unconditionally supportive husband Glen and my children Savannah, Aime, Kali and Liam, who have listened to the eternal scratchings of my pen and tapping of keys whilst I jot down another plot twist or complete 'one more edit'.

Life on earth is a magical gift, we need only see when we look.